MEAT AND BONE

By Dan Rempala

This book was printed in the United States of America.

Cover Art by Chris Claflin

Author Photo by Michelle Conley-Harada

MEAT AND BONE

CHAPTER ONE:

SCARS

Her bicep strained, and the fingertips of her left hand dug into her right forearm, but the slow, steady ascent continued. The delicate fingers of her right hand encircled the thin metal bar, and when her chin crossed the height of her perfectly sculpted knuckles, she coughed out, "One twenty-two." Her bicep slowly relaxed and lowered the rest of her body into a hanging position for yet another pull-up.

The metal pull-up bar lay over seven feet off the ground and ran like a taught chord for roughly forty feet across the left-hand side of the circular weight room. It could have held two-dozen soldiers, hanging shoulder-to-shoulder as they grunted their way through a set of pull-ups, but at the moment, it only held one. Her reflection stared out of the full-length mirror in front of her, one of the dozens that inscribed the room. Her body rose and fell methodically in a hydraulic fashion. The motion was almost hypnotic enough to make her lose count.

A battalion of exercise machines sat evenly spaced behind her, contraptions dedicated to contracting almost every muscle in the human body. She knew how to use most of them, but several looked mysterious and uncomfortable. In most cases, the machines consisted of a white, painted-metal body and royal blue padding. They all operated on computer-generated resistance, but for the time being, they sat dormant, along with the couple tons of old-timey, solid metal dumbbells in the rack against the wall. Most of the soldiers and some of the crew who normally swarmed about the ship were enjoying twenty-four hours of much-needed liberty. The main deck currently ran on a very bitter skeleton crew. Certainly, no one stuck around to lift weights when given liberty. No one except her.

The muscles of her shoulder, the one supporting her entire one-hundred-twenty-five-pound frame, bulged but showed no trace of a scar. She always knew that the anatomical reconstruction techs up at the Medical Center could fit just about anything beyond a torso with cybernetic limbs, and she knew the process was far easier than fitting people with artificial organs. Several reliable sources had told her that the techs were so proficient that, in addition to shooting themselves full of whatever muscle-building compounds they could get their hands on, many members of the Wraith Squad intentionally shot or sliced off their natural limbs at the end of missions in order to receive the mechanical replacements when they returned to the ship. She had no idea that the technicians could make the attachment look so flawless, though.

"One twenty-three," she said and released the bar. She hit the rubberized floor with the balls of her rubberized shoes, bounced once, and kept her balance. No reason to keep going. After all, she wasn't exercising the arm in the hope of building muscle; she wasn't an expert in cybernetics, but she knew that was impossible. The medic told her she would need to strengthen the connection between the remaining strands of nerves in her shoulder and the electronic relays in the new arm, though, if she wanted it to perform optimally… and she would need optimal performance if she planned to go back down to the surface.

Her pulse thumped steadily in her neck. That particular portion of the workout only winded her was because it took some effort from her left arm to keep her body balanced. You take the balancing arm for granted when doing ten or even twenty one-armed pull ups, but when you do anything more strenuous than typing over one hundred times, the repetition starts to wear things out. She planned to do twenty or so pull-ups with her mortal arm, just to balance out, but if she really wanted to exert the hunk of metal and wire attached to her right shoulder, for whatever reason, she would have to hit the side of the dumbbell rack with the 300-pound weights.

The woman bent down to get a drink from the white plastic water bottle with the blue top resting against the wall. The fact that it matched the equipment perfectly made it a little difficult to see. She tossed standard issue water bottle from her right hand to her left, just to make sure she did not crush the container when she squeezed it. The arm felt natural enough, but machines do have a statistically significant rate of mishaps. A malfunction at the wrong time, a slight flinch while touching her face or neck, could be catastrophic. *Better be careful doing pull-ups with your real arm*, she reminded herself; a little too much pressure on her forearm for a fraction of a second and her mechanical hand could turn her real forearm into cream-of-bone.

The woman pulled her shoulder-length, brown hair out of its ponytail, smoothed the strands back against her skull, and retied the elastic band. From eight feet away, her reflection showed no loose hairs. Every inch of her body was toned without enough bulk to slow her down, an impressive combination of strength and endurance that could kill 99.9% of normal humans stupid enough to face her. Above the neck, though, the illusion of invulnerability faded. The pale skin of her faced sagged around the eyes. Looking at her reflection, she couldn't decide if "weary" or "haggard" conjured a more accurate image. From the bloodshot white regions of her eyes and the baggy sections of skin an inch below, one would think fifteen years and not fifteen days had passed since the explosion took her arm. One also would think she hadn't slept in that time. On the latter point, not counting forced sedation, one would be almost correct.

As she stared into the mirror, the sterile weight room behind her seemed to dissolve, leaving her back on the dark, dirty, blue-tinted battlefield. A laser mortar explosion did the damage that night. Had to be a laser mortar. They were rather distinctive, the way they lit up the whole sky as they slid across the blackness like a cobalt-blue shooting star, almost beautiful unless they dropped into your lap. The arching, deep blue band of light made a sound like the ignition of a hyperdrive when it tore open the chunk of ground between her and the company field commander, Jervis Giles. She stood a few feet farther away from the lethal blast than Lieutenant Giles, and the distance saved her life and gave her just enough time to turn and watch the burst of light incinerate her arm just below the shoulder socket.

Giles lost a lot more. She spent a couple long seconds, maybe more, staring at her smoldering shoulder socket and did not register that the blast had hit him until the screaming started. It took her another second to realize that she wasn't the one screaming. There were so many sounds down there: the sizzle when the rifles hit a live target, the churning of the tank treads and the grinding of the loose ground… the explosions. But you couldn't see anything unless they were setting the mortars off. Dazed, she waited for the next mortar shot to illuminate her world and looked over in the direction of the screams, where little more than a charred head and torso wiggled around in the dust and the gravel. Thirteen days later, it disgusted her to think about it, but at the time, it surprised her that there was enough left of Lieutenant Giles to even scream. Thirteen days later, she could still see the ghastly scene when she closed her eyes, whether she wanted to or not.

The Battle of Coppin Bay. That's the history-book-ready name her superiors gave to that little glimpse into hell that she endured. It was supposed to end the war. The Army of the Republic suffered horrible losses over the three days in that laser-choked pit, but they supposedly won. They took the hill and supposedly scattered the last collection of Middesian forces. By the end of the next day, the short-wave reports said that the evacuation had begun. Even from the infirmary, she could hear the shouting from the hallways and the thunderous clump of heavy boots rushing in every direction. It marked the Republic's greatest battlefield victory during her lifetime... supposedly, although she didn't know what criteria they were using... and she told herself that the fact that she was part of it should make her feel better.

So why had the war continued? While she lay in an infirmary bed for two days, doped up to the point of borderline incoherence, the video monitor on the far wall showed images of the worm-like carrier ships rising from the ground and ushering the Middesian inhabitants from their home planet. According to the announcer, the members of the Vlorth, the Middesian elite class, were onboard, leaving with eighty percent of the artillery and nearly all of the soldiers. So why had the war continued? Who was left to contend with the greatest intergalactic military force ever assembled?

She didn't know, but the commanders had yet to order the launch of the occupation teams, and no live feeds from the surface made their way into the broadcasts, so some sort of action was obviously still taking place on the surface. The moment the doctors released her from the infirmary a few days ago, still wobbly from the medication, she started her rehabilitation, waiting for active-duty clearance. Her reinstatement papers came earlier that morning. She needed only to receive her re-assignment before she could return to the front, any front would do… assuming there was a front. Returning to the surface with a gun in her hands would be like mother's milk for her. She didn't want to get too used to the sterile air up here; it made the dirty air that much tougher to breathe. Down on the surface, she would be so busy thinking about surviving the present that she wouldn't have time to think about the past. When she started to think about the past, she started to hurt, and before long, the hurt became unbearable.

The eyes of her reflection stared out from the mirror. They were accusing eyes, demanding to know why she was standing around, thinking, when she knew perfectly well what she would end up thinking about. The whites had turned pink and would soon deepen into a reddish hue, while skin covering the bones of her eye sockets took on a sunken, purple quality to them. The ponytail pulled her hair back and left her forehead exposed, making visible the slight, horizontal, slowly deepening wrinkles. Weariness oozed over every inch of her body when she ran her human hand over her face, but she had to shake it off. She had to keep working. She had to get back to the front.

Her shoulders sagged slightly as she sighed and stepped up to the pull-up bar. The metal bar hovered a little less than two feet above her head while her mechanical hand rubbed her human wrist bone. The knobby little bone felt so brittle under the thin layer of skin. She could snap it like a toothpick and call it an accident. People had made that mistake before. Two superhuman limbs would make her an even better soldier. By the time the techs cleared her again, though, whatever fighting left to do may finish. Another week of the stagnant, processed air and the monotony of ship-life and her superiors might give into temptation and slap a psychiatric discharge on her. Living on the economy, with no direction... she'd be a suicide waiting to happen.

The need to get back down to the surface felt almost biological, like a fish seeking water. Standing still made what's left of her skin crawl. Beyond the crisp, scent-carrying air, she craved structure: the straightforward, shoot-anything-that-is-not-human logic of the front made sense at this point, even when nothing else did. It was the one thing she knew she could do without dissolving into an emotional mess. During moments when she could think about something other than the few seconds before or after the blue light, her thought usually involved punching her metal hand through the fleshy faces of a few of the murderous, hairy bastards who butchered her life.

She shook her head, but the black, metal bar still glowered down on her. It waited for her and would continue to do so. She squatted down, then leapt to grasp it. A voice burst over the intercom the instant her toes left the rubberized flooring. "Lieutenant Clarice Torrance, please report to the General's quarters. Lieutenant Clarice Torrance, report to the General's quarters." She pulled her hands back at the last instant, ducked under the bar, and dropped to the floor. She couldn't get used to her new title, partly because she found out about it while still doped up on sedatives and partly because it didn't seem to fit. Weren't you supposed to receive promotions for things you were proud of?

Clarice picked up her water bottle and paused for a last glance around the weight room. A hundred soldiers should have been in there, straining and grunting and getting stronger, but there was only her. The others were out getting drunk and/or laid. She snorted. Maybe that's why they were still fighting this stupid war. After she stepped out into the hallway circumscribing the weight room, she paused again. The locker room was ten paces to her right. Maybe she should run in for a quick particle shower, at least to take away any lingering stench… On second thought, maybe not. She had only met General Harvath once, but he seemed like a someone who valued punctuality over formality.

She started to turn to her left, but the sight of her reflection caused her to pause after a single step. Her eyes danced over her pale skin as she once again admired the work the technicians did on her shoulder. Flawless. Too bad they couldn't do anything about the scars the blast left on her insides.

*   *   *

Clarice lifted her right arm and sniffed at the pit as the elevator carried her upward to the General's quarters. People have trouble detecting their own stench (compared to other people's), but she honestly thought she could only smell the antiseptic scent of her anti-bacterial spray. *Good enough.* Outside of the cafeteria, that seemed like the only thing to smell on the ship. Forty-five minutes of exercise, and she barely broke a sweat. Could her new arm even sweat? Probably not. With the possible exception of covert missions, it doesn't seem like there would be a need. No doubt the mechanics had developed their own cooling system that was far superior to sweat glands, and damp skin might interfere with a soldier's ability to grip. The skin on the rest of her body had dried and grown its familiar, post-workout film, but not the "skin" of her arm.

The elevator glided to a stop, the doors silently slid open, and the automated voice announced, "Floor Nineteen." Clarice stepped into the hallway, still clad in her royal blue, elastic workout leotard. The General's quarters sat at the far end of the long hallway, a good grenade toss away. This particular hallway looked like every other hallway on every other ship. White walls and royal blue carpet, to complement with the military dress uniforms. If anything else occupied the hallways, it usually bore a shade of light gray, the same shade that the ship's crew wore. Ship, soldiers, and crew: all part of the same interlocking system.

The General's door slid open while half a hallway stood between her and it. A pair of burly laborers emerged, recognizable in their orange coverall (thankfully, none of the décor matched those). Each man carried two sizable plastic crates stacked atop one another. Those type of crates usually indicated that someone's personal effects were going somewhere, either because that someone had received a promotion or a transfer... or died.

Clarice drifted to the right side of the hall to make room for the workers but could not see inside the closed crates. The eyes of the one of the men started at her face and traveled down her body, lingering on her chest for a long second. The pair of eyes no doubt shifted to her backside when she passed by. *Yeah, keep staring, Creepy; I'll rip those eyes right out of your skull.* She could have killed him in two seconds back before she sported mechanized limbs: punched him in the throat, then snapped his neck while he clutched at his collapsed trachea. Imagine the kind of damage she could do now; the punch alone would end him.

Being ogled bothered her more than it used to. She used to rationalize it by telling herself that it meant she was keeping herself in good shape. Now, she found it disgusting... and threatening... and depressing. She should slash up her face. Then they'd stop staring. Nah, slashing up their faces would be better. Otherwise, the skin techs might give her a new, improved face: the face of a blemish-free, twenty-year-old. She glanced over her shoulder in time to see the pockmarked laborer avert his gaze. Both men were brawny specimens, each easily twice her weight and built for the slow grind of manual labor, but she could have torn through them like a Kilgore Tunneling Cannon in the time it took their crates to hit the floor.

The General's door remained retracted into the wall as she approached the doorway, and Clarice took the liberty to peer inside. The furnishings consisted of only the essentials that came standard with each room. A made bed with a royal blue blanket and tight fitting white sheet sat in the far right corner, while a gray, square conference table stood near the far left corner. Three matching gray, hard-plastic chairs sat pushed into the table. Besides the exterior view and the fact that the square-footage was about three times that of a lieutenant's quarters, it could have been the room she lived in.

Her eyes passed over him during their initial scan, but on the second sweep, she noticed a man standing in front of the window, his back turned to her. Motionless, he almost looked like one of military-issue furnishings. He wore the royal blue uniform of a soldier, and his hands lay casually linked with one another behind his back as he stared out at the endless canopy of stars. By the man's white, angular, close-cropped hair, she could tell that this was not the shaven-headed General Harvath.

"Excuse me," she said. "I'm here to see General Harvath."

The man turned and regarded her with his lone good eye. A black, cloth patch covered the left eye socket. It easily stood out as his most distinguishable feature, almost to the point of being a caricature, because with the miracle of cybernetics, no one wore eye-patches anymore. She didn't know why he wore an eye patch, but she knew exactly how he lost his eye; she read the story several times on a brass plaque that sat underneath a stone likeness of him at Camp Burden. Despite the passage of at least a decade between the creation of the granite bust and that moment, his face looked surprisingly similar to the sculpture. His actual jaw-line looked as straight and rigid as the jaw of the bust, and the left corner of his mouth turned up almost to the point of being a defiant smirk, just like the statue's mouth. No artist, though, no matter how skilled, could convey the subtle dominance of the man, like the way he waited, but never hesitated: he remained silent until he decided to speak, and then he spoke until he had no more to say. Even with the smallest movements of his body, once he started, he carried them through without a flicker of indecision. It created the illusion of grace and inevitability.

Clarice looked about her, expecting to be the victim of some sort of sardonic joke. General Garth Frusin had not set foot on an orbiting battle station in years, not since he retired from the army to accept the appointment of governor of Darrat 16. It marked his first return to that planet since he led its occupation during the energy crisis of '41. She was in secondary school at the time. The instructors cancelled class so all the students could see the parade on the video monitor.

A pair of fighters silently shot past the room's window, rocketing within a few dozen feet of the hull of the ship, close enough to shake the vessel. Clarice tensed, nearly dropping into a defensive crouch, but General Frusin showed no reaction, almost as though the fighters were operating on a timetable he had created. Fearing that the Great Man didn't hear her initial question, Clarice drew in a breath to repeat herself. Before she could unleash it, Frusin spoke. "General Harvath is no longer in charge of the occupation in Middes," General Frusin said, tonelessly, as if this were something she should have known. "I am. Can I assume you are Lt. Torrance?"

"Yes, General," Clarice said, snapping to attention. She had no idea what was going on, but if General Garth Frusin plays a joke on you, soldier, you had better fall for it.

"What's with the get-up, Torrance?" Frusin asked, nodding toward the workout clothes hugging the contours of her body. He didn't bark the question; barking was for people still trying to impress. "Somebody steal your uniform?"

Had Clarice squinted, she could have almost seen the blue and white flag of the republic waving behind him. Ever since she started thinking about the Republic as an entity, she had always associated Frusin's face with it… and excellence and duty and sacrifice and all that other good stuff. He was like a fictional character created to embody the ideals of the Republic, an impossible ideal to aspire toward, and even though they had never met, he was as much a father figure as an idol for her. With all this on her mind, Clarice's answer came a second too slow. "I came right… straight from the weight room, General."

"Punctuality, I appreciate," he said. "Sloppiness, I don't. I'm no spit-and-polish, academy-type, but I don't ever want to see you out of uniform in my presence again, soldier. Maybe someday, we'll all hold staff meetings in our jammies, but not on my watch. Is that clear?"

"Yes, General."

Frusin nodded. "At ease. Step into the room, Lieutenant, so that Major Drennon can get through."

Clarice turned and saw another blue uniformed body standing about a foot behind her. This particular uniform was spotless, clean enough to wear into surgery, and a forty-ish man wore it. He stood an inch or two taller than her, definitely the spit-and-polish, academy-type, and carried half a dozen paper folders tucked under his arm. His black hair had grown to the limit of military standards, and he wore it parted in the middle, not a single follicle out of place. He grinned at Clarice and nodded, not breaking eye contact and not betraying the impatience some officers would have in the same position. She knew that Major Lee Drennon had acted as Harvath's second-in-command since the occupation began, but she never remembered actually seeing the man.

His was a name that only appeared on forms. As a physical being, he was handsome in an unremarkable way, and he shifted into a tight-lipped smirk as he pressed past Clarice. A thick layer of cologne lingered in his wake, such that she could scarcely believe that she did not pick-up his scent while he stood behind her.

With a measured stride, Drennon strutted his way to the square table against the far wall of the spacious room and dropped the paper folders onto its surface. "Come have a seat, Lieutenant," Frusin said. "We have much to discuss and damn little time to discuss it."

Clarice followed the two men to the table. Even at his advanced age, Frusin did not move so much as flow from one position to the next. When he spoke, he said things that seemed to be stolen from the script of the movie about his life. She stiffly sat down in the seat opposite him, feeling like a child eating at the grown-up table. It didn't help that Drennon was dressed for a parade and she for a hand-to-hand combat training session.

Drennon opened up one of the files, glanced down at the top page, and when he looked up, he gave Clarice a hard stare. Paper files usually indicated serious matters because they indicated that only one hardcopy of the materials existed and it was getting incinerated at the end of the meeting. "Tell me, Lieutenant," Drennon asked, "have you ever heard of Leon Azzerello?"

The name struck her as vaguely familiar. "Wasn't he the pilot that registered all those kills during Silver Ridge?" she offered. She had no idea from what part of her memory she dredged that answer, but it sounded right.

Drennon tilted his head and continued to stare at her for a pregnant second. Maybe he was waiting for her to conclude her guess with a "sir." His eyebrows finally bobbed. "Indeed," he said. He reached forward and pushed a button on the control consul located near the edge of the table closest to the wall. A ten-inch, blue-tinted hologram materialized in the middle of the table and slowly rotated clockwise. The full-body image showed a man in his late twenties or early thirties. His blond hair showed slight signs of recession but his roundish, baby-face still made him look too young and immature for a soldier.

Drennon continued. "Ten enemy fighters in that battle alone, and while our artillery always has been better than the Middesians, they fly aircrafts similar to the Gorkam 1500s, which are on par with our own. They're still doing a postmortem of that battle, and the officers are split between several reasons we lost, but everyone who was there agrees that we would never have been able to pull our forces out in time if anyone other than Leon Azzerello had been in the air that day. Do you know Colonel Mordechai Jost?"

Clarice quickly searched her memory banks but, this time, came up empty. "Uh, I'm not sure. Is he—"

"Jost served under me during the Electronium Wars," Frusin told her. "The point the Major is trying to make is that Colonel Jost has seen a lot of flying."

"Exactly," Drennon echoed, "and he called it the most amazing piece of terrestrial piloting he ever witnessed."

Frusin shifted in his seat. "With all due respect to Colonel Jost's assessment, I don't know about all that," he said, smirking to himself as he straightened his back and crossed his arms. "I saw some pretty amazing work back on Darrat 16."

Drennon's eyes darted over to Frusin's side of the table, unsure as to whether he planned to continue. "I'm sure you did, General," he said, his tongue darting out to lick his lower lip. "I was just reading the —"

"You may proceed, Major," Frusin said, leaning back in his chair and closing his eye. Clarice wasn't sure if he was dreaming of past glory or taking a nap, but had he been paying attention, he would have seen the noticeable flash in Drennon's eyes before he refocused on the file in his hands. She didn't know what the hell was going on, which probably limited her future as an officer.

"For his efforts, Azzerello was promoted to squadron commander. His first assignment involved shooting down the transport ships that were evacuating Coppin Bay." Drennon glanced behind him in the direction of the closed door before continuing. "Azzerello's first act as commander was to take a dozen of his men, half of his fighters, and defect to the enemy."

Clarice's pulse throbbed in her neck at a faster rate than it had while she lifted weights. After the words "Coppin Bay" registered, her hands started fidgeting in her lap. The rest of the information merely helped her direct the surge of emotion. The hologram of Azzerello floated in front of her, with a moon-face she could attach her anger to. He still wore the same expression, but while it looked oblivious the first time she said it, this time it housed the blank look of a psychopath. Enemies were enemies, but traitors… they almost wriggled at a level beneath her contempt. Hopefully, the meeting would culminate with Frusin ordering her to take the next transport down to the surface and terminate the man. Until then, she slowly separated her hands and placed them at her sides before she crushed her left one into uselessness.

"They took up hiding in the Wharrib Mountains," Drennon continued, "which holds a substantial portion of the mineral and fuel deposits Middes has to offer. This is important for two reasons. First, the high concentration of Protean metals limits the ability of our instruments to locate them, unless we're down on the surface. Second, those minerals deposits are the primary reason for our presence in the first place, and if the Republic does not gain control of the Wharrib area, all those soldiers will have died for nothing." He gives that last part a moment to sink in, and sink it does, right down into the bottom of Clarice's guts. "It's only a matter of time before we get them, of course, but with Azzerello being what he apparently is, it might take an annoyingly long time. The group he's assembled has the potential to be a massive nuisance for any extraction industries who try to set up there, so Azzerello and his people have to be eliminated before we can initiate the next phase of the occupation."

While Drennon glanced down to consult his notes, Frusin opened his eye and leaned upright. "A dozen men and twice that number of ships doesn't sound like much," he said, "so General Harvath sent a sizable force to deal with Azzerello and the others. There were a small group of Middesian soldiers that got left behind when the Vlorth evacuated. Azzerello hooked up with them… somehow… but they were still out-manned five-to-one." He frowned and shook his head. "Nobody even thought it would be a fight."

Drennon found the page he was looking for, and started in when Frusin stopped. "To be fair, it wasn't much of a fight, but not in the way General Harvath expected. Unfortunately, in addition to being a phenomenal pilot, Azzerello appears to be a tactical genius. It's something we couldn't have known. His PHR Test results showed no desire to lead or any disrespect for authority." Drennon paused for a breath. Clarice didn't know what PHR stood for; she remembered taking the test, but, thankfully, no one shared the results with her. "He wiped out the opposing force and captured their artillery. Harvath sent out a force twice as large as the first. The result was the same. We might as well have just sent him a transport full of equipment and supplies with a big bow on it."

"Now Harvath's out," Frusin said, "and it's my turn to crack this son-of-a-bitch. I figure we don't have a chance in Hell of digging him out now that he's got the remaining Middesians behind him, not without razing half the planet and destroying the energy and mineral reserves. So we're sending a small ground team in, and you're going to find that hole in the ground he's hiding in and bring me his head on a stick."

"You want me on the team, General?" Clarice asked, lifting her chin skyward and pushing her shoulders as far back as they could go. She took long, slow breaths through her nose to maintain her composure. *Revenge...* even saying the word in her head brought a taste to her lips. It was all she wanted, all she had left, but she had to keep cool, because overanxious children don't get assigned to strike teams.

Frusin leaned in and set his elbow on the table, his fingers interlacing. "Young lady, I want you leading the team."

Clarice gulped. The dry mouth from the workout caught up with her. They could have thrown a rock in the air and hit someone on this ship with as much combat experience as her, and she was strictly infantry. Why had they selected her, of all people, for a covert operation? It made no sense, but she wanted... no, *needed* the position, and the only way to lose it now was to ask stupid questions. Instead, she merely said, "Thank you, sir. So, what happens next?"

"First," Frusin said tapping his index finger on the edge of the table, "you go get cleaned up and get into uniform. An officer has to command respect. Second, you pick yourself an eight-man team. You have until 0600 tomorrow morning. At that time, we'll drop you down to the surface in a T14 unit."

Clarice nodded at each point Frusin brought up. She assumed the use of the term "eight-man team" included her among the eight, but she didn't have the guts to ask for clarification.

The Great Man inhaled, and Clarice watched, wide-eyed. What else could happen? "Torrance?" Frusin continued, his tone less formal. He waited for her to nod again. "You realize you probably won't be coming back from this, don't you?" Drennon's eyes drifted from Frusin to Clarice.

She hadn't realized that, but the question actually calmed her. "I wouldn't have it any other way, General," she said, a sardonic smile crawling across her lips. Did he know about her situation? It was possible they were sending her after Azzerello precisely because of her situation, so that they didn't have to worry about some stupid, self-preservation instinct kicking in and botching a perfectly good suicide mission. Either way, did it really matter? An hour ago, she didn't think she could survive another week without sedation. Now, she might not have to.

Frusin's lips slid into a similar half-smile. He looked proud, of her and the organization that nurtured her. "Outstanding, soldier," he said. "Now go get into uniform. Major Drennon will meet you at the transport at 0600 to give you all the information you're going to need."

Clarice stood up and held her salute. "Thank you for this opportunity, General."

Frusin returned the salute. Clarice pivoted and strode from the room. On the other side of the closed door, her falling feet carried her toward the elevator without seeming to hit the carpet. Her nostrils dragged in the dry, processed air and snorted it back out. Some strange mix of rage and elation fueled her movement forward. Who knew she was still capable of feeling excited? She looked down at her right hand

and flexed it, imagining that she held Leon Azzerello's windpipe between her mechanical fingers. She continued to clench and unclench her fist as she marched down the hallway.

*   *   *

A few seconds after the general's door slid closed with a squeak, Drennon, re-organized his papers and stuffed them into the folder from whence they came. "Do you admire him, General? Azzerello, I mean?"

Frusin had draped his arm over the back of his chair stared out the window again. The base now looked out over a particularly cloudy patch of Middes. He now turned back to Drennon, squinting, as though he didn't understand the question. "Of course not."

Drennon tried to make eye contact with the Great Man, but either his eyes or his spine weren't up to the task. "It just sounds like you do, sometimes, when you talk about him."

Frusin's granite-like features shifted into a thoughtful frown. "I suppose... I suppose he interests me, as a challenge, I mean. He certainly is that." He studied the bluish, rotating image of Azzerello that still decorated the middle of the table, possibly scanning for hidden weaknesses. "I can't muster admiration for the man, but I respect his ability, the same way I respect the lethality of a dangerous animal. Respect and admiration are worlds apart, though. Ability fascinates me, but it's like electricity: aimed at the wrong thing in the wrong way, it can be every bit as bad as it could have been good."

Drennon nodded before he had time to contemplate the answer, which was his way. "Are you sure Lt. Torrance is a wise choice, General?"

"Yes," Frusin said without hesitation. His eyebrows arched. "Why? Because she's a woman?"

"No, General," Drennon reflexively spit out. Not the sort of officer to say things that might jeopardize his chance at a promotion, he took a moment to arrange the words correctly. "It's just that, with what she's been through in the recent past, I'm not at all certain that she's stable."

Frusin shifted around in his seat and grasped the back of his chair to pull himself to his feet. It took him two attempts. Standing and properly gathered, he pressed his chest forward and strode over to the window next to his neatly made bed, assuming the same position Clarice saw when she first entered the room. "Son," he said to Drennon without looking at him, "I know you've heard old men like me drone on before about war wounds, but I lost my eye during the Battle of T.C. 8. There was a direct hit on the transport's generator and we dropped like a rock. The crash was the loudest thing I'd ever heard, and something hot hit me in the eye and it just liquefied all down the front of my uniform. I wasn't even thinking about it and covered it with a rag I tore from what was left of the decapitated corpse sitting next to me. When the craft hit the ground, it felt like I'd broken every bone in my body, and I have to assume everyone who survived it felt the same. We were scared, confused, and just had the shit knocked out of us. Hiding under a rock seemed like a hell of a good idea." He paused for effect. "Yet... I gathered up our surviving crew, and we crawled our way up the side of Mount Kessle and knocked out their ion cannon. Five women and sixteen men all told, counting myself, half of 'em weren't even soldiers. We helped win the battle that turned the war around."

Frusin tasted the words as he said them, like someone reliving an event and not merely reciting a story he had told countless times before. "I noticed at the time... I'd never got that kind of reaction out of people I was leading before. They dragged themselves up that mountain and risked their lives in a naked assault against a heavily armed battalion because I told them to." He shook his head and fixed his good eye on Drennon. "The way they fought... not savage, just... hard, relentless." He faced forward again and resumed. "I always thought it was the eye. I still do. I don't know why. Might've been fear or a sense of commitment, but they fought harder. Of course, when I got back to base, they wanted to give me a new one, one that would give me telescopic vision or some such nonsense. I flat refused; no fake, new eye was going to give me what not having one did."

A couple seconds of silence followed before Drennon spoke. "Um, General, I'm not sure I –"

"I play to win, Drennon," Frusin said. "For me and for the greatest republic in the known universe. I didn't care if a fake eye gave me telescopic vision, and I don't care if Clarice Torrance is stable or one chipped fingernail away from going out of her fucking mind. Right now, I don't need stable; I need a killer to go in and root out that son-of-a-bitch. And, son, if you don't learn anything else from your time me, learn this: if you need the ingredients to make someone into a killer, have the enemy cut that someone's fiancé in half with a laser mortar while that someone is watching."

*   *   *

From the journal of Lt. Wilson Kole:

I would imagine that with each advance in interplanetary travel, children of the Republic stand a greater risk of feeling profoundly detached. Along with knowing where we are going, knowing where we are from is very important to humans; it's a major reason for the popularity of religion. Point of departure and destination go a long way toward telling us who we are, and needing a star chart to find home can't help one's sense of belonging.

It was a linear progression. First, "home planets" were no longer the planet your species originated from. Then, the occupied planets became so far away that children never saw their planet of origin. They never saw the achievements of past civilizations except in holographic projections. Home planets we never saw became home galaxies we never visited. Finally, when stasis pods were abandoned in favor of hyperdrive transports, some citizens of the Republic had the unique experience of being born, growing to adulthood, and living out their entire lives without ever setting foot on an actual planet.

I recently read a graphic that over seventy-five percent of the enlisted military personnel in the Army of the Republic were born on interstellar spacecrafts. This number does not surprise me in the least. The military serves them as much as they serve the military. A soldier is given a family, a de facto set of parents, and a very real sense of belonging. Belief in the Republic acts like a religion: with it, we have a past, and it gives us a direction and a way to be remembered. Without it, we have no reason to exist. We enlisted men and women serve the Republic as much as a chancellor or secretary, and it allows us to become part of something greater than our selves.

For some people, Clarice Torrance among them, the military provides something even greater. Clarice found love among the rank and file, so how much greater is her sense of obligation to the machine?

*   *   *

CHAPTER TWO:

AN INSTRUMENT OF JUSTICE

The little girl with the mouse-brown hair continues to wave, even after her mother and father have walked up the loading ramp and disappeared into the recesses of the vast, metal transport ship. Once the loading ramp retracts and ceases its mechanical whine, despite her fear of high places, she creeps within several yards of the edge of the floating, saucer-shaped structure upon which her school stands. Hovering several yards beyond the perimeter of the giant saucer, the massive, whale-shaped transport ship looms over the tiny girl.

She waves so hard that her tiny wrists weaken and she has to change hands every minute or so. The other children gradually drift back toward the school when all the adults are loaded and the immense ship begins to creep horizontally away from the platform, but she stays and continues waving. Dozens of windows dot the side of the five-story ship, and although she can't make out any faces of the blurry heads, she can see the waving hands of dozens of parents. She will stay and keep waving even after everyone else has gone inside. That way, she will be the only one left to wave at, and one of the people at the window seats is bound to be her mother or father, so she will know that they are waving back at her.

A coldness creeps in, and her left wrist starts to hurt, and she switches back to her right, even after the ship hurtles into the distance and transforms into nothing more than the five-pointed gleam of the rear thrusters. Unless one is partial to wispy

clouds or pink and orange sky, the ship remains the only thing to look at. She waves

until the dry, heavy hand of her teacher falls on her shoulder, and she hears the

familiar, almost masculine voice say, "Come inside, Clarice. It's time to start class."

The woman's short-nailed fingertips dig into the little girl's shoulder for emphasis. She

gradually has to apply more and more force, until she literally drags the small girl back

into the glass dome of the school.

     The little girl is five years old. Old enough to have heard the term, "mining

colony," but too young to know what it means.

*   *   *

With her skin freshly cleaned from the particle shower, Clarice sat
at the lone gray table in her cramped living quarters, wearing her full dress
uniform. The collar of her royal blue topcoat remained unbuttoned, and
she smoothed her dry hair back as she stared at the upright, flat computer
screen in front of her. The black screen showed nothing but a golden,
blinking cursor. This was not due to an inability to type. On the contrary,
her fake right hand picked up the muscle memory almost immediately and
after twenty minutes of casual use, could type as well as her real hand and
still managed not to break the console. Her problem resided within her
head; she was creating a list, but couldn't stop finding items to delete.
Minutes before, fifteen names occupied the screen, but Clarice
systematically erased each one from existence.

She drummed her synthetic fingertips on the hollow-sounding
tabletop. Most names on the list belonged to friends of hers. Well,
"friends" might be pushing it. They were people she had served with or
attended class with, back in her days at Camp Burden. Almost a decade
ago, they might have been her friends, but interstellar separation made it
hard to stay in touch and a decade is a long time. Those names lingered
on the screen for about five seconds before the reality of this particular

mission came crashing down. They would never make it to the ship in time, and she would rather not have the deaths of any "friends" haunting her conscious for the remainder of her short-ass life.

She rubbed her chin, paused to make sure she wasn't using the bone-crushing hand, then resumed. The few remaining names belonged to people she remembered from the Camp Burden who had transferred to the same fleet. She probably would identify them as "acquaintances," at best. They were options to take on the mission to the surface because (1) they were in close enough proximity that they could find transport to the command ship by 0600, and (2) she barely remembered these people; when she visualized their faces, she stayed emotionally neutral… until she saw flesh and eyes boiling under the heat of a solar ray transducer. It had been years since she knew them. They might have wives to widow or children to orphan by now. God knows it almost happened to her. How would she feel if someone had blindly selected Jervis for a suicide mission because they thought it would do minimal damage to that person's emotional state? She welcomed her own opportunity to die for the Republic, but that did not make her indiscriminate about who she dragged into the abyss with her. By the same token, the success of this mission was very important for her metaphysical well-being, so she couldn't select someone she outright hated, because she hated incompetence above all else. She definitely needed someone she could trust down on the surface.

Jervis. She always trusted him. Through the depths of the black computer screen, his bright eyes and symmetrical face stared back at her. It was his normal, confident, smiling face this time, the same face he stared at her with when they took leave to Wakkan 7 and spent most of the four days stretched out on that empty strand of beach. Wakkan 7 had blue water, several species of indigenous birds, cool days, and warm nights. They had been seeing one another for months before that, but she fell in love with him on that beach. Sitting now at the plain, gray desk, the cold, hard plastic chair-back pressing against her lower spine, Clarice's memory took her across the light-years, back to Wakkan 7. The sound of the crashing surf. The chirping of the little, gray birds with the pointy beaks. The smell of the salt water. And the warmth... the heat from the sun and Jervis on her skin.

She blinked, and the face receded. The birds stopped chirping and the waves stopped crashing and there was only the gentle hum of the computer to keep her from feeling utterly abandoned out there in space. Sitting alone in her quarters didn't keep her safe from the memories. After they returned to active duty, she and Jervis received the approval to transfer to shared-quarters; it was every military girl's modest dream. The double bed they used to make love in still sat to her left. She had only to give a slight turn of her head, just one little turn, and she could see the sheets under which they used to screw like a couple of Tradarian jungle urchins in heat.

She pressed her palms against her head, either to keep from looking at the bed or to keep her head from splitting open. If the medical technicians had equipped her with two cybernetic arms, she would have died at that moment, her head crushed like a paper cup trapped in a hydraulic vice. Clarice inhaled through her nose, but when she exhaled, the air snagged on something and the crying started. She hated that sound as it echoed through the empty room, making her wish the technicians had fitted her with two cybernetic arms.

She sobbed in the crook of her left arm, so hard that her body shook. She sobbed like a civilian, even though the Army had trained her not to. "Emotionality causes soldiers to make mistakes." So stated the Army of the Republic Code of Conduct Handbook. Instead of crying when times got tough, it advised taking Draxill LF. Draxill LF was an emotion-suppressing drug that only sounded like the name of a planet. "Relief is just a pill away," the Handbook told soldiers about this miracle pill, because it not only soothed away the ache of losing a friend or loved-one, it also walled off the guilt for a while, just in case you fired on the wrong target.

The drug techs generally recommended its use for those who survived traumatic combat experiences; the more traumatic, the higher the dose. It would keep you functional for the near future, and in certain hot spots, one only had a near future. Clarice certainly had survived some traumatic combat, but she'd known some soldiers who were still hooked on the Drax, even after years separated them from the cause. Some called the Drax a chemical lobotomy. Jervis told her on multiple occasions that the people who accepted the medication were weak, people who couldn't be trusted to do their job, counterintuitive as that may sound. What he meant was that they were relying on the drug to keep them functional, and not doing it themselves. Then again, Jervis was always good at looking into people and seeing characteristics that were invisible to the rest of the world; he believed that the people were better than the drug, but Clarice had her doubts these days.

Clarice sighed as her eye sockets swelled and her nose leaked. It would be nice to lift the burden, even for a little while, but she wasn't going to start down the pathway of chemical absolution. She didn't want to become something she used to hate. Plus, she had no objective reason for living, so her concoction of rage and survivor's guilt might be the only thing keeping her alive. If the drugs took those emotions away from her, she might find herself sucking on the dangerous end of a concussion rifle within a couple hours.

She only enlisted in the military in the first place because she had no place else to go. One of her earliest memories was the day that the

Garvey-Medford Mining Company transferred both of her parents to a colony on Alteth 4. It was a domed colony, and even before experience taught engineers the tragic flaws of designing a dome that size, safety regulations prevented children from accompanying their parents; they were more concerned about the motivations of the miners than the welfare of the minors, but it amounted to the same thing. Five-year-old Clarice kissed Mommy and Daddy goodbye when they left her at that floating boarding school on Linthal. The job was supposed to last for nine months, but the natives on Alteth 4 became restless, as natives are wont to do. The dome cracked. The miners asphyxiated. Clarice grew up alone.

She joined the army after seeing a testimonial advert that described the Army of the Republic as "an instrument of justice." Justice... she'd heard of it, like some mythical deity. She certainly had never seen it, so she decided to find out whether the advert was correct. She cruised through the training. The regimented lifestyle did not differ markedly from her routine at the orphanage, and physical fitness had always served as an outlet for her neuroses. In the end, the training did what it was supposed to. It gave her purpose and structure. She ceased to wonder what the day had in store because someone had already mapped it out on a simulation grid. A stunningly predictable life awaited her.

Then came Jervis. That ruined everything. He usurped the military family and let color intrude upon her gray little world. Emotions bombarded her that she had never felt before since she walled off that part of herself in childhood, and she didn't know how to react. Someone needed her... not a faceless sergeant, but *Clarice Torrance* in all her glory. The feeling, the euphoria of mattering, transformed her into an addict after a while. She grew accustomed to having a reason to get up in the morning beyond the fear of someone storming into her room and overturning her bed. When the working day ended, she actually relished the rush of anticipation from having somewhere to go, besides back to her quarters to clean her weapons. Feeling good became the normal way of feeling.

Now he was gone, barely leaving enough of a body to bury, and her old world clung to her like a recurrent condition, except now she could see the gray that warped the texture of her surroundings. She couldn't go back and pretend that the brightness she had grown to love never existed. She couldn't forget. Even if that were possible, even if she could have stormed down to the neurotechs' lab and ordered them to burn off the memory like a piece of scar tissue, she wouldn't have done it. Jervis had been all she ever had. Now, memories of him were all she had. The military family kept her alive long enough to find love, though, and caught her when she fell. She owed them one final duty. The familial obligation kept her breathing, that and the satisfaction that comes with killing a traitor.

In the blackness of the empty computer screen, another face appeared. The memory of the blue-tinted Azzerello hologram, with its psychotic baby-face, rotated away in front of her. Every day, Leon Azzerello killed his former comrades-in-arms. He enabled others to kill his former comrades by keeping this pointless war going. His paltry force, crawling around in the mountains, operating equipment that would run out of fuel in a matter of weeks, could not possibly win, yet he kept fighting. Each day his pointless, juvenile vendetta persisted, he destroyed more soldiers like Jervis Giles and created more abandoned lovers like Clarice Torrance. Were she able to do so, Clarice would vent her anger on God. God remained immune to concussion blasts, though, so she would gladly settle for destroying Leon Azzerello.

Clarice's eyelashes flicked away the last few residual tears, and she rubbed the corners of her eyes extra hard to teach them a lesson. The cry did her some good. The mortal body had its obligatory spasm of weakness and pushed the poison out through her tear ducts, and now the mind stood purged and ready to press on. She only had to focus enough to stay on the path her superiors laid out before her. Just put one metaphorical foot in front of the other. Her vision and thoughts cleared with each second, and her living hand steadied (the other one didn't need steadying). She was a soldier, and soldiers must perform the function of their assignments. She had a moral and professional prerogative to neutralize Azzerello and allow the occupation of Middes to roll onward with as few casualties as possible.

Her hands clicked over the keys and a name appeared to the left of the blinking cursor. The name belonged to a man she saw in action back at Camp Burden; someone that was barely an acquaintance, but who graduated near the top of the class and whom she trusted and respected. She would take half a dozen cyborgs from the Wraith Squadron down to the surface with her, but she needed at least one other person on the mission who was capable of thinking rather than shooting his way through every obstacle. Just in case something went wrong.

She searched for "Kole, Wilson" on the ship's resident database, and the man's vitals appeared on the screen. The upper half of the report dealt mainly with different technical and clerical classifications, but she already knew about his training because she trained with him. She skimmed over and found out what she needed in the lower half of the document. He was thirty-two years old, four years older than Clarice. He was single, which did not surprise her. She remembered him as rather withdrawn and serious; the kind who would prefer reading a technical manual over playing cards with the boys. He had received a couple of awards that she'd never heard of, fewer than she would have thought. A lack of awards did not imply bad soldiering, however. More likely, it implied not kissing the right asses. What the file did not say, what the computer could not yet know, was that Wilson Kole was about to be sentenced to a death in the line of duty.

Clarice printed the information on the screen and reached for the sheet of paper. With her right arm outstretched, she set her left elbow down on her knee and pinched the bridge of her nose. *Not your problem,* she reminded herself. *You could pick someone less capable, someone you feel less sure of, but it would jeopardize the mission. Everyone would still die, and the only thing it would accomplish is that Azzerello would keep piling up bodies.*

She exhaled, then jerked the paper from the tray, nearly tearing it. Kole was a good soldier. A professional. He would not pout or fuss when he received an assignment. The zombies she planned to order from the Wraith Squadron probably would welcome a fiery death with what little of a mind they had remaining. God knew she welcomed it. Clarice stood up and threw her shoulders back. As far as she was concerned, fate had selected them all. They could complain or go quietly. They could live or die. It wasn't her problem.

*   *   *

Clarice took a deep breath before knocking on a door that should have belonged to Wilson Kole. When the door slid open, the room behind it reminded her of the months she spent as a sergeant before she shared quarters with Jervis. The advantage of receiving this promotion involved moving from the barracks to private quarters. The disadvantage involved the fact that they private quarters felt only slightly larger than a trash receptacle. Kole had made his situation worse by lining his walls with shelving units to set books, *paper* books, upon. He had nearly run out of room, and in several instances, books lay horizontally atop a line of vertical volumes, wedged into the shelf in a haphazard fashion. It was possible that no one told him he could store all the information on a microchip the width of a hair follicle, but more than likely, paper books served as his little eccentricity. Up here, everybody needed their vices to assert their individuality, but this case seemed excessive; when Kole unfolded his bed at night, it must have blocked any migration from the front half to the back half of the room.

Kole answered the door in a plaid bathrobe, carrying a hardcover paper book large enough to render one unconscious if dropped on one's head. Over six years had passed since he left Camp Burden, and war can age a person like nothing else, so she expected some change in his appearance, but Kole looked *completely* different from the man she remembered. His hair had changed from brown and straight to red and curly. His complexion had improved tremendously, but a flat nose with gaping nostrils had replaced his crooked but presentable one. He must have undergone a complete facial reconstruction. A blast, either in an orbiting craft or on the surface, must have melted off his face, and he opted for a different one. A lot of people she served with had undergone facial reconstruction or something similar, and Kole was never a handsome man, so she wouldn't blame him if a bad case of sunburn had prompted the reconstruction. Still, what was he thinking when he requested that nose? If she ducked down a couple inches, she could probably see all the way to his brain. It had to be a mistake.

Kole set down his open book onto the tiny, standard-issue desk beside his left hip and snapped to attention. Clarice could tell by the words on the book's spine that it was some sort of philosophical treatise. That would figure. Only philosophers and aspiring philosophers owned actual, printed books anymore.

"At ease," Clarice said. They held the same rank, but when she wears a dress uniform and he wears a bathrobe, it feels like an appropriate thing to say. In any case, his posture remained stiff. Her eyes still darted around the ridiculously cluttered room. General Frusin would have had this guy court marshaled if he saw this place. "You are Wilson Kole?"

Kole squinted as he examined the small cluster of multicolored decorations on the left side of her uniform. "Yes… Lieutenant," he said.

"You may or may not remember me," she said. "I'm Lt. Clarice Torrance." Now that she thought about it, she had seen his face on the ship before; she just hadn't known it was Wilson Kole. Strange coincidence.

Kole provided a moment of token contemplation before shaking his head. "No, Lieutenant. I'm afraid I don't."

Honest. No pointless ass kissing. At least the in-your-face bluntness that she remembered hadn't changed. That he had no recollection of her merely sped up the unpleasant process for them both. No need to reminisce about their days at Burden, like the time a drill required her to carry him back from the river and she fell so many times that she almost broke both their necks. She didn't even have to ask about his face. If her presence triggered memories of old times later, so be it. She could handle friendships while they were down on the surface, skulking their way across the waste, relying upon one another for survival. Informing someone of his selection to a suicide squad, however, required a maximally detached relationship.

"Regardless," she said, "you have been selected for surface duty." Kole's eyes slid off her, and his shoulders visible sagged when she mentioned the surface. He remained silent, but his manner oozed incredulity. "Is something wrong, soldier?" she asked.

Kole pressed his shoulders back and lifted his gaze. "No, sir... I mean, Lieutenant."

She gave him a hard stare. "I didn't think so," she said with exaggerated disgust. In truth, she was more confused than disgusted. What was his problem? She hadn't even mentioned the specifics of the mission yet. All she said was "surface," and he started to flake out. For all he knew, they were going down to scout extraction sites. Even though they had barely spoken during their time at Camp Burden, he graduated slightly behind her and well within the top ten percent of the class. He always seemed functionally disconnected and quite the opposite of a whiner. Maybe he'd just returned from the surface, or maybe was set to take leave. Maybe she just caught him in his bathrobe while he was reading and it made him uncomfortable. The reason didn't matter... nor did anything else: this was going to happen. "Your equipment will be pre-selected for you. All you need to do is show up at Hangar 37 at 0600."

Clarice turned and strode away from the doorway in case the weakness proved catching. From the corner of her eye, before the sliding door blocked off her view of Kole's new face, his head lowered and his cheeks drooped into an even more pathetic picture. He could not have disappointed her more. Part of her badly wanted to dump him from the mission and take someone with a more positive attitude, but that seemed tantamount to rewarding cowardice. Besides, there was a good chance that the suddenness of the announcement threw him and that he'd pull together once he took his first step out of the hatch and let the training take over. If not, there was always Draxill LF.

She took a few steps in the wrong direction on her way back to the elevator, a little unnerved by her meeting with Kole. What had happened in the years since the Camp Burden that brought him to such a state? Maybe losing his face had traumatized him to the point to where the anxiety never stopped. Maybe he was mad because the technicians screwed up his nose so badly. Those weren't excuses, though. After all, she had lost so much more and could still hold together.

While watching a weakling die would not cause her to lose any sleep (and might prove perversely interesting, in its own way), there was a mission to think about. She could always pick somebody different, but who? She almost stopped in the hallway, almost turned around to tell him to forget it, but she couldn't come up with an answer. She'd never selected someone to die before, and she didn't want to go through the guilt and awkwardness twice in one night. No, Kole would have to do. He was the one she had chosen. Whatever problems he had, he needed to solve them in a hurry and rediscover the man he used to be.

Clarice shook her head as she stalked down the vacant hallway. At least she wouldn't have to worry about weakness in the rest of her landing team. Not while they were under warranty, anyway.

*   *   *

Clarice looked out over a weight room occupied by the only available members of the Wraith Squadron. On the other side of the transparent barrier, a dozen men and women stood at attention, facing Clarice. Some were more heavily muscled than others, but all obviously indulged in a rigorous weight-lifting regimen. The weight room itself looked similar to the one she occupied hours earlier, but the weight machines were bigger, there was no dumbbell rack, and the bars for the free weights were thicker, capable of holding an almost comical amount of weight.

It struck her as strange that they spent so much time lifting weights and building up their live tissue, since the raw amount of weight lifted had little effect on a cybernetic limb's functioning. Maybe they sought that slight advantage, the difference between lifting 800 pounds and lifting 825 pounds, that could help one survive certain situations. Maybe their goal involved intimidation, not function. Bigger people just look scarier, even if we objectively know better. For that reason and others, this group was plenty scary. Their eyes stared vacantly ahead, but the palpable tension of staring at organic statues proved nearly as intense as if they'd been tracking her with their eyes. In the five minutes since they had assumed the formation, not a single one had blinked.

Next to her in the darkened observation room, the commanding officer of the Wraith Squad rambled on like a salesman, "… and one's just as good as the other; fearless, obedient, and tougher than shit. It doesn't matter if you get a man or a woman, an ox or a runt. They're all the same." Clarice turned toward the shrunken, bald officer whose face had more wrinkles than a crumpled paper bag. His black pants, shirt, and cap blended in with the darkness of the observation room. Thankfully, he wore a gold vest, or else it would have felt like speaking with a shrunken, disembodied face.

The man's name was either Colonel Marcus or Colonel Marks. His name wasn't mentioned in the official ship's directory, so she had only heard it spoken by various people, and everyone seemed to pronounce it differently. Most people in that part of the ship just referred to him as "The Colonel." From the engineering room down, the people who lived and worked in that sector could not have accorded him more respect if he had been Fleet Admiral. The Colonel was no prize to look at, certainly not the sort of man one would think commanded a battalion of super-humans, but looking at him did not disturb her as much as looking at his half-human wall of underlings.

"Why are they called 'wraiths'?" she asked, regarding them only momentarily. "Other than that it sounds scary?"

The Colonel fixed one of his bug-eyes on her. "How do you mean?"

"Well, I mean, a wraith is like a ghost, right? Something insubstantial. You could barely fit two of these guys in an elevator."

"Oh, I see," The Colonel replied, nodding. "The name comes from back in the days when they did a lot of drop-in, drop-out special operations missions. Y'know: 'disappear into the night,' that sort of thing. We've become a bit more large and in-your-face since those days. Hell, if there's action on the surface, you can bet your sweet ass the Wraith Squad is going to be in the thick of it."

"Then what is this group doing up here?" she asked. "There's still action on the surface. Have they malfunctioned?"

"Ehh," The Colonel began uneasily, "we prefer to call 'em 'injuries.'" He looked up at Clarice, who stood almost half a foot taller than him, and broke into a yellow-toothed smile, as if they were sharing a sardonic joke. "But, no, they're fine. All were damaged at some point in time, but their testing and rehabilitation period is over. The one's you don't take'll be on the next transport to the surface."

Clarice tried to make eye contact with the smallest of the soldiers, a light-skinned, black-haired female with narrow eyes. In some ways, it was like staring at an over-stuffed, glassy-eyed carcass in a museum. There was something violent lurking inside, though... or something missing that normally kept the violence at bay. Instead of a soul to harness an animal desire to destroy, she had a mass of wires and a relay switch... and while people weren't perfect, neither were machines. Clarice gave up staring after a few seconds and returned her attention to The Colonel. "Were they originally assigned to the Wraith Squadron or was there a choice involved?"

The Colonel's smile broadened. "I see what you're driving at. Don't go thinkin' my people are robots. Hell, no. It's just that their extra training and the cybernetics allow 'em to do things normal soldiers can't. For instance, they can survive an airdrop with nothing more than a clip-on gravity decelerator. And since the time you got here and I lined 'em up for you, have you seen a one of 'em move a muscle?"

Clarice shook her head, unable to see how this oddity disproved her point. "Can't say that I have."

"And you won't, not 'till I give the command," he said, folding his arms across his chest. His nubby fingers were like those of a child; he probably had trouble gripping a normal-sized drinking glass with one hand. "They'd be like that until they collapsed, and that would be from dehydration because those cybernetics wouldn't let up otherwise."

That's handy, she thought, but aloud asked, "What do they run on?" She was only half joking.

"Same as anybody, 'cept a little more," The Colonel said. "We feed 'em about 6,000 calories, mostly protein, every day. In the field, they can go longer without food or water… than a normal person, because we can remotely block those signals from the hypothalamus, but you gotta watch that. They won't complain. Hell, they might not even notice, and you won't know it until they've keeled over."

"Has that ever happened?"

The Colonel laughed. "Y'mean has some of them died from exhaustion? I'm afraid so, just like a normal battalion."

Clarice nodded. It made a crude logic: you gave the best soldiers the equipment to do the most damage; every successful army did that because it was a good return on investment. Still, something about the whole operation set-up in the bowels of the ship struck her as unholy, but she could not quite articulate what it was. "So what about my other question? How did they get here?"

She expected The Colonel to accuse her of badgering him, but he merely pondered the question for a moment, as if he hadn't answered it in a long time. "Well, let's see... you got your critical injuries, of course. Y'know, where they couldn't survive otherwise. And you got your hardcore bad asses, the ones who want to be the toughest S.O.B.'s on two legs. You also get a surprising number that volunteer for the duty because it has a higher rate of survival."

Clarice's eyebrows rose at this statement, and The Colonel noticed. "Oh yeah. The Squad gets the most dangerous spots to play in, but they're engineered to be more than a match for whatever they come across." His palm pressed against his flat chest. "See, one of the first things the techs do is insert armor plating under the skin around the vitals. That makes a direct hit from just about any handheld weapon nothing more than a flesh wound. Then, we hit a button that accelerates their metabolism, and that accelerates their healing time." He shook his head. "Naw, that's all by design. The bean-counters people aren't going to spend all this money juicing 'em up with cybernetics and microprocessors just to dump 'em into a pit to get smashed to bits."

Clarice nodded. "What about a laser mortar round?" she asked, unconsciously flexing her right hand. "Plating won't do much good against that."

"Yeah," the Colonel said with a shrug, "but there are always limits. Those things can take out some small vehicles. Besides, how many people do you know that actually ever survived getting hit by a laser mortar? The number's almost not even big enough to bother counting."

Clarice gave a slow nod and continued to look at her hand. "Yeah," she said, numbly. "Almost."

*   *   *

From the journal of Lt. Wilson Kole:

I really didn't know what Proteum was or what it did; geology and mineral science weren't my area of expertise because I preferred to work with living things. The funny thing was, if you asked any of the soldiers I worked with the same questions, 99% of them would have been unable to give a decent answer, and of the ones who did, most would be guessing. Officially, it was termed an energy source, but it wasn't like our ships and homes were "Protean-powered." Maybe it was a key component in vehicle batteries. Maybe it was something that could be used in weaponry, but that didn't sound like such a good reason to wage a war. No one I know has even seen it, although we're assured that it's buried deep in the ground. So, it's conceivable that there was no such thing as Proteum, and that we just needed a reason to start a war.

That sounds ridiculous, of course, but that's a reflexive, our-leaders-would-never-do-something-like-that response. After all, if an institution ceases to be able to justify itself, the institution is diminished, bureaucratically and through its reputation. If you want to wage a war, and you are the expert on war-waging, no one will stand up and question your analysis. You create a reason, assure everyone that it is a good reason, and start the machinery.

I could be wrong… I probably am. In ten years, maybe all of our vehicles will run for a year on six ounces of Proteum. I hope I'm wrong, because my cynicism doesn't prevent the alternative from terrifying me, while waging a war to extract mineral wealth is just, sadly, normal.

*   *   *

CHAPTER THREE:
THE DESCENT

The little girl didn't sleep much at her new home. Three weeks had passed since she watched her parents fly away, but she still did most of her sleeping during the day, at decidedly inopportune times. Part of the reason was the harassment from the older girls; children can be cruel, especially to younger children. Part of it was the stress that came with threats of future harassment. Mostly, though, the girl feared falling through the cold, dark void.

She didn't understand the technology that made the floating orphanage stable. In her mind, she believed in the competence of the technologists who built the platform and the un-invested people who assured her that standing on the platform did not constitute a death sentence, but her little girl emotions prevented her from feeling comfortable. She lay awake at night, staring at the ceiling, listening to the slow breathing of those around her, but every time she dared close her eyes, the breathing turned to the rush of air as she descended through space.

In all likelihood, the platform constituted a marvel of modern engineering and technology, and she stood an excellent of surviving the night. The fact remained, though, that machines could fail, and it was childish to assume otherwise.

* * *

Clarice checked her wristclock as she paced in the shadow-heavy auxiliary hangar. She might have slept an hour the night before, but she felt the opposite of tired: she felt electric. A white light from overhead reflected off the side of the hangar's lone vessel, a small, dull-gray landing capsule, and illuminated the line of lumpy humanoids in front of her. All but one member of her team stood assembled before her, each carrying enough equipment, weapons, and explosives to snap a normal human in half. None of the Wraiths showed so much as a flicker of strain as they stared forward in the same pose Clarice witnessed in the weight room, hours before.

She carried less than half the equipment weight they did, but she still shifted it around every minute or so to avoid dislocating her spine. The backpack contained most of her gear. The smaller instruments that she used frequently (e.g., flashlight, night-vision goggles) she kept strapped to her limbs. Her black, thermally insulated covert-operations uniform would be enough to keep her warm down on the surface, but it wasn't nearly thick enough to do so while loitering in a frigid hangar. The pacing kept her warm enough.

The Wraiths short-sleeved versions of the same uniform, but if possible, they looked less affected by the cold than they did the weight. Although they came from different ethnic compositions and differed in height, body mass, and gender, each looked like a sibling of one of the others. Any number of things could have given this impression, including the black uniforms with the gold trim, the lack of expression, or the stares that fixated on nothing. The similarity was unmistakable, though: they just represented slightly different models, brothers and sisters born on the same assembly line.

Clarice took a long inhaled through her nose. The distinct odor of industrial lubricant clung to the air, not a pleasant smell, but when you'd been stuck on the ship for weeks, you began to prefer any kind of variation from the antiseptic scent of the rest of the ship. She did her best to avoid looking at her team while she waited for Lt. Kole to arrive. Each Wraith wore a cybernetic attachment over the one eye. The little black boxes left a clear view of the other eye, though, and she had to cope with the eerie stare any time she flanked them from the right. The way they stared at nothing bothered her almost as much as the way they snapped to attention like marionettes each time one heard his or her codename. It bothered her, because the things that made this lifestyle bearable where the human elements: fighting for a cause, having your brother's back. The creatures lined up in front of her were killing machines.

Instead of her unnerving subordinates, Clarice focused her attention on the fist-sized remote control the Colonel handed her when he arrived with the Wraiths she'd ordered. He only stayed a minute, and she kept expecting him to explain its purpose, but he hobbled away on his stiff, stumpy legs without doing so. Who knows? Maybe she gave the mistaken impression that she knew what she was doing.

The gray, plastic remote contained six black, numbered buttons with a larger, unmarked button below them. A plastic cover, currently flipped open, prevented anyone from depressing the buttons by accident. The thumb of her real hand caressed the "6" button, and she felt the inertia of her curiosity, telling her to push it and see what happened. She refrained from doing so, though, mainly by virtue of not being an idiot. For all she knew, the techs had packed these overstuffed bodies with explosives and rigged them to blow.

Clarice checked the time on her digital wristclock for the second time in a minute. The landing capsule departed in fifteen minutes, and she has neither seen nor heard from Lt. Kole. Granted, Hangar 37 was not the easiest to find if you hadn't visited it before. For starters, it measured less than one-tenth the size of a normal hangar and only housed one craft at a time. The carrier ship's designers also deliberately located it in an obscure area just off the infirmary so that crew members of the carrier ship wouldn't interfere with more discrete missions. Still, finding it wasn't *that* complicated if you could read a map. Kole should have arrived. She ran her fingers through her hair and retied her ponytail.

Clarice retraced her previous steps in the darkened hangar with an inconspicuous Bordick 550 Landing Capsule looming over her and half a dozen zombies that did little more than use up air while they stood in a line. "If you're worried about Kole, he's on his way," the voice of Major Lee Drennon said from deep in the shadows. Clarice gave a start because she hadn't even heard him come in. Drennon materialized in the circle of light as he sauntered forward. Maybe it was the angle of the lighting, but he cut a rather handsome figure. Clarice never noticed it before. He lacked the dazzling face or the imposing physique of a classically handsome man, but his obsessive attention to detail pushed his appearance well beyond average. Everything on his uniform and face was neat and symmetrical. Not a hair out of place. He smiled a bit too readily for her taste, though. People who went through life constantly grinning often did so to mask their true feelings and expressions. Either that or they were imbeciles. Drennon was no imbecile, but either way, one could not depend on a grinner. Drennon's standard smile remained fixed in place when he stepped in her direction. Again, maybe it was the lighting, but the smile looked smug and devoid of good intent.

Jervis smiled in public from time to time, as much as a normal human, but he didn't use it as a mask. Even when he was smiling, part of him remained vigilant. Conventional attacks didn't surprise Jervis; he was superhuman in some ways, she thought, her eyes closing for a moment. A burst of bright blue split the darkness, and her eyes flew open. He was perfectly mortal in other ways... obviously. The attack that got him was a freak thing. A blue light raining out of the sky at a random trajectory. The creature that fired it may not have even aimed. Jervis didn't have enough to scream before the bolt incinerated most of his body.

Jervis had a dozen smiles that could say a dozen different things, but only she saw the real one, the one that conveyed happiness and contentment. When they were alone together, he showed it to her all the time. She could tell it was a real smile because the eyes were alive and not hollow, searching for something. Only she could bring it out because he only trusted her. Thinking about it, she felt the corners of her mouth start to pull upward. Then she thought about how she would never see the lips, the teeth, or the eyes again and wanted to gut herself with the serrated knife strapped to her thigh. The constant shifting of emotion was making her sick to her stomach. She needed to get down to the surface. She needed to focus... on something, or else start popping pills. "Um, Major?" she asked, turning to Drennon. "What is this remote control for?"

Drennon peered at the gray, plastic mechanism she held in front of him. "Remote-destruct switch," he said. "It has a range of about a hundred yards. Just press the bottom button, the number of the one you want to dispose of, then the bottom button again. There's a delay of about two seconds."

Clarice glanced at her line of troops and noticed for the first time that each wore a different single-digit number on its backpack strap... no doubt for ease in destroying. If they overheard the comment, they failed to react. "What's the point in that?" she asked.

"Well, you never know when it might come in handy, but generally speaking, our scientists didn't want our enemies to analyze our cybernetic technology, so we fit a mechanism to release incendiary fluid into the limbs and the power source housing to dissolve the whole frame down to a big pile of metal in a matter of minutes. It used be rigged to detonate whenever the Wraith's heart would stop, but a couple times that has happened in close quarters and things got messy when the incendiary fluid contacted healthy flesh. We've since changed it to a manual process."

Clarice nodded as though she understood perfectly, even though it wasn't the sort of scenario she ever contemplated. She'd never heard of a fluid that could do what he described, but then again, that wasn't her primary specialty. She checked in the direction that Drennon came from but still found no sign of Lt. Kole. "Personally," Drennon continued, "I think the old man's off his nut. I think the whole thing is going to be a spectacular failure." He waved a hand dismissively. "Not my call, though."

"Major?" Clarice asked, suddenly feeling genuinely attentive. She'd heard more optimistic farewells in her time... although, at least he used the term "spectacular." "Why did General Frusin come out of retirement?"

Drennon's fake smile broadened to the point of strain. "Because he couldn't hack it in the political arena," he answered without hesitation. "The man hasn't commanded troops in ten years, and the Council still couldn't wait to put him in charge. Ten years... taking land vehicle speed alone into account, do you know how much terrestrial warfare has changed in the last ten years?"

Clarice shook her head. She didn't doubt that Frusin failed as a politician. That amounted to a compliment in her book. What surprised her was Drennon. She doubted that he often got this worked up in front of an audience.

"More than him, I'll bet," Drennon continued. "He asks me everything: who his subordinates are, the names of locations on the surface, where we have troops located, all the vehicle and artillery specifications… It's ridiculous."

Despite her discomfort, Clarice nodded along as her commanding officer ranted on. Her impassive subordinates remained impassive. Drennon was no more a field commander than Frusin was a politician. People in his position were supposed to stoically issue commands and inspire confidence even when they had none. Maybe that's why Drennon got bypassed in the first place. Not like she could do anything about anything, though… or would even if she could. What the hell did she know? She just did her job, and these issues were not part of that job. "Why don't they just let you run the occupation?" she offered.

Drennon drew in a deep breath, as though preparing to unleash another list of complaints. He absorbed the inhalation, though, as he scanned the darkness surrounding him. Cameras lay in every hallway and chamber of the carrier ship, with lenses that detected anything down to a body heat signature and microphones that not only picked up the most inaudible whisper, they could translate it from any known language. Drennon spent most of his life on ships just like this one and knew its surveillance capabilities well. You could whisper in a dark corner or in the midst of a fireworks show. All that mattered was whether someone viewed the monitor at the right time. Your only defense was the volume of data generated. If they were looking and listening, they would see you and hear you. Someone like Drennon would know exactly which feeds were high-priority and which weren't. Still, when Drennon spoke to Clarice, he leaned in and said in a low volume, "Except for a few brainstorms, like this one, I am running it," he said. "Most of the time, he doesn't know enough to contradict my advice… but the council needed to make a P.R. move to overshadow Harvath's screw-ups. So I got rooked out of a promotion because one of Frusin's political allies thought he'd be perfect as a figurehead."

Clarice nodded on cue. Maybe this little tiff between Drennon and Frusin had launched her and her people into a war zone to get torn apart for no reason. She almost felt offended before she thought of Jervis and the hunk of over-cooked meat he'd become the last time she saw him. After that image sunk into its customary void in her soul, she hoped the landing capsule would explode before they even detached.

The double-doors that led to the main hallway opened, and Lt. Wilson Kole shuffled toward them. He approached his mission commander fully clothed, but clutched his flak jacket, helmet, and equipment belt against his chest in a balled-up mass. When he stopped in front of her, his feet pointed outward, and he looked like a civilian attending a costume party dressed as a soldier.

Clarice sighed as Kole tried to shift his mass of equipment into one arm so that he could provide a half-assed salute. "I'm not late, am I?" he asked.

Clarice squeezed her eyes closed and shook her head. "No. Just get on board." She pointed to the Wraith at the far left end of the line, a bald, brown-skinned male and the biggest of the bunch. "Numbers One through Six," she said. A shudder ran through her as they simultaneously snapped their heads in her direction. She needed a moment to remember what she had planned to say. "Board the ship," she said. The Squad stomped toward the loading ramp in lockstep.

Clarice turned back to Drennon and found that his smile had reappeared. This one looked genuine, as though he found something humorous. "You don't have to worry about me, Major," she said in a low voice. "Our conversation will remain between the two of us."

Drennon looked over Clarice's shoulder, where Kole shuffled up the ramp and stumbled when he saw the Squad members tramping toward him from behind. Drennon let out a spurt of laughter at the graceless near-spill. "Oh, I'm sure it will," he said. "I'm sure it will."

* * *

The landing capsule lurched as it detached itself from the main ship. *This is it*, Clarice thought while her lungs pulled in and pushed out dry, processed air a few spoonfuls at a time, *there's no going back*. The transport technicians designed the thrusters of the capsule primarily for lateral movement. You could guide your descent with a high degree of accuracy, but you couldn't go planet-to-planet in one of these babies. The compressors located on the bottom of the capsule provided adequate thrust to create a soft landing but lacked the power to overcome the pull of Middes's gravitational field. So, she *literally* could not go back. *Nothing to go back to*, she reminded herself, and this helped her let go of the reflexive fear.

From the right half of the cramped cockpit, Kole swallowed what may have been a gasp as he glanced out the front window as the gray tube-shaped monstrosity that was Carrier 219 receded into the starlit sky. With both elbows locked out and his mouth hanging open, he looked so pathetic that a part of Clarice felt sorry for him. She clenched her teeth, though, and tried to become cold and objective. So strange that he'd lost the one thing she remembered about him: cool competence. He obviously wouldn't be snapping out of his spastic state any time soon, and he very likely might end up costing them the mission. "Cowards are like ticking bombs when put in positions of responsibility," Jervis once told her, long before the two of them ever made physical contact. She knew every inch of his body, every scar from every battle he ever—

The white glare of a fighter's thrusters flashed in front of her, and Clarice banked hard to her right, narrowly avoiding the larger vehicle's flight path. She had absentmindedly let the ship drift over by the main docking bay and into the path of a Heckler 470. That 470 was three times their size and would have blown their tiny landing capsule into a thousand pieces if the pilot had accelerated through them, or at the very least, the ship's wing would have torn their hull open, and she, Kole, and the Wraiths would have asphyxiated in the cold, empty space. The Wraiths probably would have remained dull eyed and unmoved as they pinwheeled through the void, but she and Kyle would have flapped about like Gelbaks on a frying pan until they froze, exploded, or suffocated. She shuddered, unable to tell which felt worse: almost sending them to an excruciating death or almost sending them to an excruciating death minutes into the mission.

Next to her, Kole stared out the front of the cockpit, his wide eyes looking like a child's. Clarice had not been much of a mission commander at this point, even before the near collision. If she glanced behind her, the six soldiers in the back of the capsule would still sit impassive as statues, but they very well might have had their ability to emote surgically removed. That made Kole the only gauge of her performance. He might have been a coward, a shadow of the man she barely knew. It might have been from losing his face... God only knew what effect that had on a person... or from something else, but she knew from personal experience that a good commanding officer could bring out the soldier in anyone.

Clarice's expression softened. She glanced over at Kole and said, casually, "Whew. That was a close one."

Kole replied with an immediate, nervous nod. "Yeah, that was some good piloting to get us... to get us past it."

Clarice shrugged off the compliment. "I should've never got that close to the docking door. It was a stupid mistake. Besides, in this thing, it isn't so much piloting as controlling the free fall. I could take my hands off the controls and the computer would take us to the landing site."

Kole nodded, no doubt hoping she would keep her hands securely locked onto the u-shaped steering system. Every click and beep from inside the pod seemed to fire a fresh bolt of panic through him.

Clarice turned long enough to look him over. "You don't remember me from training, do you?" Before they could get too cozy, she reminded herself that they were not alone in the transport capsule and took a quick look over her shoulder. Crammed into the two long benches, the members of the Wraith Squad stared mutely forward, like robots with their power supplies removed.

His dark, bushy eyebrows dove. "Training?" he asked and shook his head. "No, I don't recall seeing you there at all." Speaking seemed to calm him, or at least distract him. "I'm sure I would have remembered you," he added quickly, his eyes briefly darting in her direction.

"That's odd," Clarice said, "because I remember you pretty clearly. We even partnered up on a couple of the skill challenges."

Kole squinted. "Really?"

"Yeah," she assured him. "You looked a lot different then."

Kole looked out the window to his right, and Clarice thought she must have touched upon a sensitive topic. "I've seen a... you on the carrier, several times," he said. "You were always with Jervis Giles, but –"

Clarice whipped her head in Kole's direction. "You knew Jervis?"

Kole's confusion deepened. "Yeah, we weren't... pals or anything," he said, hooking a thumb over his shoulder. "He just graduated with me from the Academy, so I... saw him from time to time."

Clarice shook her head. "No. Jervis graduated from Flint Harbor Military Academy."

Kole nodded, quite sure of himself on this one. "Exactly. Flint Harbor. Class of '49."

An idea began to take shape, and it caused a chill to creep under Clarice's skin, despite the climate-controlled cabin. "You never went through Camp Burden?"

"No," Kole admitted. After a moment, his body relaxed, and his eyes brightened under the red-hued lighting. "Oh, I think I know what it is. You're probably thinking of the Wilson Kole stationed over in the fifty-fourth regiment. The only reason I know is because I once got his pay credits transferred to my account by mistake. I think he was in—"

"Reconnaissance," she said with a barely audible breath.

"Yeah," Kole said happily, glad to have solved the mystery. "You must have had me confused with him." Satisfied, he started to turn toward the front window, then froze. Kole's smile fell off his face as though it just got stuck in the Middesian gravitational field. "Ohh. You must have had me confused with him."

Clarice took her hands off the pod's controls and rubbed her face, from forehead to chin. Maybe if she rubbed hard enough, the numbness would go away. "Yeah," she said.

They sat in the front of the cabin, as silent and motionless as the half dozen soldiers behind them, as the capsule drifted toward the orange mists of Middes's atmosphere. The only sound came from the steady hum of the air circulator. Kole looked like he might shatter if anyone touched him. She returned her hands to the steering apparatus, to give the illusion of control. Several seconds passed before Clarice spoke. "So what is your primary specialty?"

"Botany," he said, almost apologetically.

She winced on the inside... maybe a little on the outside, too. "And your secondary?" Every soldier was required to have training in a field directly applicable to the military. Even if he needed a crash course to brush up on the basics, Kole's secondary specially *had* to be more useful than Botany.

"I have two, actually," Kole said. Clarice found her eyes rotating in his direction, hopefully. *Two chances are better than one.* "Psychology and Maritime Fortifications."

Nope. Maritime Fortifications might have been useful, if the nearest body of water didn't reside over six hundred miles away from their landing site. Part of her felt betrayed, even though she had all this information at her fingertips hours ago, had she bothered to click on the file and look at anything on the screen other than "Wilson" and "Kole." "Wonderful," Clarice sighed. "A Botanist. I didn't even know there were any plants on the surface."

"I lot of people don't realize it because it's such a small planet, but there are several spots with fairly dense vegetation, especially down by the equatorial regions," Kole informed her, nervously. As he spoke, his right knee bounced around with a life all its own. "Have you ever been down to the Korilian Swamps?"

"It's the Swamps of Korilas," Clarice corrected, her hands tightening on the controls. "And, yes, I was stationed there for a six months."

Kole shifted in his seat. "Even in the rocky areas, there are quite a few plant species. You'd be surprised."

"I'm sure I would," Clarice said in a monotone.

She let go of the controls. They drifted toward their inevitable destination.

*   *   *

From the journal of Lt. Wilson Kole:

I suppose it could be said that I was smitten with Clarice Torrance long before she graced my doorway. By civilian standards, she would have been quite plain, but in the military, with a two-to-one male-to-female ratio and a lifetime away from the civilian world, she appeared as an ethereal beauty that drifted around the ship, and whenever I would glimpse her face, it sent a surge of electricity through me. To me she was exotic, more so than most of my female coworkers, but there also existed a strange contradiction of strength and fragility about her. She seemed to be compensating, and this deep self-doubt always made her seem somehow attainable to me. Although I will never know the answer, my personal hypothesis is that she joined the military because she was too sensitive. Her sensitivity made her aware of her own weaknesses, but being alone as she was, she had no one to lean on while she nurtured this sensitivity, so she tried to eliminate it. The structure of the life in the Army of the Republic removed the ambiguity of her world, made things make sense, and made her one of the good guys. Typing the words out now, it still seems like a hypothesis, a fantasy, even. Maybe she joined the army because she was poor.

Regardless, I don't know what I was thinking when I saw her standing there. I opened the door, and there stood my Angel of Carrier 219. Life throws people and personalities at you, and while most pass over you like water, some of them flow through you, and you cannot help but feel great, sometimes uncontrollable, affinity for. I don't think a genuine bond ever existed between us. We barely knew one another. I think I wanted someone who needed me. Regardless of their opinion of the man, everyone knew about Jervis Giles' death, and even though I'm not a handsome or charming man, I thought I could help her at that time. I could see the pain in her face and how hard she tried to keep it from consuming the remains of her life. I needed to be needed. That may have been part of the reason I didn't ask any questions when she told me I had been selected for surface duty... with her.

In retrospect, I should have been smarter. I should have spoken up. I should have remained objective. Above anything else, I shouldn't have let myself want her. We both would have been better off.

*   *   *

CHAPTER FOUR:

GUTLESS

The orphan sits on the near edge of the landing platform, her arms encircling the shins of her tucked legs. The sun has receded to a soft pink glow in the western sky, and she leans back to contemplate the cluster of five stars struggling into existence above her. The pattern of the stars forms a larger star, but when she looks at it, the points of brightness remind her of the rear thrusters of the ship that took her parents away. They were supposed to be gone nine months. Then came the announcement that they were "unavoidably detained" for a "nonspecific duration," words she'd heard before but not in that combination. She waited. Messages that had arrived daily became messages that arrived weekly. Warm, personal messages became distinctly formal messages that all sounded the same.

After a few months of anxious waiting, she happened to read a personal text transmission to her friend Michelle from Michelle's parents. It read just like the transmission her own parents had sent three weeks earlier. The teachers had urged them to erase the messages, something about "jeopardizing the integrity of the mission," but she saved all of them. She checked her files. It was the exact same message, except for the name at the top and the names at the bottom.

Yesterday, the school matron called the orphan into her office. "Clarice," she said, after they exchanged pleasantries and Clarice climbed into the cushy, leather chair that sat across from the desk, "I have some terrible news." Clarice had already deduced that her parents were dead before the school matron told her. The recycled messages provided all the evidence she needed. She didn't say this, though; even for children, the punishment for disobeying orders is severe. The forewarning did no good. She remained silent while the matron spoke and did not cry. The crying would come later, but for now, it was all too much, like finding out that the world was ending. The matron noted the dry eyes and sent her out for counseling. Clarice spent her seventh birthday talking with a Mental Health Official. The only present she received was one of the many prescriptions for child-strength Draxill LF issued that week.

*   *   *

The base of the landing module slid into the dusty surface of Middes and lurched to a stop with a well-calculated thud. After conducting a cost-benefit analysis, the manufacturers of the Bordick 550 Landing Capsule decided to eliminate landing gear altogether. Instead, the pod's navigational computer calculated the distance at which to begin employing the lower air compressors, and the crew strapped themselves in. It made for a rough, but cheap, one-way landing. It was a deployment pod, after all, and no one planned to send crippled or severely wounded people charging from the Bordick 550's hatch.

The hatch swung upward on the port side of the egg-shaped pod, and Wraith One marched into the gently swirling red dirt, defying any hidden enemies to take a shot at him and expose themselves. If any enemies had lined him up in their scopes, they saw a tall, thickly muscled black man who had no hair on his body. Wraith One began removing the hair himself with an electric needle during his first week on the Squad. When someone asked him why, he said, "It slows me down." Within seconds, the form-fitting clothing that had been black inside the pod transformed into a faint, brownish-red, a camouflage feature that the clothing technicians found decreased one's chances of being shot by over fifteen percent.

Wraith One closed his eye exposed to the spray of dust. Using the black box attached over his right eye, he scanned the rocky terrain with a thermal detection system and found no other life forms on the ground or above it. The rocks and the dirt had a reddish tint to them, but since the sky did as well, the many shades of red the planet had to offer probably came more from the atmosphere and the light of the two red suns in the solar system than the actual color of the land. The first sun had already begun to set, but the second still bathed the land in a coat of crimson. Wraith One did not appreciate the landscape's aesthetic nuances, however; he was looking for something living to move so that he could shoot it. After completing a second visual sweep and giving his thermal sensor plenty of time to detect the body heat signatures of any intruders, Wraith One raised his fist to signal for the others to exit.

Wraith Two left the module next. She strode stiffly forward, clutching the barrel and the handle of her concussion rifle. A twenty-something woman with close-cropped red hair, she wore a cybernetic attachment over her left eye instead of her right. She stood almost a foot shorter than Wraith One, and was about half as thick, but she carried her pile of equipment with equal ease.

Wraith Three followed her. Deep acne scars delved their way through his profoundly ugly face. Shrapnel from an exploding hoverbike had lacerated the left half of his nose and the technicians merely grafted some synthetic flesh over the wound and closed off the nostril completely. The color match for the skin tone wasn't perfect, but at that point, aesthetics weren't an issue. He was squat to the point of resembling a hunchback, but the thickness of his arms biceps and thighs rivaled the waist of a normal human. He must have been something of a juggernaut even before the technicians crammed all that plastic wiring and metal under his skin.

Clarice and her botanist exited next, both with tentative steps. Since the Field Techs hadn't grafted a cybernetic eye to either of their faces, both wore yellow-tinted goggles to protect them from the dust and sun. Kole gingerly tiptoed off the ramp because of his minimal experience entering hostile environments and his complete lack of experience working with anything like the Wraith Squad. The two factors created a downright surreal situation for him, like strapping a saddle on a Sand Banta and fooling yourself that you had some semblance of control over the situation.

The familiar scenery caused Clarice to hesitate. The Wharrib Mountain Chain. The name came from Kartar Wharrib, the first human to set foot on Middes. Wharrib originally thought that this region of the planet was uninhabited, but soon found out that the natives lived mostly in subterranean tunnel networks. The natives probably had their own, ancient name for the mountains, but Kartar Wharrib never learned it, so neither did Clarice Torrence. The geography of most of the region really didn't resemble mountains so much as steep, red hills stretching in every direction, but as you drifted northward, you started to run into actual, craggy, steep, snow-capped mountains. Once the second sun set and a cool purple shadow slipped over the country side, this stretch of barren land would look exactly like the place she was the last time she set foot on the surface, when she lost both her arm and her reason to live. On this part of the planet, it was difficult to distinguish one locality from the next, and the odds were astronomical that it could be the exact same place, but she still reflexively scanned the ground, looking for remains of Jervis poking out of the dirt. The familiarity of the landscape cued up a series of images in her memory cells, none of which were remotely pleasant. At least it wouldn't be lit up in bright blue hues.

After the officers exited the transport, Wraiths Four through Six followed. Wraith Four was a male with high cheekbones and spiked black hair, Five was pale and had dirty, blond hair, and Six was a black woman with a flat-top haircut. Each was quite distinct at first glance, just like the first three were, but after a while, their features started to run together. They moved alike and they moved together, operated by the same puppeteer.

Machine, Clarice told herself as she fought off the emotions that came with being back on the surface. She focused on clamping her lips closed and letting her facial muscles go slack. *I'm a machine.* It looked so much like the exact location where Jervis died that, when she started to face forward, out of the corner of her eye, she thought she saw a Jervis-shaped indentation in the dust. She should have feared setting the pod down in the area, fear for her life and her sanity. All sorts of danger still lurked in the region, and if a battle broke out around her, one like the night she lost her arm, she might not be able to resist the urge to blindly rush forward in the hope of dying so that the pain would end. Fortunately, she did not feel pain or fear or emptiness, because she was a machine.

*   *   *

The Squad moved out and began their march over the blasted, uneven terrain. The thrusters of the deployment pod would never propel them into orbit, so its work was done. All the pods contained a timed implosion switch, to get rid of the evidence of a landing, but with the volume of wrecked vehicles in this region, the result of nearly four years of intense fighting, Clarice has no problem leaving their vehicle intact as long as its former occupants remain undetected. Grounded transport pods were a common sight in the Wharrib, eight soldiers marching alone was not.

The week of relative inactivity caused her cardiovascular condition to deteriorate to a point that Clarice had to jog to keep up with the Wraiths. Shifting the bulk of her rucksack to her artificial shoulder relieved some of the strain, but ultimately, her legs supported all the weight. The strain on her knees would add up, and she had to be careful exerting herself in this atmosphere. While adequate to sustain human life, the oxygen-poor environment made it common for soldiers to pass out while marching. If the environment got too rough for her lungs, she could break out the breather mask stashed in her ruck.

They trudged forward in the general direction of a chunk of land that Army Intelligence determined was the most likely site for Azzerello's base. Clarice scanned the horizon, looking for heads poking up in the distance, but most of her attention remained on the weight on her back and the ground under her feet. When the war started, there were a few incidents where heavily encumbered soldiers fell into one of the subterranean tunnels the Middesians lived in. Then, the Middesians got the hint and started intentionally digging tunnels dangerously close to the surface. Republican soldiers would fall in and get atomized before anyone even saw a target. The tunnel strategy worked well, even after the Field Techs invented the density gages, which would tell if a surface was sturdy enough to support a soldier's weight. The strategy backfired, though, after the advent of the Hellhounds, these mean, little, metal, four-legged… creatures the weapons techs designed to burrow into the tunnels and discharge poison gas. Then, of course, the Middesians just packed the tunnels full of explosives, abandoned them, and waited for the Hellhounds to trip the detonators.

Wars characteristically featured those back-and-forth strategic adjustments. The bottom line: Clarice worried that, with the weight most of these Wraiths were packing, they might break through at any moment. It would be the easiest way to kill them. It's what she would've done... were she fighting a Wraith Squad. Someone up in the ship surely thought of that earlier, though, and had taken the necessary precautions. Maybe that was one of the functions of the cybernetic eyes.

An hour of marching passed, following Wraith One to the destination zone, then another hour. Two hours that, to her knowledge, they might have spent walking in circles. Everything certainly looked the same. Her legs churned away, far beyond the point she would have thought possible, given her conditioning. Her knees, ankles, and hips engaged in a race to see which would give out first. Thankfully, Kole saved her the humiliation of announcing a rest. While completing their descent of one of the larger hills, she felt a tapping on her shoulder. She turned to find Kole barely keeping pace to her right, his clear plastic breather mask in place, its hose dangling in front of him like an insectoid proboscis. "Can... we... stop for a minute?" he begged breathlessly.

Clarice narrowed her eyes and pretended to weigh the matter before holding up a fist. "Halt," she called out. At the sound of the command, the Wraiths stopped marching, gravitated into a semi-circle, squatted on their haunches, and dug through their rucksacks with no further prompting. They made each movement in eerie unison. No one could mistake Kole for a well-oiled machine, though: he all but collapsed backward into a seated position, his legs splayed out in front of him.

Clarice eased her pack off her right shoulder, then felt her stiffened vertebrae pop as she threw her shoulders back and overcorrected to her left. Her back always seemed to get stiff in the exact same place during marches. Maybe she should see the marching therapist about her form. *Yeah*, she thought wistfully, *you do that right as soon as you get back to the carrier...* She drew in deep, deliberate breaths as she ran the corner of a small rag into the crevices of her goggles. To her right, Wraith 3 (the one with half a nose) squeezed his high-protein paste from a silver, foot-long tube. He sucked on the open end like a breast-feeding infant, slurping at the tube's contents and lapping up the stray bits with his long, thick tongue. The others ingested calories in a similar, albeit slightly more refined, fashion. For a moment, they looked less like machines and more like livestock at a trough.

Clarice would ingest the contents of her own protein tube later. The tubes she carried looked a lot like the paste the Wraiths consumed, but the formula provided nutrients more suitable for a normal human. It tasted like modeling clay and looked like infant defecant, but it provided a lightweight source of vital nutrients, nourishing the body, if not the soul. After witnessing the Wraiths chow down, though, loudly smacking their six sets of lips with each bite, she doubted her mind could handle ingesting the thick, chewy paste. Her original unit commander, the late Lt. Dontz, used to say, "If you aren't in the mood to eat your protein paste, wait an hour. At some point, you'll be hungry enough to chew wet sand."

Several feet away, Kole still lay flat on his back. Clarice took a few steps in his direction and leaned over him. "Think you'll make it?" she asked, more curious than concerned.

He paused from his hyperventilating long enough to tilt his green eyes in her direction and give her a sober look. "Would... it ... matter... if I... said, 'No?'"

She shook her head, feeling oddly refreshed after basking in Kole's sorry state. "Not for your situation," she said. "That transport isn't coming back for us until the mission's done."

"That's... what... I... thought," Kole said before lifting his mask, twisting his head to the right, and expelling a thick, white glob of spit onto the red dirt. He drew in a couple labored breaths before continuing. "How do they know when the mission's done?"

"My understanding is that Major Drennon has cameras hooked up to the Wraiths' cybernetic eyes," she said and tapped her right eyebrow to indicate the location of most of the cameras.

"What if they all die before we do?" Kole asked. He said it quietly, but all six Wraiths turned in his direction. Though their faces remained impassive, Clarice could detect a glimmer in each of their organic eyes that conveyed a very real danger. It was moments like this that made her wonder if she really was in charge. Kole lacked the nerve to look in their direction, but surely he could feel every ounce of their punishing stares. He swallowed the lump in his throat and returned his attention to Clarice.

Clarice pulled the top of her left boot tighter and pushed the steel clamp down around its rim. "I think they would assume that without the Wraiths, we wouldn't last very long."

Before she could see Kole's reaction, she shifted her gaze to the rapidly darkening horizon. A few stars glimmered in the dark violet overhead, a familiar, five-pointed pattern among them. Clarice didn't delude herself into thinking that it was the same cluster she stared at as a child, but she still averted her eyes. Her team would have to switch to night vision soon, and that prospect made her uneasy. If anything more than a spark flashed in front of somebody using night vision, it could blind the person for up to a minute. The Wraiths remained equally susceptible, since most of them failed to upgrade their organic optical structures. A massive headache accompanied the condition, as well, but headaches in the field rarely killed a person. Blindness did it like clockwork.

Clarice slid her thin, black gloves off of her hands and shook them to get the dirt and sand out. Enemy lines did not exist in a guerilla war. Collections of combatants randomly ran into other collections of combatants, both above the ground and under it. The preceding years of war had all but eliminated the indigenous population in the area, not that civilian casualties prey heavily upon one's mind during a war of occupation. While following a policy of conquest, the Republic had the luxury of engaging in planet-wide genocide. Survivors of the war probably would succumb to genocide-by-neglect. Only Middes's natural resources were important, anything else was a nuisance, at best. It was heartless, but not without reason: the Republic badly needed those resources. In particular, they needed something called "Proteum." Clarice didn't know what it was, but she wasn't a geologist. It supposedly could be used as a power source, and without a power source for the vehicles and machines of the Republic, humans could die, more humans than the entirety of Middes's sparse population. Either way, good or evil wasn't for a soldier to decide.

If enemy lines did exist, Clarice and her collection of soldiers would have crossed them moments after landing. During the real war, the hunk of land they had marched into saw some of the hottest action, and enough crashed vehicles, mangled skeletons, and discarded weaponry dotted the landscape to prove it. Intelligence had triangulated Leon Azzerello's location based on his verified activities of the last few days, and Wraith One steadily led them toward the middle of the triangle. As they encountered enemy combatants or individual aircraft (hopefully not directly), they would plug that information into the equation and narrow down his whereabouts further.

Clarice unscrewed the top of her canteen and took a sip of the carbo-fluid. She glanced behind her, toward the direction they had come from. Their tracks remained etched in the dirt, despite the intermittent wind gusts. It wouldn't matter if the enemy troops saw their tracks: they were maintaining a hell of a pace. How far had they marched? She had no idea, but she could continue marching through the night if she gave herself a break every couple hours. Kole, though, would only last a couple hours, total. He rose to a sitting position a few paces behind her, his shoulders sagging forward as his breathing finally receded to a normal rate. Wouldn't they all be safer if he were dead? The answer, of course, was "yes," but she refused to shoot him… for the near future.

Wraith Four's spiky hair faced her. He sat a few paces in front of her with his legs crossed under him, his head bent toward the ground while he munched on a mouthful of paste. *Those things can keep going until their organs implode*, she thought. The propagandists advertised the Wraiths as half human. Watching them masticate in unison on a substance that could probably clog a fan blade made her think boasts like that were massive overstatements. She once heard a rumor that the Wraiths were developed as a substitute in the field for cyborgs. Adding to an existing skeletal structure and nervous system supposedly cost less than growing your own organic tissue and relying on artificial intelligence. She never found any confirmation of this rumor, but one rarely did on those sorts of things.

Wraith Four noticed her staring and glared back in a way that a soldier should never look at his commanding officer. His eyes narrowed to slits as though trying to bore their way through her. She did not look away, but she did get the impression that he was considering all the ways to kill her with his bare hands. After a few seconds, Clarice broke eye contact. She wouldn't win a stare-off with one of these things, not if she valued her eyesight. The image from back on the ship, when The Colonel lined up all the unblinking drones he had in stock, stuck in her mind. They could probably keep staring until their eyes fell out of their heads. *They are good soldiers*, she reminded herself. *Superhumanly good. And they made a choice to be that way.*

She pinched her right forearm with her left fingertips. It felt like flesh. At some point, the electrical signals in the limb are transferred to electrochemical signals so that the brain can read them. It was part of her body now… so why does it feel less like an arm and more like a weapon strapped to her shoulder? She could never see herself doing a mass replacement like the freaks over there chewing their cud. They weren't really human anymore, just… human-ish. Maybe something bad happened to them, though, something they wanted to forget about. Maybe the Republic was all they had, and they wanted to do their best to see it preserved. From *that* point of view, she could certainly see –

The low hum of an engine cut through the rush of the wind and scattered her thoughts. Clarice's eyelids spread, and she spent two seconds listening and staring at the sky before she could determine the direction of the sound's source. East. It was coming from the East. "Incoming!" she shouted. "Three o'clock!" She need not have yelled; the Wraiths had begun to take evasive action before she even spoke, and Kole had no idea what she was talking about. Essentially, she warned herself.

Clarice reached behind her to the lower corners of her rucksack and grasped the plastic rings waiting there. In a practiced motion, she dropped to her knees, pressed her face in the dirt, and brought her hands and the retractable wrap over her head as the low flying craft shot across the darkening sky. She gulped. *Don't flake out, don't flake out*, she told herself, but this was her first action since… well, her world ended. The distinctive whine of the vehicle's engine identified it as a well-maintained

Heckler 452, but since Azzerello's defection, it could belong to either side. One side could kill them as easily as another, since only the highest of the Army's higher ups knew about her mission; on the instruments, they would look like just another group of heavily armed soldiers in enemy territory. Feeling somewhat safe under the wrap with her hands stretched over her head, Clarice counted silently. *One one-thousand, two one-thousand...* Kole interrupted her count, though, when he asked, "Hey, what's going on?"

The anti-thermal wraps looked like large, brown, camouflage sheets. Nearly weightless, they pulled out from the bottom of a soldier's rucksack. A soldier merely dropped into a crouch and pulled the wrap over their head. The Army issued the wraps to small groups of soldiers for this very reason, so that during reconnaissance missions, Republican soldiers could camouflage themselves from enemy aircrafts. A low-grade circuitry woven into the cloth dispersed body heat and made it much more difficult for the craft's thermal sensors to pick up the signature of the soldier under the wrap. They proved quite effective when every soldier in a platoon used one. How effective could they be, though, when seven members of a team covered up and one stood gawking with his thumb up his ass? With any luck, the pilot or anyone else on the Heckler 452 that spotted Kole would mistake him for a lone, incredibly stupid soldier separated from his unit. Certainly not a threat.

Beneath the cover of her wrap, Clarice gritted her teeth and listened to the receding sound of the engines. It would have been convenient to blame Kole in this situation; he was not much of a soldier. Had she bothered to ask him back on the ship whether he was at least semi-competent, though, he probably would have told her the truth. He had never served in a combat situation on the surface and, since they become standard issue only after he left the academy, had probably only heard of the wraps in passing conversation. Most of his equipment had been issued to him that morning, not self-selected, so he probably didn't even know he had one. Kole clearly would not live through the mission, and Clarice again wondered if the good of the many did not outweigh the temporary good of the few, especially when deaths far, far more painful than a concussion blast to the temple lay in wait for all of them.

*   *   *

Clarice kept her elbows locked and her head between them for several long seconds as she reminded herself to keep breathing. She pictured the Heckler 452 barreling into her back, or the side of the hill collapsing on her while she sat there like an idiot. Back in her early school years, the "lights out" hours frightened Clarice, but so did the probable reprimand she would receive if she brought the issue up with any of the personnel. Instead, she pulled the covers over her head, rationalizing that the monsters that lurked in the shadows might miss her and move on to the more visible members of the ward. The strategy must have worked well enough; she survived her school years. The downside to this experience was that, while no longer afraid of darkness, Clarice had developed a rather persistent case of claustrophobia.

The instant the engines became inaudible, Clarice released the corners of her wrap and let it snap back into the bottom of her rucksack. Kole stood in front of her, vulnerable as a newborn babe, his shoulders drooping and his right hand scratching his stubbled cheek. The index finger of his left hand hung limply from one of the plastic rings. The look on his face reminded her of someone in shock after surviving an explosion. He knew what he did, and even though Clarice tried to get angry, she couldn't. This moment resulted solely from her decision; she pulled him into this by selecting a complete stranger, because it was easier for her than killing someone she knew, and a complete stranger was what she got. Now, not only was Lt. Kole doomed to die, he might end up crippled or brain-damaged before he reached that point.

"Lt. Torrance," a deep voice said from behind her, causing Clarice to unsnap the Rivo 40, standard-issue concussion laser on her hip and spin around to face the speaker. A massive chest hovered at eye level. Clarice's eyes traveled upward to see Wraith One's hairless face glowering down at her. His voice surprised her more than if one of the small boulders dotting the landscape had spoken. "May I have a word with you?" his granite-like jaw barely moved when he spoke. It didn't sound like a request.

Clarice looked back at Kole, whom she could have knocked over with a nudge from her human arm. Maybe she should take a moment to give him a few words of instruction, if not comfort. Wraith One's glare on the back of her head seemed to generate a palpable heat, though, and she decided against ignoring him. She stepped forward to take his council.

Wraith One turned so that both of their backs faced Kole before speaking. "Lieutenant," he said, his voice even, "the Squad and I are concerned about the danger Lt. Kole poses to the mission."

The visible eye of each of the Squad members looked identically cold, and they all aimed at her. *The Squad and I are concerned?* she thought. Hopefully, it was a figure of speech and that Wraith One, as the group leader, merely assumed that he spoke for all of them. None of them had uttered a word in her presence, and she preferred to think that they were incapable of communicating through low-grade telepathy. "What do you suggest?" she asked in a low voice.

"That we shoot him in the head and bury the body," Wraith One said almost before she finished her question. His voice wasn't particularly quiet when he said it.

Clarice's eyes dropped and rested on the base of Wraith One's throat. He was right, of course. His dead, psychotic eye stared down at her, and the contempt that lingered there betrayed the malfunction in his mental wiring, allowing human emotion to taint his thoughts, but that did not make him any less correct. She had the same thought several miles ago, long before he opened his mouth, and it seemed like an unfortunate, but undeniable reality. Wraith One seconding the idea, however, made her reconsider. He was the machine, the blunt instrument that allowed you to get from Point A to Point B. She was the thinker, the one who saw the bigger picture, which was why General Frusin put her in charge. Which raised another issue: Wraith One was her subordinate. What the hell was he thinking, telling her to kill another member of the team? Jervis would have slapped anyone that said that into submission, even this monstrosity… maybe. Still, for the good of the group, Jervis also might have taken the unsolicited advice.

No, she decided. *That isn't an option.* She planned to die in the next couple of days and refused to leave this mortal coil with Wilson Kole's tainting the last days of her life. Despite her best efforts to convince herself otherwise, she was no machine. She had emotions and she had a conscious, and those struck a delicate balance with the more calculating parts of her being. Although her arm would beg to differ, the parts that made her Clarice Torrance were meat and bone. Maybe that was why she never made it past lieutenant.

"Negative," she said. "Suggestion noted and denied."

"Yes, Lt. Torrance," Wraith One said. He pivoted and returned to the other members of the Squad, who looked as fresh as ever (Did they even breathe?). While he turned away, though, she thought she saw another flash of emotion in his eye. It was not one of the gentler emotions.

Clarice snapped her hand laser back into its holster. "Be ready to move out in five minutes," she said in the most commanding voice she could muster. "We'll be heading East in the direction the Heckler came from. Slower pace this time; we don't want to walk into a trap."

The Wraiths scrambled to their feet while Clarice turned and took a couple steps toward Kole. He looked better, by virtue of the fact that, a couple of minutes ago, he could not have looked worse. "Thanks for keeping the pace down," he said weakly. "I don't know if I could have kept up."

Over her shoulder, the entire Squad pinned Clarice down with their stares. She ignored Kole's comment. Receiving thanks for her weakness failed to improve her feelings about the situation. "How are you feeling?" she asked.

Kole's eyes hovered in front of her, their rims red either from the dust or the stress. He ignored her question. "He wanted you to kill me, didn't he?" His tone was more glum than panicked.

Put you out of your misery is more like it, she thought. Aloud, she said, "It was more like he wanted permission to kill you."

"Why don't you?" he asked.

"Because I'm a soldier," she said automatically, "not a murderer." Although she never remembered him speaking those exact words, they reminded her of something Jervis might have said when he was trying to instill confidence, something subtly inspirational. He never endured a situation quite like this, though. He could afford to remain the consummate professional because he never descended into soft, disgusting underbelly of the war machine. No covert operations, assassinations, or political rivalries. How far would he have gone to avenge her death, especially when dealing with a doomed man like Kole? Would he have abandoned his newfound cause or his soul? She started back toward the Wraiths before they could bounce more invisible thoughts amongst each other.

"I had ten days to go, y'know?" Kole said.

"Pardon?" she asked, turning.

"My commitment to the military was up in ten days," he said, absently checking one of the pouches on his belt. "Nine days now, I guess."

"I didn't know that," she said, pulling her skin-tight gloves tighter and snapping them at the wrist. *Shut up shut up shut up...*

He gave a humorless smile. "No. I guess you didn't. I mean, you didn't do the background check. Obviously."

Clarice kept absently tugging on those gloves and tried to think of an appropriate response but doubted that one existed... because just like Wraith One, Kole was *right*.

Kole shrugged. "I... I shouldn't have brought that up... when you were at my door. I don't know what I was thinking." He shuffled back over to where he had dropped his canteen before pausing. "At the time, I just thought you needed a botanist for something. We aren't exactly trained to question orders." He reminded her of a man she once saw stalking around the medical ward, while she was getting fitted for her new arm. The man would stare at the ground as he slid his feet across the carpet, probably never lifting them more than an inch off the ground. For a while, she thought the man had sustained profound brain damage. She later learned the techs had just diagnosed him with terminal radiation poisoning.

In that barren stretch of ground, Clarice literally stood between the subhuman super-humans and the luckless botanist, unable to please either. She still had a couple minutes before the scheduled march time. She slid her Helix-Gort Laser Assault Rifle off her shoulder and started an equipment check. If time remained when she completed her check, she would start another one.

*   *   *

From the journal of Lt. Wilson Kole:

Amid all of the unsettling aspects of life in the Army, the Wraith Squad has always stood out as a particularly unsettling enigma for us normal, enlisted humans. I know they started out as a covert mission team that saw a lot of action behind enemy lines during the Krynan 4 mess of a few years ago. In that fight, the enemy used a lot of hand-held incendiary weapons, so, while those-who-would-later-become-the-Wraiths sustained a lot of bodily damage, the wounds were cauterized almost instantly, and many of them lived. I don't know if a conscious decision was made by some of the higher links of the chain of command or if it was something that happened organically, but it seems that every time some medical breakthrough came about in the field of body reconstruction, it was first tested on a Wraith.

Whoever picked the name "Wraith Squad" did a nice job of summing up the feeling one gets in their presence. Despite their being larger than normal humans and being packed with muscle and metal, they move with minimal noise. Up in orbit, they didn't eat in the regular mess hall, and it never seemed like they left their section of the ship. Still, sometimes they would show up in the engineering deck, skulking around among the pipes and the wire panels in their black uniforms. They were one step away from being a bedtime warning for adults: "Be a good soldier, or the Wraith Squad will get you." I never had the guts to ask any of the ones I saw what they were doing. In my defense, though, I don't know of anyone else who did, either.

Entering down into their dank little section of the ship seemed like an even more absurd idea. A person might disappear down there, the victim of an unbalanced, overzealous killing machine. Rather than throw away in upwards of one hundred pounds of expensive metal and circuitry, the brass would probably decide to just shoot the body into space with the rest of the garbage and chalk it up to a chemical spill or something similarly innocuous. "Machinery malfunction" might have been more appropriate. This is all speculation, of course.

*   *   *

CHAPTER FIVE:

COLD, COLD GROUND

The young woman stands in front of the school's eight-lane swimming pool, rubbing the satiny strap of her dress between her fingers. So delicate. Too delicate. Delicate enough that it broke when Dar Ellington pulled on it, out in the hallway. He tried to lower it over her shoulder, she pushed him in the chest with both hands, and the strap broke.

She stopped crying several minutes ago. Now, breathing through the post-tears congestion, she stands alone in front of the swimming pool, not sure what to do. The only sound comes from the pool water lapping into the water filter. Down in the water, her wavering reflection shows a plain girl with all the accoutrements of a beautiful person. The school's staff transported in a professional hairdresser to arrange the girls' hair for them. Her physics teacher loaned her the beautiful, midnight blue dress that his daughter had worn years earlier. She wouldn't have been able to go to the Founding Day Dance otherwise. It was the nicest thing she'd ever worn until Dar put one of his busy hands on it. "Let's go for a walk," he said, and she liked him enough to trust him. Even after he broke the strap, after she almost started sobbing, he still tried to force himself on her. His big, foul-smelling maw opened up, as if he wanted to inhale her instead of kiss her. She kneed him in the groin and ran away before she could find out the extent of his intentions.

She was having a nice time at the dance, pretending to fit in. She and the rest of the orphans pretended that, since they didn't belong anywhere else, they belonged together. It doesn't work that way, though. A chain of islands may form a pattern from a distance, when you stare at it long enough, but each is still an island.

She pinches the two severed ends of the strap between her thumb and index finger and presses, hard. She opens her fingers and the piece of strap attached to the front of her dress flops forward. They remain two, separate pieces, and that makes them useless.

She doesn't go back to the dance. She tells her friends it's because the dress tore. She knows it's because she can't pretend anymore. She stops going to dances.

*   *   *

When the march resumed, the pace slowed to more closely resemble a leisurely stroll. Clarice considered that, if indeed the Wraiths possessed a sense of humor, the plodding might constitute a poor joke on their part. She could have ordered them to speed up, of course, but they still advanced at a steady rate. Also, factoring in the fact that they didn't know where they were going, any time they saved by doubling their pace would have been lost if someone overheated and collapsed.

After an hour of walking, as the distant foothills began to turn into dark, craggy mountains that punctured the low-hanging clouds, Clarice found herself leading the line of black-clad soldiers up a steep incline. Even stranger, Wilson Kole occupied the second slot of the marching order, ahead of all the Wraiths. He trudged forward on soft legs, his lips pressed into a line of effort. If he maintained his version of steely determination, she might have to break down and admire the man, someday. His movements were sloppy and inefficient, and while those certainly were unfortunate qualities for a soldier, he continually seemed to muster forth a level of effort far beyond what she expected. At various points, it probably required considerable focus for him to keep from having a complete emotional breakdown, because… again… *he wasn't trained for his.* As a man, he also possessed a visible sensitivity that probably made him a good person. In another time and place, that would be admirable, but their current situation didn't exactly lend itself to depth and morality.

On her way up a steep slope, Clarice's foot landed on a stone and knocked it loose. Her oversized rucksack tugged her toward the ground, and she stabbed a hand at a chunk of outcropping rock in attempt to arrest her momentum. The stone skipped past Kole's shoulder. Her hand found purchase. Luckily, it was her right hand. Clarice pulled herself upright, shook her head, and kept going. Keep going. It was all she could do. Jervis once told her that when everything breaks down, only two things matter: the quality of a person and the quality of the person's training. When you didn't have time to think, the latter became more important, but when fully aware that you face the worst of situations, only the strong rise to meet the challenge.

Clarice stopped looking at her feet long enough to gaze upward. Two of the three moons of Middes occupied the pink canvas of the sky. Full-on night had fallen. At this time of the year, they would only have to wait a couple hours before the first sun poked its way over the horizon, but the steep, rocky terrain would get downright unforgiving before then. Adding to that, six robot killers stalked over her trail, wanting to make her their next victim as surely as not. Adding to that, her lone ally probably could offer assistance only as a target or if plants attacked them. Circumstances certainly appeared to be at their worst, so according to Jervis, this provided her with a chance to prove herself.

The path started to level off, such that Clarice had to contort her neck to see the sky. She shortened the length of her steps until Kole walked even with her. Thankfully, he initiated the conversation. "I've never been on this part of the planet before," he said, slightly. "How cold does it get at night?"

"The days get hot, but the nights are pretty moderate, even though there aren't any substantial bodies of water for a couple hundred miles," she hooked her right thumb under the strap of her rucksack. "I don't know how or why, but I fought in this region for the past two years and never needed so much as a coat at night."

"Yeah, given the size of the planet and the two suns, it just doesn't stay dark long enough for the land too cool off," Kole said, nodding. "That's one good thing... I guess."

Clarice returned his nod. "Yeah, I guess. One good thing and a million not so good ones." She checked behind her. The primary not-so-good-thing, Wraith One, still plodded onward, relentless as death. The red light from his cybernetic eye gleamed in the darkness. Ten normal-human paces separated him from her; properly motivated, he could probably clear the distance in three. All six members of the Squad probably had enhanced hearing. Hell, they probably all volunteered to let the medical techs rip out their auditory innards through a tiny, surgically drilled hole and replace the ear guts with a mass of wiring. Her "command" seemed tenuous, at best, and it felt important to not show weakness in front of them, even though the conventional rules of morale probably didn't apply to a platoon of cyborgs. They may hate her. They may regard her as a weak human, but they always followed orders. They had to. Her eyes drifted down to the remote control hooked to her belt. One way or another, they had to.

Clarice glanced at Kole's slackened face, then turned forward. Even though the Wraiths probably could hear her as well as if they were standing two inches from her face, she needed to lower the wall for a moment. She licked her lips and cleared her throat. "I haven't apologized to you yet for pulling you into this. It was a mistake on my part, one I wish I could take back. I knew this would probably be a suicide mission. I may have been counting on it…" Her voice trailed off. *Probably shouldn't have said that,* she thought, *no matter the audience.* "Regardless, I didn't want to take anyone close to me. I'd attended the Camp Burden with Wilson Kole… the other Wilson Kole, and even though I barely knew him, I respected him as a soldier." She took a couple seconds to listen to the pebbles grind under her boots with each step. "Like I said, a mistake."

Kole nodded but remained silent. His reaction struck her as a bit mopey, but what was he supposed to say? "Heyyyy, it's okay"? "Shhhh, don't worry about it"? "So what if I had a few days before I went to back to a real life with people that love me. It's not your fault"?

Technically, she had nothing to apologize for. Technically, Kole was a soldier enlisted in the army, and one week left or not, he was every bit as expendable as the next grunt you shove out the door to get blown to bits. One can only hide behind technicalities for so long, though. Eventually, you run into fundamental ways of treating people. You don't try to kill people, nor do you ask them to do more than they are capable of. For Clarice, the trip was not long at all. Technically, Jervis was a soldier, too, and soldiers die. Dying violently somehow never made it into the job description during recruitment, but everyone knew that stark reality. Jervis was also a part of her, though, and when he died, a part of her died with him. It didn't disappear in a brilliant flash of blue like her arm did. It festered and died and decayed, leaving a heart-sized, sucking hole behind it. By selecting this particular soldier, she'd hoped she would not subject someone else to the same torture… and she undoubtedly failed in that regard, as well.

"So you were, um, close to… Giles?" Kole asked.

Clarice stared at him, feeling a mixture of confusion and alarm. For a moment, she feared that he had read her thoughts but realized that he was merely trying to change the subject.

Her stare made Kole uncomfortable, and he averted his eyes. "Sorry. I know you were close. Um, I just heard he got, um, he died on the surface during Coppin Bay, and didn't know if you wanted to talk about it."

Clarice did not want to respond; as far as she was concerned, the damage that Jervis' death inflicted on her life had no resolution and, thus, in its own way, was resolved. For the time being, though, talking kept her from feeling like she was on a death march. Wilson Kole may be the last creature with a soul with whom she ever held a meaningful conversation, and he almost certainly... meant well. "Yeah," she said and coughed into her mechanical fist. "Yeah, we were very close." She felt like continuing, but not here. Not now. Not with those machines tromping away behind her, with their superhuman hearing and circuitry where their soul should be. "So what about you?" she asked, trying to sound casual. "Anyone waiting back home?" The question left her lips before she remembered that she preferred not knowing.

"Naw, not really," Kole said. Clarice felt the hither-to-unnoticed tension leave her muscles in a sigh. The focus was off her, but she didn't want to hear a story involving deep, green eyes, farewell kisses at the transport dock, or locks of hair stuffed in care packages. "No one in the 'significant other' category," he continued. "I've been kicked around for four or five years, from planet to planet, transport to transport, so I never even made many friends. Not having anybody back home was one of the main reasons I enlisted. I figured I'd save up some money, get some experience, and make a go of it in the civilian sector."

Clarice pushed her shoulders back and adjusted her body lean as they descended the back of a steep hill. *Almost a perfect five-year plan,* she thought, *unless you ran across a jackass lieutenant who didn't bother to read your personnel profile before sending you into combat.* The light breeze blew against her exposed face and forearms and felt soft and strangely soothing. She never thought this place could be soothing. She did appreciate the available smells, though. Even windblown dirt smelled better than the antiseptic air of the transport ship. She shifted her rifle to her real shoulder. "Botanists do quite well for themselves financially from what I hear."

"Oh, absolutely," Kole agreed, nodding. "As long as you don't mind the interstellar life. The Republic's expanding at such an obscene rate that they're always looking for people who can find food sources for colonies. It can't go on for a whole lot longer, not without a change in consumption habits, but that's hardly my problem. The Republic will be around in some form or another long after my ashes have been scattered." Kole paused, probably realizing that the current situation had drastically accelerated his hypothetical timetable. "That was the plan, anyway, before I became victim to a complete lack of serendipity." He rubbed the corner of his eye. "What would the converse of serendipity be?"

Clarice shook her head, relatively sure of what he meant by "converse." "I have no idea. I suppose one of us should invent a word if there isn't one."

Kole looked over at her, and his expression lightened. "Don't go thinking I'm mad at you. I'm just mad at circumstance. I mean, Wilson's a popular name, or at least it was a couple years ago. Kind of like how, these days, everybody seems to be naming their kids Brice if it's a boy and Helen if it's a girl. Kole's even a popular last name in some sectors, so to run into another Wilson Kole or two at some point was probably inevitable. But to have everything shake out the way it did," Kole shook his head. "It's not only enough to make a person believe in a higher power, it's enough to make one believe in a higher power with a really sick sense of humor."

"Maybe you did something in a former life," Clarice said, wryly. "Maybe we both did."

Kole scoffed. "Yeah, well, I hope it was worth it. I hope I had one hell of a time accumulating all that bad karma." He looked at either side of the invisible path they followed. Clarice could not imagine what he thought he might be trying to detect; the shadows were condensing to the point to where she could barely see him walking less than two feet away. The sky on the horizon had turned a deep shade of purple, and they would have to switch to night vision in a matter of minutes. Wraith One stomped rhythmically behind them. In the darkness, she could be fooled into thinking it was her heartbeat.

Clarice performed a slight bend to her right while she marched and slipped her fingers into the deep pocket on her right thigh. On her first attempt, she pinched the heavy plastic, night-vision goggles and dragged them out of the pocket. While she unfolded them, Kole asked, "So what about you? Any plans before you got sucked into this maelstrom?"

"*Maelstrom.* There's another word I haven't heard in a while," she said, rubbing the thumbs of her gloves over the green lenses of the goggles. "You read a lot, don't you?"

"Just about anything I can get my hands on," he said. "I like the old style books the best. The paper books."

"Yeah," Clarice said, affixing the goggles into place over her eyes. "I saw your room, with the books. What about them do you like?"

Kole shrugged to the maximum extent that the forty pounds of equipment strapped to his shoulders would allow. "I don't know. Tradition, maybe. Being linked to something great from the past." He kicked an unseen pebble in front of him and paused as it trickled away into the distance. "Everything's so efficient these days; every act is engineered to be as inconsequential as possible. It's like people live their lives and disappear from existence and there's nothing to mark that they were ever here."

Clarice flicked a switch on the side of the goggles, and the formless void surrounding her transformed into a world of bright green. She'd contemplated the things that Kole was talking about, but she had resolved the matter in her mind: the Republic would serve as the evidence of her existence. Not just plaques and medals, the entire entity. She was sacrificing her life for the principles that the Republic stood for. In front of her, the path had leveled out, but unfortunately, she could only see more barren, rocky hills. At least now, she could turn and see the stomping, shadowy forms following her.

Kole must have decided that Clarice wasn't going to respond, so he added, "Well, nothing physical, anyway. I suppose we impact the people around us, even if it's temporary. When we have an interaction, it's our obligation to do our best to make it a positive rather than a negative one." He shook his head. "Now I'm just rambling. I'm sorry. Attitudes like that might get me kicked out of the military."

Maelstrom. Clarice still pondered Kole's use of the word as they continued into a shallow ravine. For Kole, the maelstrom started a matter of hours ago, with the selection for this mission. For her, it started the instant she lost Jervis. The mission was her angel of mercy, pulling her out of the awful abyss of confusion and pain with the promise of structure and peace. Kole probably did not appreciate finding out that she dragged him into the midst of a well-choreographed suicide. He probably thought she whined too much. He didn't understand, though. He admitted as much. He did not know what it felt like, to form a link, body and soul, to another person, or the resulting agony when something severed the link. How many people truly did? She never should have involved another real human in this mess, though; she had all but assured that Kole never would find that connection in his life. That was a mistake. The cast of her little melodrama should have consisted of her and a group of thoughtless, emotionless Wraiths hunting Leon Azzerello.

"I try not to read into things too much," she said, which was true in its own way. "The military's a lifetime occu—"

"Incoming!" Wraith One bellowed.

*　　　　*　　　　*

The roar of the aircraft's engines hit Clarice's ears only after she extracted her wrap. The deafening sound made it feel like the ship flew right over the top of them. Night fighting limited the effectiveness of the thermo-flage because the temperature of the surrounding land dropped drastically without either of the suns radiating it. Still, the wraps distorted the scanner image such that only the very best pilots could identify the targets properly. Of course, this was only the case when a target actually used the wrap.

Kole swaddled himself in the camouflage wrap a full second later than anyone, but even Wraith One, with his enhanced sight and/or hearing, ducked and covered far too late. The concussion shells flared up everywhere at once. Clarice peered out from under her wrap in time to see a shell explode several yards in front of her. She lingered just outside the blast radius, but a flash of pain bored into her eye sockets and ripped through the center of her skull. Instinct told her to tear off the night-vision goggles and press her palms into her eye sockets, but her training refused to let her release the wrap.

As the concussion blasts peppered the dirt, the part of Clarice's mind not in charge of taking action began to piece together a theory as to how the pilot caught them off guard so badly. From the sound of the engine and the type of ammunition it unleashed, the attacking craft seemed to be a low altitude fighter, in all likelihood, a Kechlet 840 Sprinter. The pilot must have taken the vehicle to its highest cruising altitude and shut down the engines. The momentum of the Sprinter would have carried it for several miles and allowed said pilot to drift silently over to their position. Of course, the ship would have dropped almost to the point of crashing before the pilot kicked the thrusters in, but the strategy could work... in theory. It was risky as hell, and a Republican pilot pulling it would have faced severe disciplinary action, but by the time the Sprinter roared to life again, the heat patters of the eight bodies would have lit up the targeting screen like a pack of Mibusu Glow Worms.

Masterful, Clarice thought as she slithered her way toward the wall of the depression, her hands still clutching the nearly useless wrap. A fantastic plan, if you could pull it off. Not many could.

The last of the concussion blasts scarred the ground, and with her goggles still in place and a pain spike digging its way into her brain, Clarice released the ends of her wrap. The snap of her wrap retracting and rolling itself up at the bottom of her rucksack mixed with six other identical sounds. She rolled to one knee and scanned the western sky for the rear thrusters of the assault ship. The white flame from two thrusters receded into the bright green distance. *Probably was a Sprinter*, she noted with only a flicker of satisfaction.

The butt of her rifle pressed into Clarice's right shoulder. The Wraiths would assume a similar defensive position without instruction. She turned the expulsion knob up to full power, listened to the weapon hum, and waited for her attacker to turn around and try to finish them off. Assuming that it was a Sprinter that unleashed those concussion blasts, the ship's hull couldn't shake off a direct hit from a Helix-Gort Laser Assault Rifle without sustaining damage. One hit would hurt it. Seven direct hits would shred the vehicle's hull and bring it down into the side of a mountain.

Clarice propped her head against the metal stock of the rifle and tried to blink away the lingering effects of the night-vision mishap. She inhaled and held the air in her lungs while waiting for the off-white vehicle to emerge from the solid green of the night-vision sky. Ever since the blue light took Jervis, she had waited for her chance to hit back and expel the built-up poison in an explosion of rage. She could compose a long list of acts more satisfying than blasting apart an 840 Sprinter from a hundred yards away (ramming Leon Azzerello's sinuses through his warped brain would rank at the top of the list), but it beat the hell out of smacking around an inanimate punching bag for an hour. Clarice released her breath and took another. And another. And another. Silence. She removed the goggles and only a black void greeted her. The Sprinter was not returning for a second pass.

Her hands started shaking. Clarice set her rifle down so she wouldn't accidentally fire off a few rounds and began clenching and unclenching her fists. She needed to hit out. She wanted to turn her rifle on the side of the mountain and carve it open until it bled. An outburst like that, though, would make them conspicuous prey if a ground party happened to be hunting them (which now seemed extremely likely). Capture and incarceration would ruin any chance she had for real catharsis. Instead, she picked up a fist-sized stone with her gloved right hand and squeezed. The rock made several brief, popping sounds. She opened her hand and let the gentle breeze carry off the small pile of red powder in the same direction the Sprinter disappeared. Clarice rubbed the bits of former stone off her black gloves and turned to regard the others.

Six forms stood in a loose circle, looking down at the single form that writhed on the ground. Someone shined a circle of light down on it. Clarice took a few steps toward the shadowy casualty. She fully expected to see Kole lying on his back, covered in his own guts. Instead, the supine form belonged to Wraith Two, the pale woman with barely any hair. Clarice leaned in and squinted, but saw no blood, missing limbs, or even an expression of pain on the woman's face. Still, Wraith Two's arms and legs milled about with their own agenda, like a marionette with tangled strings, rhythmically scraping against the dirt.

Clarice scanned the grim, shadowy faces until she found Wraith One. "What's wrong with her?" she asked.

Wraith One pivoted the entire front of his body toward Clarice and answered in his normal speaking tone. "Her cybernetic relays have sustained damage. It does not happen often, but it does happen. She needs to be put down."

Clarice held up her palm to signal a slowdown. "Hold on here. I didn't catch that first part. Damaged cybernetic something or other. What does that mean?"

Wraith One paused. He stiffened and drew in a slow breath. Frustration lingered in his deep voice and made him sound almost human. "Cybernetic relays are like motor neurons. They control movement in the cybernetic limbs."

Outside of the circle of light, the darkness swallowed everything. Wraith One's voice seemed to come from nowhere. She could barely make out the outline of his body, and the only part of his face she could see was the red dot on the cybernetic eye. They, on the other hand, all five of them, no doubt could see her thermal signature better than if she stood in an open field on a sunny day. Clarice shook her head. "I thought the cybernetics were hooked over the existing muscle structure."

"Yes, in some cases," Wraith One said. He scanned the sky and waited for his commanding officer to digest the information.

"Are they in her?" Clarice said.

"Yes, I believe so," Wraith One said.

Clarice expelled her idea slowly. "Then can't you close off the power supply so the cybernetics shut down and she can just use her muscles?"

Wraith One did not respond. He showed no signs of hearing her as he continued to search the star-choked sky.

"Well?" Clarice snapped. Her tone sounded especially sharp to her ears, and she instantly remembered that three quarters of her team probably wanted to kill her. Not only that, she realized the reason Wraith One was staring at the night sky; collectively, they had not moved ten feet in any direction since the Sprinter attack. They both knew that, while they spoke, the Sprinter might be silently falling out of the sky again, hot to finish the job. Even when she stared at Wraith One, the perpetually moving form of Wraith Two invaded Clarice's peripheral vision. The woman-cyborg looked to be peddling an invisible bicycle. Too many distractions. Clarice closed her eyes, but even that couldn't block out the rhythmic scraping sound.

"In theory," Wraith One said. "I would not recommend it, however. I think you should use your remote control to put her down."

Clarice's hands patted down her beltline and couldn't find what they were searching for. A bolt of panic shot through her until her hands fell across the small, plastic remote tucked into a pouch on her right hip. She must have absently moved it to a more secure location while marching; it was the one piece of equipment she didn't have extensive experience with, so her reflexive considerations failed to include it as a factor. Her thumb brushed over the surface of the seven buttons. Could Wraith Two hear them talking about her? Probably. Clarice briefly considered the advice before regarding Wraith One's dark outline. "No. Do like I said. Shut down the cybernetics."

"Lt. Torrance," Wraith One said, his tone overly stern for a subordinate, "I strongly suggest you reconsider."

Clarice glared across the circle of figures at the larger, darker man. He really was huge. If they were both normal humans with normal muscle structures, he could still snap her in half like a twig. Then you throw in all that machinery... it would be like fighting a tank. "I just gave you an order, Wraith One," she growled. Her thumb gingerly tapped the remote. "I suggest you follow it." To her right, someone gasped... had to be Kole.

The red light on Wraith One cybernetic eye gleamed in her direction for a long second before he turned, dropped to one knee, and leaned over the gyrating woman on the ground. Wraith One's crowed into the circle of light and reached for his fallen colleague. Despite the bulky form in her way, Clarice could still see Wraith Two's slack, hollow expression. Wraith One's massive shoulders and back eclipsed her view of the woman from the neck down, but the series of clicks and squeaks indicated that he was manipulating the main power lead in Wraith Two's circuitry. The main power lead probably sat housed in the back of Wraith

Two's neck; that was where the Med Techs told Clarice hers was installed, anyway.

Of the five humanoids that remained standing, four stood rigid as rocks. One, small shadow on Clarice's right shifted his weight from one foot to the other. Clarice folded her arms and looked on, ignorant of the purpose and process of Wraith One's actions. She knew barely anything about how her own arm worked. Kole probably knew more about it than she did, solely due to random knowledge he seemed to absorb by virtue of being a scientist. She did not know what form of energy powered the cybernetics or why they didn't need constant replacement. She never claimed to be a Med Tech, though, or an electrician.

No final, ceremonial click of a switch initiated the screaming. It started all by itself. Wraith One rose from his crouch and showed no alarm amid Wraith Two's shrill keening. He kept his cybernetic eye's red light pointed at his fallen comrade as his lips shifted into a self-satisfied smirk. Clarice barely noticed, distracted by the fact that the woman's scream sounded a lot like Jervis's.

Like an asphyxiating fish, Wraith Two arched her back to an unnatural, painful angle. "Wha – where am I?" Wraith Two moaned in between wails. "Who are you people?! What's happening to me?!" She growled the words through clenched teeth. Her facial muscles contracted so that the audience could see her bulging veins. Her hips and shoulders continued to press in opposite directions, like a worm trying to burrow into cement.

Clarice whipped her head around to Wraith One, who stood beside her, still wearing an I-told-you-so look. Unprompted, he asked, "Do you want me to shoot her? Or would you prefer the remote?"

Wraith Two's eyelids spread to their widest point, and she inhaled with a series of short squeaks. Clarice's jaw went rigid, and she scolded

Wraith One with her eyes. He could not have cared less. Kole continued to dance from one foot to another, his pace having increased since the screaming started. "Lt. Kole," Clarice said, "might I have a word with you?"

Wraith Two let out a yelp and started screaming again. "Hyaaaaahl!" It kind of sounded like she was calling for help, but the pain mangled the sound before it left her lips.

Kole took a pair of hesitant steps away from the circle of Wraiths, who stared down at their former comrade like ignorant children regarding a mortally wounded insect. Clarice grabbed Kole's arm and dragged him about ten feet from the circle before stopping. The ones with enhanced hearing could still hear every word she and Kole had to say, but hopefully Wraith Two's second round of screams would drown out some of their conversation.

"Well?" Clarice asked.

Kole shook his head but his eyes remained locked on the squirming woman. "Oh, you've got to kill her."

Clarice nodded. "Yes. Yes. Absolutely." She made no movement back toward the fallen body.

Kole looked away from the morbid display long enough to regard Clarice. "So what's the hold up? I'll do it if you don't think —"

"I can do it," Clarice snapped. She bit her lower lip. "I just... don't want him to win." She tilted her head in the general direction of Wraith One.

"Win?" Kole asked. "That woman's in horrible pain, and we have no way of getting her medical attention. You can't let that psychopath—"

Clarice cut him off again. "He's trying to undermine my authority every chance he gets."

Kole leaned in and when he spoke, his attempt at a whisper came out in a hiss. "You're doing it to yourself this time. The enemy knows our general location, and her screaming is going to lead any search parties right to us. Besides, who cares if they think you're a complete twit? The Wraiths don't follow conventional authority, anyway; they follow whoever's holding the self-destruct switch."

Clarice nodded, her gaze affixed to the ground. "You're right. He's right." An involuntary shudder rippled through her. "But remember, he recommended I off you for the same reason."

"She's already dead —"

"I know," Clarice snapped. "I know. That's my point." She turned away before she had to see or hear Kole's reaction.

The remote felt like it weighed ten pounds, even in her right hand. Clarice pulled herself to her full height and marched back over to where the five passive observers stood over the wailing curiosity. "Okay," she said, "everybody take a step back." All the coherent members of the Wraith Squad looked at her in a synchronized motion. Each of their left legs reached behind them and carried them exactly one standardized step backward.

"Wha-what's h-happen—arrrrrh!" Wraith Two moaned.

Clarice kept the remote in her right hand; her gloved left had begun to sweat. She could only imagine the woman's expression because she kept her attention on the remote. *Focus on the two buttons you have to push*, she told herself, *not on what they'll do*. Her mechanical thumb did her bidding and pressed the narrow, unmarked button at the bottom of the remote, pressed the "2" button, and then pressed the unmarked button the second time.

Even with the deed finished, Clarice's eyes remained locked on the remote. The "1" button beckoned to her. She could off that mechanical monster in less than a second. For the sake of the mission, she let go of the thought and her hand dropped to her side. No matter how much his presence irritated her, she was down there for the mission and for the Republic. The same probably held true for Wraith One. He no doubt hated her, along with anyone else who wasn't stuffed with at least sixty pounds of circuitry, but he would not do anything to jeopardize the mission. She always had the remote as an option, just in case the appeal to his patriotism did not work.

The screaming stopped in mid screech. A second later, the left side of Wraith Two's neck blew open as though rigged with a small firecracker and pulled Clarice's attention away from the piece of plastic in her hand. The poor, incoherent woman's eyes turned glassy, and real death registered on her expressionless face. Her body seemed to dissolve from the inside out, which, in fact, it did. Her skin bubbled and hissed before opening up in several points at once, like a plastic bag held over an open flame. Thankfully, the chemical stench overpowered the burning flesh and kept the effective area smelling like a factory instead of a crematorium.

The analytical portion of Clarice's mind informed her that the main storage battery must have caused the release of an incendiary liquid into the woman's body and ignited it. The liquid, in turn, proved hot enough to melt the metallic portions of Wraith Two's skeletal structure and render the expensive hardware useless. The part of her mind that felt, though, the part that training and life experience had yet to corrode, told her that a woman was melting to death in front of her. Skin, tongue, and everything else dissolved like a wax candle. The woman's right eye swelled and burst, sending vitreous humor down the front of her black uniform. Despite her extensive experience dealing with dead bodies, Clarice had never seen someone's skin boil and collect in puddle on the ground, and that sight, along with the smell of liquefied flesh and industrial lubricant made her turn her head and vomit.

The reflexive gag didn't amount to much more than a mouthful of stomach acid. She hadn't eaten anything except protein paste in the past day, and the body absorbs that stuff ten times faster than normal food. As the telltale headache began to build in her temples, Clarice blew her nose on a rag and wiped the regurgitant from the corner of her mouth and turned toward the members of her team. Seven left, including her. The flesh fire illuminated the frozen faces of all the Wraiths. Thankfully, they continued to stare at the fire and showed no reaction to her fit of nausea. Kole didn't get sick, but he glanced over at her, his face more drawn and worried than ever. If his eyebrows arched upward anymore they might have slid off the sides of his face. She did not need his pity. She really didn't.

"Let's move out. Same marching order," she said in the strongest voice she could manage, through a throat raw with stomach acid. Her gaze tried to wander down to the blackened hunks of metal lying in the dust... the fire had consumed the entire body alarmingly fast... but Clarice marched past with her face turned to the right. She noticed that her hand still clutched the remote, and instead of returning it to the safety of its pouch, absently hooked it on the inside of her belt.

The Wraiths instantly shouldered their rifles and marched due east, the direction from which the Sprinter descended. The humans had to hustle to keep up. Kole sidled next to Clarice and set a hand on her shoulder. The sensation sent a jolt through her body as though he had pricked her skin with a needle. He pulled his hand away on instinct. "Are you going to be okay?" he asked.

The burning taste of her own vomit still lingered in her mouth. Clarice worked her jaws around to collect some saliva and spat it to the right of the path. "I'm in charge of this mission," she said in a clipped tone. "I would not have been so delegated if I couldn't handle any possible situation. I'm fine." She glared at Kole as though he had insulted her lineage.

"I didn't mean that," Kole said, apologetic. "I have the utmost confidence in –"

"You should," she said, patting down her thigh pocket in search of her night-vision goggles. They were not there. Her other hand gave her other thigh a good frisking. Both hands worked their way up her body until her fingers danced across the hard plastic of the goggles, clipped to her rucksack strap. She ripped them free. "And you should be devoting all your attention to keeping the same thing from happening to you." She hiked a thumb in the direction of Wraith Two's remains without looking at them.

"I can't," he said.

"What was that?" she snapped. She twisted her head toward him without breaking stride.

"The same thing can't happen to me," Kole quickly explained. "I don't have any cybernetics in me."

She fit the goggles into place before flipping them on. The green image of Kole and his pug nose hovered in front of her, and she noticed again how ugly he was. He might have been more attractive than the original Wilson Kole, but the contest was close. Can something about the quality of a name make someone ugly? No one would ever mistake him for the tall, square-jawed form of Jervis Giles. Just an ugly, little man. He was correct, though, and not for the first time. It might have been an offhand remark. He may not have known about her extra-human improvements, or he may have seen her crush that stone into powder. Either way, she stood as a good a chance as anyone remaining in their detachment of dying from a fast boil. God only knew what they inserted under her flesh while she lay unconscious on that Med Tech table.

"Of course you don't," Clarice said before re-focusing on the bright green path in front of her. Clarice blinked and the image of Wraith Two's face popped up in the blackness, the way it looked after that section of her neck exploded. She had a delicate nose, high cheekbones, and a remarkable set of straight, white teeth. Wraith Two must have been a beautiful woman once, a long time ago, but you can't tell that when someone's face is immobile as a gargoyle's. The image replayed in Clarice's mind, from when the woman's lips liquefied and seeped through the slight gap between her central incisors.

*   *   *

From the journal of Lt. Wilson Kole:

I find the Republic's treatment of death in recent military undertakings interesting. In earlier days, the body of a soldier was a valued thing. Having a body dictated what group a new recruit would be assigned to, and it gave the soldier's family some modicum of closure. Nations made real concessions to one another in effort to get the corpses of their sons and daughters returned to native soil.

With modern advances in technology, if a soldier falls in the field of battle, someone will always hear it. That has come to mean that a soldier's own platoon scavenges the body for useful equipment and destroys the remains with a low-grade explosive or abandons it to rot. Most soldiers not having what is commonly considered a home, and for those who do have a home, that home is so far away from the field of battle that the army cannot economically transport a corpse. So, even if they do exist, the distant family rarely lodges a complaint when Johnny's carcass is blown to bits on the furthest moon of Alpha Centuri.

This hyper-efficiency is best exemplified by the members of the Wraith Squad. The body is digested by a horribly corrosive, flammable acid charge in a matter of seconds. The exact chemical combination is some macabre trade-secret, but whatever it is, the substance burns through metal almost as easily as it does skin and organs. Once released, it burns itself out in about 30 seconds; that way, it doesn't eat through the hull of a ship. In the end, the body is completely and efficiently disposed of. It is appropriate, I suppose, since the Wraith's soul was just as thoroughly destroyed years earlier when the body was the only thing deemed worthy of keeping... but maybe I'm just being sentimental.

*   *   *

CHAPTER SIX:

BONE CRUSHER

The hologram hovers in the middle of the hallway, rotating clockwise. The student watches, clutching her notebook computer against the front of her light-blue uniform. The pupils of her eyes grow large and lock onto the top of the image.

The full-body projection shows a person with a young, hairless face. The androgynous face levels an unflinching gaze out at an invisible target on the horizon, its proud chin lifted high in defiance of any danger. It wears a blue and white uniform with the high, flat collar that circumscribes its neck. The familiar "R", with a golden sword constituting the lone vertical line of the letter, adorns the jacket's left lapel.

The student feels a light tugging on her arm. "C'mon Clarice. We're going to be late, and I know you can't take another tardy."

Clarice turns toward her friend with the raven hair cut to regulation length. The friend carries a computer model under her arm two years newer than the one Clarice clutches, and wears pants and a jacket exactly like the ones Clarice wears, except that they are orange instead of blue. "What?" Clarice asks. "Oh, yeah, sorry about that."

They walk down the hallway for a few paces. A handful of students wearing yellow, green, or blue uniforms rush through the wide, high-ceilinged hallway, hurrying in one direction or the other. None of the red-uniformed students streak through the hallway. The Reds always get to class on time; that's why they're Reds. "You were staring at the guy in the hologram like you were on drugs. Did you think he was hot or something?" her friend asks as they scurry along.

Clarice furrows her brow, glances behind her at the proud soldier, then looks back at her friend. "You think that's a guy?"

Her friend shrugs, indifferently, as she quickens the pace. "I don't know. You were the one gawking like an idiot."

"Do you think all the Republican soldiers wear the exact same uniform?"

The friend rolls her eyes. "Duh. Didn't you see the film we watched in History last week?"

Clarice wrinkles her brow, thinking.

"You've really gotta start paying attention, girl," her friend says, shaking her head. "Look, the recruiter's supposed to be in the cafeteria at lunch time. You should ask him." They make a sharp right turn and enter their civics classroom. "I still think it's a guy."

Clarice sits down in one of the three seats available at the back table, with the rest of the Blues. Her friend continues up to the second row of tables, right behind the row of tables filled with bright, attentive Reds. They both reach their seats as the electronic bell starts to ring, announcing the start of class. Clarice hears it, but her mind stays on the soldier, wearing the same uniform as every other soldier.

*   *   *

Stomp.

Stomp.

Stomp. Clarice's heavy legs churned beneath her, methodically pushing her up the hill. Behind the night-vision goggles, the green-tinted, rocky scenery only varied by the angle she traveled. She had no idea how much farther they had to go. Not even the Wraiths knew that. She assumed the ship that hit Wraith Two came from Azzerello's main camp, but even if she was right, it was an aircraft, and distances in aerial terms simply did not translate to overland travel on foot. Given minimum fuel efficiency and speed levels, they might walk for a week and not reach it.

Another issue was that Azzerello would keep a mobile base of operation, so they were not necessarily walking toward a fixed point. His side fought a war of attrition, and no matter how many "battles" he lost, as long as he could minimize his personnel and equipment losses, he could continue to fight. There were no supply lines to cut, since most of the Republican vehicles commandeered by Azzerello's group were smaller, lighter machines that ran on solar or magnetic cells. Clarice had to admit: so far, the man had lived up to his reputation. He obviously anticipated Frusin's assassination attempt, and the only encounter with him thus far involved a five-second, surprise attack that they could neither defend nor retaliate against. Clarice's team's days were numbered, and everyone knew it.

Clarice braced her hand against her knee as she straightened it atop an outcropping rock. Her fondest wish at that point, beyond having Azzerello's face in front of her to pound into paste, would have been a pair of cybernetic legs. Her knee and hip joints ached so badly that she could not see how hacking off the offending limbs with her Strontium survival knife could inflict any more pain. If fate sent her to die in a puddle of flesh, anyway, she might as well attach the maximum number of mechanical super-limbs to propel her along during her journey. That would have to happen when they returned to the ship, though… so it probably wouldn't happen at all.

They traveled through the brief Middesian night. She never remembered getting cold on Middes prior to this mission, but she never reached their current elevation before. Thankfully, the constant movement helped those of the party who still felt temperature extremes from getting too cold. At first light, they each slept under the cover of their wraps for exactly one hundred and twenty minutes. Wraith Six kept watch, standing in the middle of their circle, clutching her rifle and scanning the horizon for the duration. She would sleep the next night and show no ill effects. Clarice found it difficult to refer to Wraith Six as a "she," and not because she was overly masculine (although she was). After seeing Wraith Two's sixty pounds of blackened metal and circuitry lying in the dirt, it seemed akin to assigning a gender to a moisture evaporator.

The midday suns now beat down upon them. Middes's first sun had passed its zenith, but the second, brighter of the red orbs still strove to reach its peak. It got hot in the daytime, mostly because, with two suns blasting you from different angles, there isn't much shade to be had. The sunlight struck your skin and stayed there, hour after hour, pulling sweat from your pores. Clarice knew this because, other than the upper atmosphere of Linthal, where she spent her formative years at the floating orphanage, she spent more time on the surface of Middes than any other single planet.

The troops had traveled for four consecutive hours and failed to encounter anything resembling a humanoid. Clarice cast an occasional glance behind her to check on Wraith Six, but the woman's scowl remained locked into place, and she did not behave any differently than the day before. Kole dragged himself along, exhausted, looking incrementally worse every time she turned around. He probably hadn't exerted himself like this since basic training.

To his credit, Lt. Kole never complained, nor did he appear on the verge of cracking up. The other Wilson Kole might have maintained a better marching pace and doubtlessly would have provided more help in a firefight, but he would have resented her for effectively ending his life and would have second-guessed Clarice every five minutes. This Wilson Kole definitely knew two things: (1) botany and (2) how to shut up. Neither talent brought much to the table in the current circumstances, but at least they didn't take anything off the table. Otherwise, the man was so useless he might as well have been a pacifist.

Wraith One's disparaging remarks and hard stares ended with Wraith Two's life. He did nothing but stomp forward at the front of the line like a good machine. In turn, Clarice found she could perform her job infinitely better without the fear of one of her subordinates turning around and punching a hole through her ribcage. Of course, the cooperative attitude might have evolved less from a sense of duty and more from the presence of the destructive charge that lay lodged in Wraith One's neck. Seeing Wraith Two liquefy might have helped boost the morale of the rest of the team, too. Clarice had seen the same thing happen dozens of times to one-hundred-percent natural soldiers. Petty rivalries and jealousies fell away when the first casualty hit the ground in a heap. When that happens, reality gets up in your face, blocking out everything on the periphery, and forces you to realize that the survival of any single component of the unit aids in the survival of all other components.

She not only saw the phenomenon happen, she experienced it first-hand. It was the first lesson Jervis taught her. Her assignment involved nothing more than guarding the rear of the formation, and at the time, she thought she received that duty by virtue of being the physically smallest member of the unit. As they marched through the dense, swampy underbrush, she muttered under her breath and stared at the back of Lt. Giles' head as if it had crosshairs painted on it. She stopped doing both when a Korilian Serpent Beam swept past her shoulder and sliced in half the soldier standing immediately in front of her. His name was Lorent Norce, and although she had never spoken to him directly, she would remember his name for the rest of her life. The top half of the Corporal Norce died screaming because she had not paid attention. Her attitude toward duty improved exponentially after she helped set fire to the body of her fallen comrade in an unmarked spot somewhere in the Swamps of Korilas.

Jervis never talked about the incident, even after they became intimate. He really didn't need to. Clarice thought about it a lot after it happened, and the sounds and images of the event never totally left her. Just when she thought she was rid of the memory, the image of the red, curving band of light materializing over her should and slicing through Corporal Norce right below the rib cage, jumped back into her thoughts. It could have been her... or Jervis... instead, it was Norce. In retrospect, Jervis must have believed in her enough to entrust her with guarding the rear of the formation in a potentially lethal situation. He believed in her, and she failed him.

The two halves of Norce faded back into her memory banks, but Jervis's face remained. He hated his light, patchy facial hair so badly that he always brought his shaver with him on missions. He obsessed over traveling light, not taking any unnecessary equipment, but he always brought along that shaver. He had no hair on his chest either, but that was mostly natural. It felt smooth, like a teenager's. She remembered sliding her fingertips over the skin of his chest and the way it felt on the skin of her back as he held her in bed.

Clarice shook her head and allowed the pain in her knees and the red dirt scenery to once again consume her reality. She wished she could stop thinking about him for a while, not permanently, but just for a couple hours, like a vacation. If she did that, though, when the memories returned, they would land ten times heavier. For years, in her more quiet moments, the image visited her of her parents walking up the boarding platform. She could even see her little, waving hand in the image. Now, the serial invading images belonged to Jervis: Jervis in bed. Jervis the first time she met him. Jervis dying. Two weeks ago, he was the only thing good in her life. Now, the memories of him were the only things good in her life.

Letting go of the memory would prove difficult, but in time, the memories would start to dull around the edges, like memories always do, and so would the pain. Even now, she could not remember what he smelled like. He always smelled good. She remembered that. Even when drenched in sweat, he seemed to have a force field that kept out the repugnant odor that clung to most normal humans like a Galbakian Roundworm, but her nose had forgotten his particular aroma. Someday, if she lived long enough, the only memories of his face would be reconstructions from photographs and holograms she owned. So, part of her refused to let go out of fear... fear that the best thing in her life would fade into nonexistence, leaving her with nothing. For a few seconds, she still could lose herself in the memory, but just like losing herself in her work, when the awareness of the reality she occupied returned, the pain had metastasized. Like an addict, though, she always returned for more.

She felt worse when it got cold. Last night, while she marched through the world of bright green and black, a stiff breeze picked up, and the cool, thin air slithered between her segments of body armor and across her skin and made her acutely aware of her isolation. It felt like marching alone through a graveyard. She spent most of the night, step after endless step, wishing for his warm arms to encircle her, and his lips to whisper in her ear and remind her that she wasn't alone. The person she used to be, before she knew what it felt like to have someone care about her, would have laughed at the idea, but that person was ignorant about life. At daybreak, when Clarice slept for most of her allotted one hundred and twenty minutes, she dreamed about him. In the dream, he still had skin and pulse. When she awakened, she had to cope with the loss all over again. The dream lied to her. Jervis was gone and he was not coming back.

Her eyes itched, and a something wet trickled down into the crook of her nose. *Great*, she thought, *I'm crying*. Nothing major, just a couple tears trickling out from the crevices of her dusty goggles and down her cheek. Assuming the Wraiths couldn't hear the sound of the descending tear, if she smudged the dirt on her face and kept from sobbing, no one would know. Clarice shifted her grip on the strap of her rifle and drew some of the dirty air into her lungs. It seemed like a distinctly bad idea to let the Wraiths catch her crying. They detected fear like predators in the wild, even if they didn't show it.

Her gloved left hand deftly rubbed the underside of her nose. *Nothing to be ashamed of*, Clarice reminded herself. Crying did not make her weak or a bad soldier. She was not some hysterical bundle of female hormones. As long as displays of emotion did not affect the mission, she felt no guilt. It might even be adaptive. She was not made out of steel (not all of her, anyway), and a harmless, ten-second spate of crying might keep her from exploding later.

*   *   *

The jagged tops of the barren, black peaks loomed thousands of feet above Clarice. They were in the mountains now, the real mountains, and it wouldn't be getting any warmer in the near future. They had dipped down into a crevice, and the steep rock walls cut off the wind. That made it a little less frigid, but they had found a little shade, and at least Clarice could see without the goggles. She lifted them and let them rest at her hairline. "Such an ugly planet," she muttered under her breath.

She could not imagine a worse section of a worse planet to spend the final days of her life.

Wetness still clung to her eyes several minutes after she silently leaked tears. Maybe the goggles had trapped in the moisture or something. The shoulders of the blurry silhouette dragging over the ground in front of her bobbed with each step. She followed for several paces without being conscious of her direction. Her gloved hand drifted up to her eyes and wiped away any tracks her tears had sliced into the thin layer of red dust coating her face. The wetness probably caused her eyelashes to clump together. Hopefully, no one would notice.

Clarice lifted her eyes and blinked twice. Something was not right about their location: Wraith One had led them on a descending route with sheer, ten to fifteen foot high walls lining either side of the wide path. The negative elevation and the lack of escape routes would classify it in infantry terms as a classic "Killing Box." It was exactly the type of place you learned to not go during your first day of training.

Panic hit Clarice as she tentatively glanced up at the rim of the small canyon they had descended into. Shadows shifted and a gust of wind brought the red dust curling over the lip. Was something moving up there or was it just her paranoia?

"Wraith One," Clarice called out before looking ahead and noticing that he had stopped marching. He faced her now, and his right hand rested on the small laser pistol strapped to his belt. The weapon remained in its holster, and Wraith One's manner was not overtly threatening, but he certainly was closer to firing on her than she him. Thankfully, Wraith Three's squat, lumpy form still stood between the two of them; his shoulders were broad enough for two Clarices to hide behind.

"Yes?" Wraith One asked, almost casually. Still, his deep voice rattled through the canyon. Everyone else stopped marching.

"What were you thinking bringing us here?" Her eyes darted to the left and the right. Maybe that exact moment in that exact place was not ideal for having a discussion. Granted, if an enemy force sought to ambush them, though, it would have done so long before Clarice and company had walked three-quarters of the way down the hundred-yard crevice. This logic provided her with little comfort.

"I brought us here so you couldn't escape," Wraith One said.

In between drills, some of the cadets at Burden used to engage in quick-draw contests with their stun pistols. Clarice was never the fastest on the draw and never thought the skill would come in handy, so she never worked at it. Add to this deficiency the weight of a rucksack, the awkwardness of wielding a rifle instead of a pistol, and the fatigue that results from a day of hard marching, and she essentially had no chance. Wraith Three silently dropped to the ground, leaving his commanding officer exposed and with a full view of Wraith One pointing a laser pistol at her.

"Drop you rifle, Lt. Torrance," Wraith One said.

Clarice hesitated for only a second. She considered shouting a command to the other Wraiths, but after Wraith Three's treachery, she had to assume they would react in a similar fashion. It seemed *possible* that Lt. Kole might *try* to do something constructive, but the chance of him successfully executing such a strategy seemed equal to the chance of the sky raining vanilla pudding in a desert on a clear day. While wishing again that she had picked the other Wilson Kole, Clarice set the stock of her rifle on the ground, then let the rest of it drop into the dust. Her thoughts immediately shifted to finding a way to get the little, black remote tucked into her belt.

"Are you going to tell me what's going on?" she asked. "Or are you just going to execute me?" Wraith Three rolled to her left, stood up, and joined his fellow squad members behind her. In truth, she really didn't care about the reason behind the mutiny. She was just stalling.

"Execute you," Wraith One informed her. "You, too," he said, gesturing to Kole without taking his eye off Clarice.

"Me?" Kole protested. "What'd I do?"

"It's nothing personal," Wraith One assured him, tonelessly. Wraith Four, the man with narrow eyes and spiky black hair, turned toward Kole and ripped away the rifle that Kole held gingerly in front of him. Resting a hand on Kole's shoulder, Wraith Four forced the smaller man to his knees. "Get to your knees," Wraith One said to Clarice.

Clarice began to lower herself to the ground, but with her knees bent, she sprung forward. A red laser beam flashed past her, within inches of her stomach, and burst against the ground. Her hands flew to her right hip and grasped the remote as she somersaulted over the loose dirt and rolled into a crouch. Almost as though she'd trained them for the occasion, her fingers nimbly pounced down upon the buttons necessary to send Wraith One into a meltdown. Both thumbs simultaneously clamped down on the unmarked command button, and she looked up to view her handiwork. Another red energy beam exploded in front of her face, incinerating the remote control, knocking her against the rock wall, and singeing her real hand. Wincing, Clarice cradled her gloved left hand and looked down at Wraith One's boots. Her eyes traveled up the length of his mountainous body until they spotted the laser pistol extended toward her. He seemed fine, certainly not on the verge of liquefying.

"If you move one more inch, Lieutenant," Wraith One said, "I'll start breaking one bone at a time, starting with your ribs. This doesn't have to be personal, but you're making it that way."

Clarice remained frozen, more confused than afraid. "What the hell just happened?" she asked.

"You tried to kill me," Wraith One said, his voice untainted by emotion. "It didn't work. Now get on your knees." Clarice shifted to her knees, one leg at a time, mostly because she didn't know what else to do; the gambit with the remote really was her best shot. Wraith One waited until she complied before approaching.

Clarice's hands hung limply while her eyes shifted to either side of her. Jervis once told her that a situation only becomes hopeless when one gave up hope. According to his way of thinking, there was *always* a way out. Everything had limits, though, even maxims. Had Jervis ever found himself staring down five Wraiths, unarmed, with only a botanist to guard his back? Probably, she decided, and he probably found a way out. He was much better at his job than she could ever hope to be. Even before she wanted him, she wanted to be as good a soldier as him.

Kole was not visible, but the sound of his uneven breathing came over her shoulder in a series of long, creaky sighs. The mission should not have ended this way, not exactly. She did not want to die a fool and did not want Leon Azzerello left alive to continue his psychotic, useless little war, but at the same time, a wave of relief rolled over her. She tried her best to complete the mission, and after the ensuing laser discharge blew her brains all over the red rocks, she would not have to deal with this soul-crushing emptiness anymore. She would not miss Jervis anymore, and on the offhand chance that the afterlife existed, she would join him there. She supposed she could live with that... figuratively.

The cold metal barrel of a laser pistol pressed against her temple. *This might be the last sensation you ever feel,* she considered. Wraith Four grabbed Kole by the strap of his rucksack and dragged him a few steps closer, into the edge of her peripheral vision. He gave Clarice a sad smile, as if to say, "Well, it was a good try." It was a good try… her whole life seemed like a constant series of good tries that never quite succeeded. She just hoped that when the concussion blast cleaved her skull apart, there would not be enough of her left to assemble into a Wraith.

She blinked and stared down the rocky corridor that would serve as her open grave. She should have never let Wraith One lead her down here. She just got momentarily distracted; human error, but it was totally unforgivable. Only a couple seconds had passed from the time she felt the metal barrel against her skin. Even that seemed too long, though, for someone as efficient as Wraith One should have been. He should have popped her while she was fooling around with the broken remote, just kicked her in the stomach and blown a hole right through her back. She could see lining up her and Kole to kill them, execution-style; that way, you only had to use one incendiary grenade to dispose of the bodies, but why the delay? Wraith One still stood silent as an obelisk on her right, but she could not see the expression on his face because his massive chest blocked her view. What was taking him so long?

Clarice's heart pounded against her ribcage, and the euphoric rush of rage flowed through her. *He's doing it precisely because he knows I hate it*, she realized. Whether he hated her personally or merely despised her human frailties, he wanted to do more than merely kill her. He tortured her because he could, because she was helpless, and that made him something less than a machine; that made him a sadist. She wanted to die, but not by his hand. She wanted this mess to end, but not if that meant he won.

The instant Clarice decided not to give up, her right hand darted upward to the side of her head. It was a reflex. If she'd stopped to think about it, she wouldn't have tried because she had no idea that her hand could move that fast (although, really, what did she have to lose?). The circuitry bolted to her right shoulder instantly translated her thought into action. Her fingers closed around the middle of the hand laser and flinched, crushing the metal weapon like a paper cup. It took Wraith One by surprise... the cybernetic limbs gave off a thermal reading similar to the flesh and blood ones, so maybe he didn't know about her arm replacement... but he recovered admirably. She hopped to her feet in time to catch a mechanical knee in the middle of her very human solar plexus. Wraith One's attack came almost too fast for her to see it and it landed like a sledgehammer. Doubled over, Clarice had time to blink away a legion of spots before a closed fist came crashing down between her shoulder blades. The ground slammed into her face and chest so hard that she bounced.

Dust flecks flew everywhere. Despite his previous threat to take his time if she moved, Wraith One took an efficient approach in killing her. Clarice only had time to draw in one dry, burning breath before a boot pressed into the base of her neck while two sets of fingers dug into the underside of her jaw bone. The punch in the back left her so dazed that she barely realized that he was about to rip her head off.

Damn, she thought as the tendons in her neck strained beyond the point she thought possible. *This is so much worse than getting shot.*

"Hailt!" a vaguely human-sounding voice shouted.

The fingers curled under Clarice's jawbone eased off the pressure until they merely held her head. She grimaced and strained to resist until Wraith One's fingers pulled apart and let her face drop into the dirt. By the time the boot lifted off her neck, Clarice had sucked in another dusty breath and begun to take inventory. Since she still could think, that probably meant that her head still remained in its proper place. Her breaths came rasping out, along with stray flecks of spit, as she took a couple seconds of random wiggling to make sure Wraith One had not caused any spinal trauma or torn any body parts loose. Even her inhalations and exhalations began to comport as though she were a professional breather. Her spine felt as though a cargo door had closed on it, but Clarice seemed to have survived the ordeal without sustaining any permanent damage. Her arms of varying strengths pushed her back into a kneeling position.

"Hailt!" the same voice screeched.

Still on her hands and knees, Clarice obeyed the command, happy for the moment of rest. Whatever happened in the near future had to beat having her head torn off. She rotated her eyes skyward. At least a dozen Middesian males lined the tops of both canyon walls. A tall Middesian with one visible ear stood atop the left wall and appeared to be the one who spoke. Half pointed incendiary rifles down into the crevice, while the other half carried sharp rocks. Given their superior position, though, one soldier with a rifle on burst-setting could have wiped out the Wraiths in a matter of seconds.

A thick fur covered the body of a Middesian, except for its back, where the fur takes the form of long, spiny quill-like extensions. Their noses extended to a slight snout, and this feature, combined with their beady eyes, betrayed their subterranean lifestyle. While they walked erect, their stubby legs severely limited their upright running speed, as Clarice knew from experience; they didn't retreat much in battle because they were terrible at it. She did not know how many clawed digits sprouted from their hands, only that it was enough to work the trigger mechanism on a rifle… or a laser mortar. These, like all Middesians, wore clothing similar to that worn by humans, only shabbier: tattered brown and grey rags with a thin coat of red dust. Often times, Clarice could only distinguish the males from the females by knowing that males tended to wear clothing comprised of darker tones and heavier material.

A scratching sound emanated from over her shoulder, and Clarice assumed that a Middesian or two were scrambling down each of the walls. The large, one-eared leader squeaked instruction to others in the garbled Middesian language. Behind her, the furry creatures frisked the Wraiths and relieved them of their arsenals. When the creature got around to patting her down with its stubby digits, Clarice realized that, despite spending almost two years on the surface occupation, this was only the second time she had ever made physical contact with a Middesian, or at least one that had not previously had its chest cavity cauterized by a laser blast. The first time had been a rather bloody, savage affair that involved two combatants meeting in an underground tunnel after having run out of ammunition.

The band of Middesians fell to either side of the line of Republican soldiers. Although neither side spoke the other's language beyond a few rudimentary commands, the behavior of captors and their captives forms a rather universal standard. It took at least two Middesians to carry the weapons and equipment that one Wraith had toted, but this proved easy enough given their superior numbers. When the Middesians started marching, Clarice, Lt. Kole, and the Wraiths followed suit.

The muscles of Clarice's stomach cried out as she pulled herself to her full height and continued to ache as she walked. Painful as it felt, she knew that cramps would soon arrive that were every bit as intense. Otherwise, she felt surprisingly functional. Her neck seemed weak and strained but relatively unharmed, and her back only hurt when she walked over particularly uneven terrain. On a couple of occasions, though, Clarice's foot landed in a slight hole or depression, and the jarring sensation felt as though someone had struck her in the spine with a hammer. Thankfully she didn't have to carry that damn rucksack.

Some of the smaller Middesians grunted and strained as they climbed the steeper portions of the trail. They marched at probably half the rate the Republican soldiers traveled earlier in the day but it seemed even slower, mainly owing to the hundreds of pounds of equipment the Middesians dragged behind them. Republican military code dictated that, unless explicitly instructed, the belongings of an enemy soldier were to be incinerated. She doubted that many situations in the annals of Republican military conflicts required its soldiers to forage for survival, however. In this place, she would bet that anything not comprised of stone or dust had value.

This can't be good, she thought as they marched to the north, toward the first of the setting suns. She was still alive, though, with most of her mind and body intact, so it could always be worse.

*   *   *

From the journal of Lt. Wilson Kole:

The leadership of the Republic never cared whether the Middesian population survived the occupation. In fact, they probably would have preferred to rip apart a barren planet. Despite the overall cavalier attitude toward the indigenous life-forms, the Republic's Subcommittee on Resource Acquisition initially dispatched a couple dozen cultural anthropologists to Middes to learn what they could about the natives, in the event that negotiation proved a more cost-effective strategy than occupation (of course, the resulting information ultimately proved useful in either case). The anthropologists found that, with very little variation, the Middesians lived in a rigidly structured, highly stratified social structure. When the anthropologists submitted their report to the Subcommittee, they estimated that the entire Middesian population was a little bit north of 25 million. Following the flight of the Vlorth, a report by the Occupation Council estimated the adjusted population at roughly ten million Middesians lived on the entire planet, almost two million having left on the transports (comprised mainly of the elites and their security teams, servants, and staff), and the rest dying as a result of the occupation. These numbers do not refer to soldiers only, but also, non-military, children, and the elderly.

By all accounts, the elites considered the turn of events (i.e., losing the war) a decided inconvenience, but not a catastrophe. They had, after all, taken with them on the transport virtually everything of value that did not first need to be mined or refined. With enough wealth, technology, and military might, they could find asylum on nearly any habitable planet they wished.

The Middesians on the lowest, most populous strata were considered little more than beasts of burden. What I find fascinating is that, after generations and generations of living in this specific caste, these hither to disposable Middesians managed to find enough worth in themselves to throw in their lot with Azzerello and continue fighting for their physical survival when no collective existential goals remained. It's hard for someone from a completely different culture to understand the subjective experience of another, but consider: the utter destruction of their culture stripped the meaning of their lives from them, leaving them in highly anomic circumstances. Nothing meant anything anymore. They basically had to re-construct their own meaning from nothing, and I have to wonder if humans would have been capable of the same reinvention under similar circumstances, or if they would have curled up and let fate run its course. Thankfully, it remains an open question.

*   *   *

CHAPTER SEVEN:
THE BELLY OF THE BEAST

Thank God they aren't making me wear my school uniform, *the recent graduate thinks as she steps onto the loading ramp, onto a newer, smaller version of the transport ship that took her parents away from her thirteen years before. Thirteen years, and she had hardly ever left the floating orphanage/school. Strangely, the threat of homesickness once she left the ethereal environs of Linthal failed to imbue her with a sense of dread. Part of it comes from the fact that a full one-fifth of her graduating class either has enlisted or plans to enlist, so she is bound to have some acquaintances in her training group. Mostly, this lack of sentimentality comes from never really having a home to miss.*

Finally, she can sit anywhere she wants, so she takes a seat near the front of the transport, right next to the window, and looks out at her school. Three stories high at its highest point, it stretches into the distance so that she can't even see the dorms. It looked so huge when she was a little girl, but even with the edition of the new gymnasium they built five years ago, it seems only slightly larger than a refueling station. She will never see it again; she knows it in her heart.

A dozen or so faculty members stand just off the loading platform, waving to the students they had nurtured for over a decade. Grey-haired Ms. Hatcher feigns happiness, behaving as if she has helped prepare the graduates for adult life by teaching them about the history of the Republic. For some, that may be true, but there's a hollowness behind Ms. Hatcher's eyes, because, as a non-delusional teacher of history, she can estimate with startling accuracy how many of the teenagers on that transport ship are going to be left to rot on a foreign planet. Several other members of the faculty don't bother to hide their somberness. They are the closest thing the young woman has to parents, but that really isn't close at all. Caring is part of their job, and when she and her classmates blast off, never to be heard from again, they will treat a new set of students the same way. It really is all that they can do, but in the end, it isn't very much. It fails to provide even the illusion of permanence.

She and her physics teacher, Mr. Gemmel, make eye contact through the layer of unbreakable glass. He has played the role of her father for these past five years, she remembers him better than her actual father, and he will perform that role for someone else, now. He's a pudgy, balding man who stands several inches shorter than her and seems to shrink every year, but he never ceased to show warmth to her and her classmates. He smiles and waves, mouthing some unintelligible farewell. "You can do anything you want," he once told the young woman during one of her deeper fits of melancholy. To how many other similarly limited students had he offered the same platitude? Maybe it held true, but only if she desired something within her station; you can do anything you want, but only so long as it involves, at most, administrative assisting. *If he thought so highly of her, why didn't he ever make dinner for her the way he did for some of the students with the brighter uniforms? She waves back, thinking,* I hope I never see any of you again. *It's time to move on.*

*   *   *

They marched through the setting of the first sun, deep into a mountain valley. The red sunlight grew deeper over the next hour as the second sun began its downward path, changing the landscape from red-tinged to positively crimson. The hue of the Republican uniforms changed along with it. Clarice marched in the oversized footsteps of Wraith One, well aware that only the presence of the enemy soldiers and their weapons prevented him from turning around and finishing the job he started back in the Killing Box. As impotent as her captive status made her feel, she gained some satisfaction in knowing that these same circumstances must have infuriated the colossal cyborg's remaining human parts. She still watched him closely, just in case he wanted to risk his own life to end hers. *Thank god he didn't know about the fake arm*, she thought for maybe the tenth time.

On a couple of occasions, Clarice risked a glance over her shoulder to check on Kole. He walked behind Wraith Three, the troll with half a nose, and in front of Wraith Four, the one with the narrow eyes. Without the bulky equipment to encumber him, Kole strolled more than marched, and wore a curious, easy look on his face, as though he were about to smile. More than once, Clarice glimpsed her second-in-command gazing up at the pink sky, his hands linked behind him. Given the context, she found it slightly unnerving; his mood seemed far brighter than anyone else, including their captors. It certainly wasn't a typical reaction to being captured by a hostile force, but Kole wasn't a typical soldier. Maybe he'd gone crazy. Maybe he considered himself already dead, and any stretch of life beyond the canyon constituted a gift. She had heard of things like that happening to captives in hopeless situations: they let each moment wash over them, milking the passing seconds for whatever small sensations they had to offer.

While she envied this feeling, of appreciating life's nuances again, Clarice had not reached that point. Not even close, because the longer she remained alive, the more pain she endured. If death became inevitable, she intended to take as many members of one group of enemies or the other with her. She intended to kill Wraith One, and if she survived that, she intended to kill Leon Azzerello. Revenge was still her driving, burning desire that gave her the motivation to continue moving forward. Even if one courted death, it feels better to believe that your death served a cause. Hopefully, they would find Leon Azzerello before her thirst for vengeance dried up and she went full-on suicidal.

The Middesian waddling along to her left carried no visible weapons. The pair of rucksacks it lugged nearly dragged on the ground. The creature wore a dirt brown tunic that it had tied at the waist with a length of frayed rope. A rather runty looking specimen, even for a Middesian... almost half the size of the Middesian carcasses she gutted and left on the battlefield. Perhaps the Middesian in charge of the ambush stationed this particular male next to her because it considered her relatively harmless. Perhaps she could prove it wrong...

Even with deadly weapons held in their claw-heavy digits, Clarice failed to find any of the Middesians too menacing from up close. Physically, most Middesians looked rather clumsy and pathetic, and this particular group bore a far more ragged appearance than those she fought during the "official" war. The ones she had fought were highly trained, well-equipped, physically fit soldiers, more than capable of tearing apart a human in unarmed combat. These creatures were none of those things. Some wore ratty clothes in dire need of mending. Others wore sections of cloth that they had converted into clothing, probably with little more than a knife and a rope. The most plentiful color was a brownish-red, either because that was the color of the material or because it had so much dirt clinging to it that red might as well have been the original color. For those whose torsos remained visible, their ribs visibly protruded through their skin, and all of them sported the occasional patch of scarred, bare skin where fur should have been.

Thinking about the Middesian soldiers used to terrify her to the point where she would have nightmares the night before a campaign. Granted, those were a faster, stronger breed, but it seemed laughable now.

In her young, inexperienced mind, these horrific, shadowy creatures only surfaced at night and could tunnel under you and drag you into the pits of that scarred little planet. Sometimes on the battlefield at night, she could only see their eyes: beady, red dots poking out of the darkness. When she marched past the blasted bodies of fallen enemies, her eyes always lingered an extra-long time on the thick, black claws that could dig through all but the densest rock. Beyond anything physical, though, they were the ones that sent the blue lightning raining down on her and those she loved.

Lying on her stomach, with Wraith One preparing to decapitate her with his bare, mechanical hands, Clarice could scarcely have imagined that things would have worked out so well (relatively speaking...). Her enemies had all exposed themselves, and now she knew whom she could trust (even if that lone person was utterly useless). It seemed likely that these furry foot soldiers would deliver her to a Middesian base, perhaps the one where the treacherous, elusive cause of all her pain resided. Even Kole had survived up to this point, which was no small feat. Keeping him alive had come to represent an added, moral victory for her: a mission within a mission... the proverbial cherry on top. If she could overcome her now obvious obstacles from without and within, kill Azzerello, and keep Kole alive so that he could tell the tale... well then, she could leave this pathetic universe a legend of the Republic. Maybe they'd place a hologram of her in high schools across the cosmos.

Roughly one hour the second red son crossed the craggy horizon, as the three parallel lines of marchers came over a rise, the wrecked hull of what appeared to be a Middesian PT-417 Transport consumed their path... or at least half of a wrecked hull. The front half of the great, white ship sat propped up against the side of a cliff wall. Except for the missing tail, it looked ready to blast off. Judging from the regularity of the cut, the damage hadn't been inflicted by multiple attack ships; a single shot from a laser cannon on the surface must have torn the monstrous ship apart. The rear half, with the engines and fuel tanks, would have struck the ground and exploded somewhere within a few miles of their location, while the wide, flat nose portion lay dormant before them. The one-eared Middesian that led the group veered toward the shell of great ship.

The wreckage grew larger as they neared it, until it consumed Clarice's vision. The thought of the hundreds of decayed bodies waiting inside the ship sent a shudder down to the heels of her boots. Hopefully, they would veer off before they got under the behemoth. Decayed Middesian bodies were still decayed corpses. Republican soldiers quickly and efficiently disposed of casualties on both sides, occasionally by burial but usually by manual incineration. So while she had seen her share of dead bodies during her time with the military, Clarice's nose had minimal experience with the odor of rotting flesh. She chanced a look behind her at Kole, and while he still looked mighty chipper for a prisoner of war, his expression leveled off as he eyed the broken ship, the same thought no doubt drifting through his mind and his nasal cavity.

The musky odor crept up on them soon after the wreckage became visible and thickened with each step. When they were within a few dozen paces of the ship, the thick, fetid stench hit like a wave. Still, the Middesians seemed intent upon entering the mass grave, and Clarice could not imagine why. Certainly there were other areas that would provide shelter with a less pungent downside. They did not need to stop there for the night, or anywhere for that matter, since Middesians in that part of the planet were nocturnal. And why lead them through the wreckage at all? The putrescence must have been even more intense to the well-developed Middesian snouts. Maybe they weren't offended by that particular strain of stench. Maybe they *ate* their dead. It was possible; Clarice simply didn't know much about the Middesians except where to shoot them when she wanted them to stop charging.

Even in its partially intact state, the hull of the PT-417 must have stretched five hundred feet up the cliff wall, higher than any Middesian-made, above-ground building on the entire planet. The Middesian in the lead continued toward the jagged, shadowy hole that used to connect to the back of the ship.

Clarice felt faint. The weight of the stench settled over her like a soiled blanket and pulled her down. She did not know anything, even rotting flesh, could smell that bad. It hit her on a biological level; even if she had no experience with corpses or a fully developed concept of death, something in her nasal receptors would tell her to avoid the thing giving off that scent. Thankfully, she had already emptied her stomach the previous evening. Kole made some uneven gagging sounds from several paces behind her. *When was his last meal?* she wondered. She attempted to breathe through her mouth, but the air had a thickness and taste to it. The Wraiths appeared immune to the stench, plodding along the same as they would when stalking prey through a flowery meadow, which seemed odd, since the technicians had probably enhanced all their other senses. Their condition must have either kept the smell from affecting them or kept them from reacting to it. They probably could push a button on their wrist units and close their nasal passages or disconnect their olfactory bulbs.

The group slipped under the mouth of the wreckage and into thick shadows. Even if she could have reached her night-vision goggles and switched them on, Clarice would not have done so. The only sight to see would be an endless line of corpses in various stages of decay, hovering over her, stretching toward the sky. Passengers, mostly civilians still strapped into their seats, killed by decapitation, fright, or man-sized debris crushing the life out of them. Given the thin upper atmosphere of Middes, though, most of the decaying bodies probably died from asphyxiation. They probably clawed at the windows, each other, and themselves for a few minutes, trying to get air. They must have sat in the same position for weeks, at least since the mass evacuation, their bulging eyes staring down the long tunnel of blackness.

Her eyes rotated upward, slightly, but only found blackness. They told her... the people at the school told her that her parents died from asphyxiation. She shuddered. Human miners trapped, miles under the ground, for minutes or hours of terrified contemplation. Some going mad and scratching themselves bloody on the rock walls. Not the kind of images she wanted in her head. At least Jervis's remains got a decent disintegration. At least his death came (relatively) quickly. The weight of the hundreds of dead eyes fell on her as she passed beneath, because there weren't enough carrion-eaters in this part of the world to remove them. It was not something she wanted to look at, even if they were Middesians.

Once the shadow of the ship consumed the entire group, a grinding sound echoed through the void, followed by a sharp click. A sliver of light split the blackness and slowly, mechanically widened into a square of light. The light emanated from a sliding panel in the side of something that looked like a ten-foot-high mound of scrap metal. The panel slid to the right to reveal a dimly lit passage angling sharply downward. The Middesian at the front of the column motioned for its prisoners to walk down into the tunnel.

The small circumference of the tunnel actually helped to offset the almost vertical angle it took into the ground. Clarice braced her hands on either side of the rock passage and allowed gravity to escort her downward a few inches at a time. Even with her gloves protecting it, the rough surface abraded the palm of her hand… her left hand. The grooves on the wall indicated that the Middesians dug it. How long had it taken them? Hours? Weeks? The descent ended after about twenty feet of slow, controlled sliding, and Clarice found herself inside an enormous, natural cave.

Several dozen Middesians milled about inside the dank, gray cavern. Given their variance in age, size, gender, grooming, clothing, and activity, that seemed the most accurate way to describe them: a bunch of Middesians. The cave obviously acted as a base of sorts; Clarice had hoped her captors would take her to a place like this when they ambushed her "team." Over in the far left corner, Middesians tended to the arsenal of hand-held Republican weapons they had stockpiled. Over in the far right corner, Middesians tended to the wounds of other Middesians. Dead ahead, against the cave's far wall, Middesians lined up in front of a large table, waiting for their turn to dine on bowls of something that, from a distance and to the untrained eye, resembled hot mud.

The one-eared Middesian, the only one of the group to vocalize in Clarice's presence, steered them toward a conspicuous cluster of humans assembled atop a raised, wooden platform to the immediate left of the tunnel opening. They all sat around a large table and looked up when they saw the line of Republican soldiers. The humans wore the tattered, white uniforms of Republican aviators and looked so ragged that at first Clarice thought they were fellow captives. She counted eleven of them, four women, seven men, and one person wearing a helmet with the blast shield down. One of the women had no left arm. One of the men appeared to be missing a left arm and a right leg.

Clarice watched closely as she neared them. It soon became clear that these were not captives. The ones who looked at Clarice and her team didn't make eye contact or look in their direction for more than a few seconds before their gazes fell away. A large, sturdy piece of paper lay draped over the edge of the wooden table at which they sat. Even though Clarice couldn't read the writing on it, she could identify it as a map. The humans milled around the platform and spoke to one another with the ease of free individuals. One, a young, blonde-haired girl that looked like a teenager, even smiled. None of the Middesians in the area targeted the group with a weapon. As she looked on, a Middesian that looked like little more than a mound of fur with a snout approached one of the humans. The human, a thirty-ish male with thin, blond hair, put his hand on the Middesian's shoulder and whispered in the creature's ear. There was a casual familiarity in the movement. As the Middesian left, the human patted it on the shoulder, like one would a friend. It seemed that, despite all the mistakes and obstacles, she had found Azzerello and his nest of traitors.

*   *   *

Clarice's pulse throbbed and her breathing quickened. One of the people standing or sitting in front of her rained down the concussion blasts that damaged Wraith Two the previous night. The memory of Wraith Two and the confused look that fell across her face when they cut her power sent another shudder through Clarice, and she pushed the image out of her memory as fast as possible. It was terrible and disgusting and whoever did it pushed a button and zoomed on by without sticking around to witness the carnage. Any of these treacherous psychopaths could have done it, since they had all effectively denounced all allegiance to the Republic and everything it stood for… but she would show them all that actions do have consequences.

Her eyes slid to her left, toward the runty Middesian that stood about three feet away with it head turned away from her. It held the two rucksacks in one appendage and an incendiary rifle in the other. She could punch the Middesian with her right arm, grab the rifle with her left arm, and fire from the hip in a right-to-left arch across the group. She liked her chances of taking out a few of the standing traitors, but first she needed to find out for certain which one was Leon Azzerello. After all, even if fifty Middesians, ten traitors, and (maybe) five Wraiths protected him... even if he could mock the gods behind the controls of a spacecraft... down on the ground, he was still a flesh and blood meat-bag. One shot from an incendiary rifle turned up to its maximum setting would cut him in half, just like one punch from her right arm would crack his skull like a nut.

The armed Middesian captors motioned for Clarice and the rest of her group to step forward, toward the platform containing the band of traitors. Wraith One wanted her dead, for some reason. Did they even *want* to kill Azzerello? Maybe, but they certainly weren't a commodity that she could count on. For all she knew, Azzerello somehow engineered their mutiny. *At least I know what to expect from Kole*, she thought, with a slight internal smile, *honest effort and zero output*.

Clarice scanned the traitors as she continued to shuffle forward. A brown-skinned woman, roughly Clarice's age, stood opposite the map table. At first, the woman reacted to Clarice's glowering visage as if Clarice were some curiosity from an intergalactic freak show, but as soon as their lines of sight connected, the woman's eyes dropped to the ground. Clarice shifted her glare to an older, bald man on the brown-skinned woman's left, but he looked past Clarice, as though he did not even see her and the others enter the cavern. *So, cowardice is catching.* A few of the pilots still wore the designations of rank from before they decided to betray the Republic. Others seemed to have removed theirs on purpose.

Two blond men stood on the platform. Which one was Azzerello? She would bet on the one on the right of the cluster of traitors, the one that patted the Middesian on the shoulder; he looked a little more fresh-faced, and Azzerello supposedly looked ten years younger than his actual age. Battle has a way of aging a person, though, even when floating around in the sky, so either one could be the Head Traitor, or neither. She only saw the slightly blurry, blue-tinted hologram for a couple minutes as it rotated above table in General Frusin's quarters, and she could not be certain how much his appearance had changed since they scanned the image for his personnel file. If she jumped the guard, she probably had one chance to aim and get off a shot before her assorted enemies tore her apart. There was still the person wearing the helmet; that could be anyone. And Azzerello could have shaved his head... no, strike that: the bald guy was a little too old and a little too subordinate-looking.

The Middesian that spoke back in the ravine held up a clawed fist, the armed escorts stopped their captives' forward movement at the base of the platform, right in front of a set of recently constructed wooden stairs. None of the traitors stepped forward to initiate the parlay, so Clarice took it upon herself to do so. The instant she cleared Wraith One's bulbous, right shoulder, half a dozen Middesians shoved gun barrels in her face. All of the humans except three took at least one step back toward the table: the one-legged man merely leaned, the person in the helmet nearly fell over a chair, and one of the blond pilots held his ground.

The blond male human, seemingly in his late twenties, stepped forward to receive her. He had a small frame, like most fighter pilots, and delicate features that seemed almost fragile despite his longish, unkempt hair and light beard. She noticed these features but passed over them until she reached his eyes. They had such a deep blue color that, even from ten yards away, they were almost annoying to look at. They gave him an aura of serenity. He looked like a painter, or someone who should have served as the battalion chaplain if he ever entered the military at all. A twinkle lingered in his eye, and he actually smiled at her. "Hello," he said as though they randomly had bumped into one another on the street of a planet not involved in a war. "Who might you be?"

The guns pointed at Clarice from every angle, enough guns to utterly atomize her if they were turned up to maximum power. Her target still stood about ten feet away, at the top of a platform, and unless she could take him to hell with her, this would be a useless death. Azzerello leaned in, though, bringing his face a few inches closer in search of an answer. "I'm Lt. Clarice Torrance," she said. "I've been sent here to find Leon Azzerello."

Azzerello linked his hands behind him and gave a toothy smile. The bright white grin reminded Clarice of Drennon, except this one seemed genuine. That somehow made it worse. How the hell could he smile like that? After what he did to her life? Maybe he was a simpleton, or a savant, or worse. Maybe all psychopaths smiled like that. "You mean 'kill me,' don't you?" he asked.

"Yes I do," she said without hesitating. The bluntness didn't faze him. His slight grin clung to his face and threatened to make her do something rash. *How... dare you stand there smiling?* she wanted to yell. By virtue of existing, he had killed so many people, better people than him... and would continue to do so... yet seemed so content with himself. His idiotic actions sucked the meaning and purpose right out of her life. He might as well have fired the mortar that destroyed the only man that ever cared about her. How could he do that and still occupy her reality? How could he stand there, grinning that stupid grin, as though he was an embarrassed stranger and not the man who crushed her soul?

From atop the five-foot-high platform, in front of the set of four stairs, Azzerello nodded. He seemed oblivious to the anger pulsating in her and showed no more alarm than if she'd told him that it had started raining outside. The other traitors eased their way out of hiding and congregated behind their leader like a set of wary pack animals, but he ignored them. He lifted his thin, pointy chin and regarded the other members of her assassination squad. "Let me guess... he's the only one that's totally human," he said, pointing to Kole's rigid form. "The rest of you are..." he turned to his human comrades for help. "Specters?"

Both of Azzerello's shoulder blades momentarily faced her as he turned, and Clarice leapt forward. The Middesians juggled their rifles and tried to track her as she lunged for the steps. Although they had enough battle experience to fire a rifle, none of them were soldiers, so they didn't respond reflexively to her attack, and she caught them off guard. The pilots, who normally pushed buttons from a comfortable chair and observed the results of their handiwork from a mile away, froze in the face of actual combat. She caught everyone off guard... everyone except Wraith One. While the others fumbled with their weapons or gawked, Wraith One's left hand lashed out and grabbed Clarice by the nylon shoulder strap that crossed her body. At the top step, Clarice's feet lifted out from under her, and she braced herself for the crash against the rock floor. She would have made it, too. Azzerello had just started to turn around, and a single fist to the back of his skull would have ended this entire mess. Betrayal stalked her path like an Olmarian Carrion Hawk.

"Don't shoot!" Azzerello commanded anyone with a gun.

Clarice's tailbone slammed into the ground, and she reflexively backward-somersaulted into a crouch. The world around her shifted and spun as the Republican and Middesian soldiers drifted away from the two combatants and formed a makeshift skirmish circle. Clarice barely registered the movement, because while she tried to blink away the assorted spots and draw breath, Wraith One set upon her like an avalanche. His right arm snaked around her neck, its massive bicep muscle smashed against her throat, and before she even has time to regain her balance, her feet lifted off the ground.

She surprised him with the cybernetic arm last time, but Wraith One had learned from his mistake. His bulk prevented her from reaching anything particularly vulnerable with her right arm, while he... he could do a lot from that position: choke her, break her neck, or try to rip her head off, again. Her feet flailed helplessly, several inches above the ground. Clarice dug her fingers into his right forearm, trying to pull it an inch or two away from her throat as its owner momentarily deliberated on how to end her life.

Clarice kicked out, for an instant, shifting all her weight forward. She barely budged Wraith One, but "barely" allowed the ball of Clarice's right foot brushed the ground. With a half-second, at best, to act, she planted her heel between Wraith One's feet. Fortunately for her, the newer-model cybernetic limbs of Wraiths were constructed almost entirely from plastics with lightweight metal casings. This accounted for the Wraiths' inhuman speed, but it also kept their weight under 150 percent of a normal human with a comparable build. Clarice stepped back into her massive opponent and twisted at the waist, flipping him over her shoulder.

Wraith One hit the stone floor, skidded for a couple feet, and spun into a crouch with the unsettling quickness of a Prothold Jungle Cat. Clarice clenched her teeth. Killing him would be impossible unless she used her right arm, and he wouldn't be stupid enough to make that mistake twice. Azzerello could kill him if he ordered the Middesians to open fire, but only an idiot would kill someone who just saved his life. If she could get to one of the –

In the second she spent strategizing, Wraith One sprung forward, his thick arms spread wide. The tree-sized forearm slammed into her abdomen, and Clarice spun inward, toward his midsection. The two mechanized arms smashed against her back, pinning her against his massive, armored chest. Her brittle spine would shatter in two seconds.

Her eyes rode slightly below his chin. The arms squeezed her torso like a pair of bellows. Clarice's mouth popped open as a hiss of oxygen rushed out of her. At eye level, Wraith One's all-too human Adam's apple bobbed once before she chomped down on it. A sharp crunch split the shocked silence, and she nearly gagged. Instead, she kept pressing her jaws closed until her teeth met. The Wraith's arms released her, but the gloved fingertips of both his hands pressed against her face and launched her backward. In a way, his pushing her away helped her finish the job; she probably never would have torn away all that connective tissue, otherwise.

Bright red blood arched after her as flew backward toward the ground. Clarice hit the floor and skidded to a stop against the base of the platform. She sucked in air through her nose, but her jaw still refused to let go of the chunk of flesh. Wraith One fell to his hands and knees, gushing blood from his neck like a normal human. Were he not making gargling sounds, he might have sobbed like a normal human. He staggered around in disconnected half-circles, his eyes rotated word the ceiling. His hands pressed against his missing hunk of neck, as though if by pressing hard enough, he could regenerate a missing trachea.

From the platform above her, Azzerello's deathly pale visage slowly came into focus. He looked down at Clarice, slack-jawed and wide-eyed, as though she were some sort of terror from a children's story.

A blood mustache probably stained her upper lip, but at least she finally got that stupid grin off his face. She staggered to her feet like a battered pugilist and spit the hunk of throat out onto the stone floor. It bounced once and landed next to Wraith One's boot.

Wraith One continued to wilt. He was built to level an enemy bunker, but blood was blood: he needed it, and it gushed between his massive fingers. He fell to his knees, fell forward in slow motion, then rested his forehead on the ground.

Azzerello visibly shuddered from atop his pedestal and turned his head away from the slowly shriveling cyborg. Clarice kept her gaze locked on him as she braced her back against the rock wall, savoring the reaction. *Nothing like a hard dose of reality to shake this piece of shit out of his delusion.* She could chomp out a dozen throats and still wouldn't have caused a tenth of the suffering he had.

When Wraith One collapsed onto his side and finally stopped moving, everyone else came to life. Two Middesians grabbed Clarice by the arms. She let them drag her across the main floor of the cave, toward a side tunnel; her work here was done, for now. Among the traitors, the dark-skinned woman and the other blond man tromped down the wooden steps to make a token attempt at saving Wraith One. Azzerello remained motionless. Despite her rough escort, Clarice's eyes stayed locked onto him. "That should've been you!" she barked over her shoulder. Part of her saw acting crazy as an effective intimidation tactic, but at that point, she honestly didn't know if she could have stopped if she wanted to. "That should've been you!"

Azzerello remained silent. He watched his henchmen drag her away, his empty expression equal parts confusion and horror, as if he had never been hated before.

*　　　　　*　　　　　*

From the journal of Lt. Wilson Kole:

I don't know what makes one person chew out the throat of another. I certainly doubt that such an action would never occur to me and if it did, I think, on some level, I would prefer death over actually carrying it out. I think it's safe to say, though, that Clarice and I were cut from different cloth.

I never spoke to Clarice before the blast took her arm. I don't know if she was a throat-chewer at heart, but somehow I doubt it. At the time she did it, she already considered herself dead. The mission had become the single motivating factor that she fed upon, and killing Azzerello would give her vengeance and what she hoped would be peace. Whether it would have or not is irrelevant; the thought that it would motivated her.

As such, I didn't lose respect for her as a human being while watching her kill Wraith One in such a manner. On the contrary, I saw someone with such a desire to continue living that she would overcome any obstacle in order to pursue the goal that gave her a reason to live. Compared to the numbing malaise that enveloped me, it seemed like she was franticly trying to dig her way out of her grave while I surrendered prematurely to mine.

I never confused her with a normal person, and I say that as a compliment. I posit that her hypersensitivity made her more alive than anyone I knew, for better or worse. It drove her to these excesses of bravery and madness. I had been smitten with her from the moment I first saw her walking shoulder-to-shoulder with Jervis Giles down to the officers' quarters… her looking up at him as if he were the most important person in the world… but maybe it was then, as they dragged her away with a cluster of bright red arterial blood dots decorating her cheeks, that I truly felt love for Clarice Torrance. War is such a strange endeavor…

*   *   *

CHAPTER EIGHT:
SMELLS LIKE GIRL

The trainee falls on her face for the third time. "Damn, Torrance," the slightly older, male trainee groans from atop her. "You're going to break my neck before we get to the finish line."

She scrambles out from under him while the unsettled dirt still levitates in the air. "I'm sorry," she says, breathlessly, wincing as she pushes him onto his back. "I'll make it... this time." She turns around and leans her shoulders against his supine form. Her right arm snakes between his thighs, and her other arm around his right arm. He's supposed to stay limp, like an unconscious person, but he keeps his arm rigid to help her out. Otherwise, the film of sweat coating her arms would cause her to slide right off. "Hrrumf!" she grunts and jerks herself to her feet.

Her left foot slams into the dust. The other eighteen cadets cheer in the distance, a blur of gray jumpsuits caked in mud. Her right foot slams down. All the others had crossed the finish line over a minute ago. All the other women. Hanna, Rendiela, Natali... they all clap, shout her name, and pump their fists. Hanna's shoulders are as broad as a man's. From a distance, with her ponytail tucked into her collar, it is hard to tell the difference. The others almost look like men, with their forearms like I-beams and their thighs like tree trunks. Most of her fellow cadets are twice her size, even if she never understood what physical strength had to do with firing a concussion rifle. Kole carried her all the way down to the river without falling, though. The least she can do is bring him back without killing him.

Her left leg plants, wiggles, and buckles. Kole's midsection lands on her head. Her nose doesn't break. Kole actually laughs. "At least you have the decency to break my fall," he says.

"I'm glad you think this is funny," she snorts as she drags herself to her bloody knees.

She takes a second to survey the remainder of the course: fifty yards of wet, brown sand stretching in front of her. "Stoppin' for a rest, sweetheart?" the mustachioed drill sergeant barks, his face inches from her ear. She never even saw him approach. "You ain't got time to stop! You gonna stop and take your sweet-ass time when you're in the middle of a firefight and you got Kraltian death-rays cookin' your buddies?"

"No, Drill Sargent," she coughs, rolling Kole onto his back. "I can make it."

"Can you make it without falling, sweetheart?"

"Yes, Drill Sargent!"

She does… fall that is. Half a dozen more times. The last time, though, she falls on the other side of the finish line.

*   *   *

The pair of mangy Middesians dragged Clarice down a dark tunnel in a series of steady jerks. They were larger than her and far from weak, but she continued to resist as well as she could. She wasn't trying to get away, because killing Azzerello was temporarily impossible; she took her shot, and now there were fifty guns between the two of them. Besides, she really couldn't escape in any meaningful way, even if she wanted to; it's hard to generate much force when your arm is cybernetic and nothing else is, and if she got away, where would she go? No, she just resisted for the sake of resisting.

The dry, abrasive pads of the Middesians' "hands" pressed against her wrists and elbows and made her skin crawl. The moldy smell that enveloped her could have come from either her captors or the cave. Unlike the walls of the larger cave, the surface of the tunnel walls appeared too smooth to be natural. Someone had probably bored out the tunnel with a cutting-laser; either that or some of the Middesians dug it with those bone-shredding claws and paid extra attention to refining their work. After fifteen paces, the tunnel emptied into a dimly lit, cramped chamber that featured six, steel-barred cells lined up against one wall. The uneven walls indicated that nature had undertaken the job of carving this room out of the bedrock. An oversized, key-operated padlock hung from each door, for use in keeping the cell door closed. No prisoners currently occupied the cells, and the Middesians shoved Clarice into the first one.

When the door slammed shut behind her and the lock clicked closed, Clarice immediately spun around and grabbed two bars of the cell door, coldly staring down the two departing Middesians. "Are these supposed to hold me?" she yelled, jerking manically on the bars.

One of the Middesians, the smaller of the two, pivoted long enough to shake its snout. Its claw pointed toward the slit in the wall opposite the cells. The slit measured about six inches by eighteen inches, and the black barrel of an incendiary rifle extended out of it. The shaggy, shadowy form of a Middesian hovered at the opposite end of the weapon, no doubt under orders to burn to the ground anyone attempting to escape. Clarice nodded to herself as the two Middesians shambled back into the shadows of the corridor, but the sight didn't discourage her.

She paced around the cell, patting her thighs with her fingertips. The bars weren't perfectly straight or uniform, and their worn, ragged surface belied the fact that the Middesians probably cut them out of the wreckage of the ship on the surface, but they were solid and ran from the floor to the ceiling. If Clarice decided to escape, if she knew exact Azzerello's location, she had only to place her right palm on one bar and her right elbow on the other and twist to create enough space to step through. That was the easy part. Not getting killed in the two seconds that followed would provide the challenge. Several fist-sized or smaller rocks littered the cellblock floor. Her right arm undoubtedly could toss a hard projectile at a lethal velocity. All she had to worry about was accuracy. That slit wasn't very wide, and the angle was terrible; she would either have to backhand the throw or toss it through a couple layers of cell bars. Her eyes darted around the floor of her cell. No stones. In fact, the floor was immaculate. *Great...* Several suitable rocks lay about in the other cells but they sat far from her reach. There had to be another way out. If the events of the past couple minutes served as any indication, Azzerello seemed particularly inept when it came to covering his ass.

Alone, with the exception of the guard in the makeshift pillbox, Clarice alternated between pacing about the cage and rattling the bars. She felt... *up*, like she had loaded herself with stimulants before a shift as the night watch. The adrenaline rolled its way through her veins, and her pulse bounced along at a nice, elevated rate. She could chew through one hundred throats as long as one of them belonged to Azzerello.

After a few minutes, she clutched the bars and let her head rest in the crook of her arm. Her eyes closed and her last look of Azzerello drifted into view. He wore a wide-eyed, dazed expression, some combination of fear and confusion, when his goons hauled her away, like she was an unclassified alien that had shambled out from the depths of the cave. Working in infantry, Clarice witnessed far worse deaths than the kind Wraith One endured... mortal injuries that took hours to die from. Hell, she *caused* deaths worse than that.

She witnessed one death in particular that always stood out in her memories as being particularly cruel and surreal: her company was engaged in an urban firefight in Trilton. She was taking cover from behind a ground transport and saw a male private who she didn't know run past her, clutching his rifle in one hand and his quickly escaping entrails in the other. Everyone on both sides stopped shooting for a second and watched him run. He loped along, probably thinking that, if he just ran fast enough or long enough, he might travel back in time, back to when his guts were still in the right place. Ground fighting was nasty. On you ground, you got your hands dirty, and you only got good at it after you got used to it.

Pilots, on the other hand, never saw real fighting or real dying. They danced around on colored winds in an existence that mimicked art more than life. In bombing runs, the victims lingered too far away for you to witness the actual carnage. Your navigator might see a pillar of fire or a plume of smoke out of the rear window as the ship zips away. The pilot sees even less. The people marching behind the attack, the ones on the ground, are the ones who see the ripped and burned parts of bodies that the pilots left behind. Air-to-air combat was even cleaner. In dogfights, the explosive, brief confrontations generally ended with a cinder hurtling toward the horizon and left no mess to mop up.

It was hard to perceive someone who caused so much pain as being oblivious, but in that moment, Azzerello certainly looked more like a dope than evil incarnate. Maybe... despite his disgust or because of it... maybe witnessing Wraith One's bloody demise piqued Azzerello's curiosity. Maybe he would request audience with Clarice so he could ask where all the rage came from and try to understand it on a philosophical level. If he let her get close enough, she might explain herself in a whisper before she takes him to hell with her.

Her hands wrung the bars of her cell and her shoulders bobbed in rhythm with her heartbeat. She was still up, so up she could not remember the last time she felt so up. Her emotional rocket leveled off while her brain coughed up the appropriate memory. *Oh... yeah... of course.* The last time she felt that high-energy surge of emotion must have been right after she saw Jervis's charred body fall in a heap. The rocket shifted its course and hurtled groundward.

During the two weeks that followed the ruination of her life, she never let herself remember much beyond the flash of blue, the pain, and the screaming, but now, alone in her cell, she forced the gates open. She closes her eyes again, folded her left hand around her right hand, and let the scene form in the blackness. Jervis lay on the ground, little more than a blackened mass that made gurgling noises. The one-armed Clarice of her memory stared and screamed until she realized that it was doing no good. She turned away from her mortally wounded lover and ran over the hill, cradling her rifle with her remaining hand and firing it at the shadowy figures that charged toward her. She didn't even know she lost her arm until the technicians told her the next day. What did she think happened to it? No good answer. There wasn't much logic going through her head at that point, just overwhelming, animal emotion. Some toxic mix of fear, hopelessness, helplessness, and anger welled up inside of her and needed purging. Her remaining index finger squeezed the trigger every few steps, blasting flaming holes in a couple of the enemy and dispersing the rest.

Thick fog clung to the specific details, making them more like chunks of scattered, barely related images. She could remember some things very clearly, though. For one, as long as she ran, she felt good. Running saved her from the entropy that followed her. Part of her brain insisted on the idea that, if she chased off the aggressors, the medics could get to Jervis and save him. That argument now seemed empty. She knew on all important, rational levels of her mind, that Jervis would die. She could tell just by looking at him; the lifespan of people with all their flesh and most of their limbs burned off numbered in the seconds. There were still options available to her, even if none of them were pleasant. She could have stayed with him and held his charred hand while he died, or she could turned her rifle on him and mercifully ended his pain. Either would have kept him from dying alone. Either would have done him more good than running over that hill, blindly firing like an idiot. She received a promotion for it, but it was wrong, and there was no way to justify it, except to say that her mind wasn't strong enough to force her body to perform the necessary action. Her weakness forced her to run away: she had to move and kill and get out of there, or else fracture into madness.

Clarice's eyes opened, and a blurry view of a series of makeshift bars greeted her. With the last vestiges of her adrenaline evaporating with every step, she walked the three paces to the far end of the cell, to the uneven, rock wall and slumped against it. The frighteningly clear image of Jervis's burned-beyond-recognition body couldn't cling to her thoughts for too long before her head started spinning. An urge took hold, just like it did the night she lost him, telling her to get out and do anything but sit there. She had no energy left for mindless action, though, so instead of trying to rip the door of her cage off its hinges, she clutched her real forearm with her fake hand.

Don't break your arm, you idiot, she reminded herself and switched the positions of her hands. It was easy to see why she reacted the way she did out on the battlefield; it was... *understandable*. She doubted that anything could have set her off the way that... what she saw... did, but that series of horrible events did happen, and now she was left living in their aftermath. Weakness was never an acceptable excuse for stupid behavior in the past, though, and she refused to give it quarter now. Fear, sadness, horror… these were emotions, not excuses. A strong person can master her emotions. She left Jervis to die, alone and in pain. Left him alone in the dirt of a foreign planet. Alone. Abandoned him.

Clarice buried her forehead in the crook of her real arm, but did not cry. The numbness penetrated far too deeply for that. She would soon, though, probably with long, embarrassing, gut-wrenching sobs. Hopefully, her only audience would be the Middesian on the other side of the gun pointed at her. She could accept that scenario; Middesians probably had no idea what it meant when humans cried.

As if on cue, the lock on her cell door clicked open. Clarice's head jerked up and saw that she was mistaken; the sound did not come from someone unlocking her door. Rather, a Middesian had entered the prison and began to unlock every other cell door, starting with the cell to her immediate right. The four remaining Wraiths stood in a line that trailed into the hallway. Their flat affect made it difficult to tell that they were the prisoners and impossible to tell how they felt about that status. Two armed Middesians nervously stood to the rear of the group with their rifles trained on the cyborgs, while a third Middesian fumbled around with a ring of iron keys to unlock the giant padlocks. As each door swung open with a loud creak, the runtier of the two armed Middesians stepped forward and motioned with the tip of its laser rifle. On cue, each Wraith took a turn shambling into his or her cell individual cell. Only the cell furthest from Clarice remained unoccupied. Clarice craned her neck as far as she could without standing up, searching the hallway entrance for Lt. Kole, but found only stationary shadows.

The doors slammed shut, and Clarice started absently rubbing the bloodstain on her mouth. "Where is --" she began to ask the Middesian with the keys as it passed her cell on its way back to the hallway, but remembered that even if it understood her human dialect, its limited vocal capacities only allowed it to produce a handful of human speech sounds. She turned to the Wraith in the adjacent cell, the male with high cheekbones and black hair (Wraith... Four? Maybe? She couldn't tell with the backpacks removed.). "Where is Lt. Kole?"

Strangely, she wasn't certain she would get an answer from him, either, but Wraith Four's head snapped toward her. "I am not certain, Lieutenant," he said. "The humans detained Lt. Kole and appeared to be questioning him." He rotated his head forward again.

Clarice nodded. The fact that one of the Wraiths responded to her question with the usual brevity and tonelessness gave her a flicker of satisfaction. At least the message didn't contain any malice, or any other undertones. Dealing with automatons beat repeating the drama with Wraith One by a wide margin. Maybe he was the only one that malfunctioned, and the rest merely followed his lead. Maybe after witnessing the bloody mess she made of their squad leader, they were ready to give her some respect. This, of course, assumed that whatever brain matter the medical technicians left them with still allowed the Wraiths to respect people and things. On some level, they still valued their own life, though; if you take away the self-preservation instinct, your machine becomes a distinctly worse investment. That left them with at least one thing in common with their fellow soldiers. In truth, she had no idea how a Wraith's mind worked, or how much of a mind they had left, but if they were taking orders again, it would take them less than five seconds to break out of this holding chamber.

As for Kole, she could think of dozens of people who she had served with over the years that she would rather have facing an interrogation. Poke him with a couple needles, and he'd probably admit to injecting female hormones. That said, she doubted he could provide any useful information. What did he know? That General Frusin sent them to kill Azzerello? That was already obvious, as obvious as the fact that they'd failed. If Clarice stood in Azzerello's position, she'd send a Middesian with an incendiary rifle down to the holding cells and just start blasting away at the occupants. Azzerello didn't striker her as the type who could handle blood on his hands, though. He'd take an alternative route, but whatever happened from that point on depended on Azzerello's next move.

*   *   *

Her eyelids grew so heavy that they required effort to keep them open, so Clarice pulled herself to her feet and paced her cell. Soreness had to crept into her body during the minutes of sitting, but she had to stay awake, had to keep thinking about how to get out of this cell. What would Azzerello do next? After he finished extracting the limited information Kole had to offer, he probably wanted to find a way to contact the Army and arrange to release the prisoners in exchange for some concessions. Of course, the Army would deny having sent her team to the surface, so she probably didn't have much time before Azzerello decided to execute them. The next nap she took could be her last, so she began pacing again. In the shadows, the furry guard still hovered behind the laser rifle pointed in her direction, seemingly as alert as ever. The Wraiths sat still as corpses, their backs pressed against the wall and their hands resting on their knees.

Clarice kept moving. Actual, physical confinement was a new experience for her, and she hated it. While in basic training on Ultory – 11, a little, smarmy trainee named Barth Kitridge used to catch harmless flying insects in his hands, cup them, and slowly press his palms together. Bouncing off the walls of its flesh prison, the insect would flit around more and more frantically the closer it got to death. She'd seen children do things like that before, but when performed by an adult, the spectacle made Clarice a little ill, more so from the gleam in the sadistic creep's eyes than from the terror it caused the mindless insect. Kitridge only picked the kind that didn't sting to torture, and after he was finished, he would grin, wipe the bug guts on his pants, and search for another one. Clarice rarely empathized with insects, but her current situation had brought her to that point. If she was an insect, though, she was the stinging kind.

In the next cell, Wraith Four's eyes fixed their gaze on the far wall. Clarice ran her dry tongue over the cracked, jagged skin of her lips while she considered commanding all the Wraiths to pry apart the bars in the hope that one could make it out of the holding chamber. The rifle the Middesian carried looked to be a smaller caliber, maybe a XRL-180, or something similar. At its most focused, it could generate a narrow beam that would burn right through the Wraith's hides, but it would be so narrow that it would take several seconds to completely kill the target. At least one of the Wraiths would make it to the main chamber. It would never make it out of the main chamber, though. Even without an alarm system, the sound of bending metal and discharged weapons would alert the legion of enemies waiting there, and since most of them were armed, they would cut the escapees apart. It would almost be worth it, though, to keep her skin from crawling.

The experience made her feel so weak, so... helpless. Almost as helpless as the night when Jervis... *Don't go there.* Clarice pressed her palms against her temples and kept pacing. *This has to end soon.*

Minutes or hours later, after time in the cage ceased to hold meaning for her, one of the humans and an emaciated Middesian escorted Kole to his cell. "Escort" is completely accurate, too. They did not drag him, carry him, or even lead him in shackles to his cage. The human walked behind Kole and gripped Kole's shoulder as they walked, but Kole's arms swung freely at his sides. He still strolled along when he walked, just like he did on the walk from the Killing Box. Clarice's hands wrung the bars of the cage, and her eyes locked onto Kole and tracked him as he passed. He returned her gaze with a nod and a slight smile. She drew in slow, deliberate breaths, trying to check her anger until they were alone. Kole might not have betrayed her. Azzerello and his people might just be stupid and overly trusting. *What are you worried about?* she reminded herself. *Kole doesn't even know anything useful... neither do you, for that matter.* In any case, she remained silent, because drawing attention to Azzerello's lax security could rob her of a future advantage.

The cell door on the far side of the chamber closed with a click, and the two captors retraced their steps toward the exit, the human trailing the Middesian. Clarice shifted her glower from Kole to the tall, blond haired man with the patchy beard as he passed. This must've been the other guy she thought might be Azzerello, back when she first entered the main chamber. He was taller, and his hair was a darker blond and not as wispy as Azzerello's. The patches of his beard were thick, like he'd been living in a cave for a year, not a little over two weeks. Black grease streaks marred his face and uniform, as though he had just finished performing maintenance work... perhaps on a ship. There were no ships visible in the cavern, so there might be a passage to a different cavern, one with a ship-sized exit. This information could prove useful in a variety of ways. At the mouth of the tunnel, he stopped in mid-stride and stared back at Clarice while the Middesian continued out of the prison chamber. "Can I help you?" he asked.

"You can let me out of here so I can break your stupid neck," she hissed. As long as she stayed angry, she could avoid the crushing fatigue and lurking depression. So, she spared no effort in viewing these men and women as the lowest form of scum.

He scratched at his chin hair as though actually considering the proposal. "Tempting... but no. No, I think you'll just have to wait for the boss."

"What's your name?" Clarice demanded. "I see you've removed your name and rank from you uniform, so maybe—"

He took a step closer. "My name is Stevin Rich," he said, his voice devoid of sarcasm, "and I can write it down for you if you want. My bars and name badge got shipped back to Republic headquarters along with my letter of resignation." His eyebrows dove into a "V" as he regarded Clarice. It only took a couple seconds for him to shift from casual indifference to full-blown rage. He looked angry enough to shoot her if he had the means. He wore no visible weapons, though, and if he recently had played mechanic, he probably wouldn't carry a gun.

Clarice worked to keep her voice even. They could yell at each other for a satisfying five seconds, but in her experience, nothing infuriated the furious like someone that sounded impassive and condescending; that worked on her, anyway. "Tell me, Mr. Rich, what made you throw your lot in with a psychopath like Azzerello?"

The left side of Rich's mouth flinched into a snarl-smile, as if he recognized that she was trying to talk down to him. He seemed like the complete opposite of Azzerello: a tightly wound ball of emotion instead of a flat-line. Clarice found him infinitely more relatable. Maybe he contained enough rage for both men. For a second, she thought he might order the guard to shoot her, and she took a half step away from the cell door. He let out a snicker, even though his mask of anger remained in place. His eyes regarded the floor as the laughter built for a couple seconds, as if he was indulging in a private joke. It created an eerie enough scene for all four Wraiths to turn to regard Rich. "Have you ever heard, in your diligent study of the war, of a liquid chemical called Xellion B?" he asked Clarice.

She wrinkled her brow. *What does that have to do with anything?* "It's a defoliant," she said.

"That's what I thought, too," Rich said. "That's what they said about Xellion A, but they could be lying about that one, too. I just assumed they were the same thing until I thought about the topography of the area I was dumping it on." He frowned and stretched his arms out to indicate the area surrounding this base of operation.

Clarice stared blankly. She was physically and emotionally exhausted, and instead of jumping through the mental hoops required to follow his argument, she found herself wondering what rank he held while serving the Republic. He seemed a little high-strung for an officer...

His eyes widened in exasperation. "Nothing grows here!" he said. "This is the Wharrib Mountains. Before the war started, no one even lived here. This is where they fled because it's easier to hide. The only thing there is to eat is some root they have to dig down five feet to get to. It would have to rain Xellion B for a couple days to reach those things, and we were only dumping a few thousand gallons over a fifty-square-mile area."

"So what was it?" Clarice asked, not really caring. Even if Rich's payload consisted of a bio-engineered disease, they were fighting a war, and in war, you did whatever you had to do to destroy the opponent. Even if one side officially decided to play "fair," evil, horrible things naturally trail in the wake of war; it creates such an ugly context. Soldiers slaughter, rape, and perpetuate assorted other crimes that they would not normally do were they not placed in the bleeding, screaming hell of battle, so playing to win meant winning as fast as possible, and that justified some awful things.

"It was a chemical sterilizer," Rich said. "Strictly for animals; it had no botanical uses. We dropped it in containers on nights when the wind was blowing. The containers would burst a couple hundred feet from the ground, and it was supposed to make anything that breathed the fumes or made contact with the liquid sterile... anything." His eyes took on a distant, hollow look while waiting for a reaction. He apparently expected this information to horrify her.

Clarice's head tilted to a condescending angle. The strategy made perfect tactical sense to her, a stroke of brilliance, in fact. One never knew how long a war of occupation would last, but if you planned to occupy the area for more than a decade or two, and it helped to limit the supply of future opponents. Considering that the occupation of Middes involved setting up an elaborate mining operation, the Republic probably would maintain a long-term presence. It would prove beneficial to prevent generations of natives from sabotaging the operation. There had to be something else, something personal, maybe. "So... you betrayed the Republic because they made you sterile?" she asked. "That's weak."

"No," he said, sharply, "because it was wrong to do. Because we were doing it for the Republic. We work and kill all the time... we exist to feed this non-living, destructive thing. It doesn't do anything except expand and consume and occasionally enrich the ones who are pulling the levers. We chew up other people and chew up ourselves for the almighty Republic."

"Oh, spare me the platitudes," Clarice began. "Would it have made you happier if you'd been dropping bombs? Wake up. If you hate the Republic so much..." she stopped, realizing her mistake.

"What? Then leave? I did! I..." Rich licked his lips, trying to come up with the perfect thing to say to make her understand why treachery was worth more than the sum of his entire life. "I... I don't even know why I'm talking to you about this. If you haven't figured it out by now, you never will."

Clarice's eyebrows arched for a moment. *Dear God! Of all the people to talk down to her...* "Well, I appreciate the effort," she said, clasping her hands behind her. Her fatigue and the headaches it produced made it difficult to control her emotions, but she did her best. In this case, it wasn't enough. "You know, if you'd shown this much conviction while you were—"

"I'll leave you with this," Rich said, cutting her off. "I didn't know it at the time, but the chemicals I dropped did more than sterilize. There were a lot of Middesian females fighting on the front lines, even pregnant ones. Fighting against a genocidal occupier kind of makes you desperate. To pregnant females, the Xellion B stopped the fetus from fully developing. Sometimes that means stillbirths, but most of the time it's worse. Middesians are more developed when they're born than human babies, and their lungs develop pretty quick. When the babies exposed to Xellion B are developed enough to scream, they never stop." He licked his lips. "For this camp, I'm the one in charge of taking the babies from their mothers and... putting them down."

Clarice's mouth dropped open, and she stopped fidgeting. Okay, she had to admit: that was a bit beyond the pale. "You mean to tell me that Azzerello assigned you to kill those babies? That's psychotic. You couldn't have known."

Rich snorted out a humorless laugh. "He didn't assign me to it as punishment. I volunteered." He looked down, and his hands crawled into the pockets of his uniform. "It won't make amends for my mis—"

He took a breath and tried again, "... for my willful ignorance. Nothing ever will, but it's what I deserve. It's how I get through my day." He glanced up at her for a second with reddening eyes. No doubt the image of a wailing, mutated Middesian newborn danced in his head. When Rich spoke again, his voice cracked. "It was my fault. I pushed the button. Just think about that, will you? Next time you think about calling someone a traitor, ask yourself what exactly they're betraying."

Rich stalked away without waiting for a response. His shoulders rode at ear level. He probably wouldn't run off to a corner and start sobbing, but it would take him a minute to two to re-pack all that baggage and regain his composure. Clarice wanted to snap off a reply on general principle, to get the last word in as the lone representative of the Army of the Republic, or as a rational human being. Her heart was not in it, though. Rich lumbered down the tunnel looking like a man who was contemplating gutting himself, and she was no sadist.

The eyes of the Middesian guard glowed from the shadowy pillbox as Clarice turned away and resumed her pacing. Could it understand a word they said? Probably not, but emotions are hard to miss. Rich did not strike her as a bad man. On the contrary, he seemed like a sensitive, conscientious sort who, in a different capacity, really had something to offer the Republic. He certainly was unfit for soldiering, though. He couldn't subvert his own sensitivities in favor of the big picture. He could not see that a very real, very noble goal existed beyond the atrocities that occurred on the surface every day. The many needed the few to serve them and achieve this goal, though, and that dirty job fell to soldiers.

Clarice ran her fingers through her dirty, greasy hair as she shook her head. Her fingers failed to make it all the way through on the first time, probably because some of Wraith One's blood had snuck in there and coagulated. *The Aviation Council should schedule a flogging for whoever made the decision to let Rich become a pilot,* she thought. *Just put it on the books right now.* Even with the distance from the fighting that being a pilot afforded him, he clearly lacked the stomach for even that sort of work, and lacked the responsibility to be in charge of a few tons of government technology. The personality profile failed to catch his obvious deficiencies, and now the entire Republic was paying for it. Stupid bureaucrats. They should have assigned him to a safe sector, like Kole, away from the type of experiences that could activate his obviously anti-authority inclinations.

The tunnel remained black and silent. No one was coming. The guard pointing the rifle on her probably could not understand human speech. Clarice had to stay active, so she adjusted her head so that she could see Kole's crouching form through the multiple sets of bars separating them. He leaned against the far wall with his arms folded across his chest and eyes tilted toward the rocky ceiling. He frowned, deep in thought.

"Kole," Clarice called out. His head weaved in and out of view among the bars as he searched for a clear visual path. She tried not to sound too threatening when she asked, "What did you tell them?"

His response came quickly, and did not betray any more nervousness than usual. "Um, just basically everything that's happened over the last couple days, from my point of view. Y'know: who I am, the mix-up that got me here. Things like that."

"What else?" she asked. God... even from a dozen yards away, she could almost look up those nostrils of his and see his brain.

Kole shook his head slowly. "What else is there? He knows we came to kill him and that General Frusin is in charge of the army now. I guess I told him about Wraith Two dying and Wraith One trying to kill you, but I didn't see any harm in that." The Wraiths showed no reaction to the conversation taking place across the cells, even when the topic involved fallen comrades.

Clarice scratched her cheek with her human hand while considering the point. "No. No harm, I guess. What else? Didn't they ask about advancing formations or other assassination parties?"

"He asked," Kole said, "but I told them I didn't know."

Clarice's mouth shifted into a wry smile. "And they believed you?" she scoffed. Azzerello extracted information by... what? Just casually asked questions and accepting the answers at face value, as if they were chatting in the mess hall? How bizarre. She was gradually accumulating a list of her opponent's weaknesses, but turning them to her advantage would be another matter.

Kole nodded. "I guess. I mean, they didn't torture me, if that's what you mean."

"That's what I mean," Clarice said, then shook her head in disgust. Either Azzerello was an uncanny judge of others or a complete sap. Granted, he correctly assumed that that Kole did not know anything about Frusin's overall military strategy; she didn't and she was commanding the mission. Still, if she ever found herself in Azzerello's position, she would at least threaten a man like Kole with torture; that's just common sense. Maybe they wanted Kole to trust them. Kole still leaned against the wall, thinking. His expression made her wonder if their ploy was working.

Clarice bit her cracked lower lip. Maybe they were trying to use Kole to extract information from her. That was an unwelcome thought. Which cause he ultimately sided with was immaterial in and of itself. In military terms, he held little value except as a target. Hell, he probably couldn't even shoot another living being except by accident. Still, it benefited her sanity to have at least one person that she could let stand behind her without her wondering if he would try to kill her. After the drama that unfolded with Wraith One, Wilson Kole looked like her only prospect for filling that role, and she didn't want to lose that.

*   *   *

From the journal of Lt. Wilson Kole:

I'd never met anyone like Azzerello. That's an easy thing to say, and many times you do meet another person that's distinctly unlike anyone else you've ever met, but rarely do you know it within five seconds of shaking his hand (yes, I shook his hand), and even when you do experience the feeling, rarely are you right. I suspected his uniqueness when we first entered that cave, right before Clarice killed Wraith One in that awful way that she did, and history proved me right.

Azzerello had an eerie calm about him, where I wasn't sure if he was mentally retarded or twice as smart as me. "Simplicity." That's a better word: it felt like everything was simple to him. Physically, he had these light blue eyes that constantly gave the impression that he was dreamily staring off into the distance, and he always seemed on the verge of smiling. The way he moved is what really got me, though. Everything was easy. Everything would happen in due time. It reminded me of the monastic subcultures that some societies produce, where the members are so well-versed with their religion and finely tuned to their environment that they have all the answers, or at least all the answers they need to coexist with the rest of the world. I envy that disposition. I don't even have that kind of confidence when I'm talking about plants.

As we talked, I tried to imagine what his life must have been like in the Republic, how he ever got selected to run bombing missions against a civilian population. The story he described made me stop envying him: he was selected because he was so good at flying that the Army thought they could endure the "defect" of his potentially problematic moral code. He must have walked a lonely road during those long years, skulking around in the aircraft hangars with the legions of soulless zombies who also had all the answers, except that their answers had been selected by someone else and were contained in the Republican Army Code of Honor.

Years ago, I found myself in the unenviable place between those two poles, and I still haven't resolved the issue. I flatter myself into thinking that I know something of isolation, but the only answers I have in life are the ones I read in books, which represent the fruits of someone else's philosophical labor. Azzerello found the answers out by himself, and he forged his moral code the hard way. When you have figured out all the answers for your life, I would imagine that you can't simply teach them to others and have it hold true for their lives. I would imagine that they have to bleed, the same way you bled, and not many have the strength and the will to do that. Unfortunately, I know that I don't.

* * *

CHAPTER NINE:

SMOKE AND MIRRORS

"Leave the bugs alone, Kitridge," the female trainee says to the red-haired, male trainee as she runs a forearm across her sweaty brow.

"They're just bugs, Torrance," Kitridge replies, his malicious grin breaking into a slack-jawed glare. "What are you? My mom?"

The rest of the lightly armored recruits stand around them, amid the lush greenery and vines, but they are all busy drinking from their canteens or quietly engaging in their own conversations and pay no attention to Kitridge's antics. "Don't you think it's a little juvenile? I mean, didn't you get enough bug-killing done when you were a kid?"

He rolls his eyes in disgust. "Killing 'em isn't the fun part," he informs her. "Watching 'em bounce around and freak out. It's hilarious." He refocuses his barely adequate attention on the twig-like, multi-colored targets drifting through the air. His hands snap around a yellow and black, inch-long, flying insect, and a toothy smile spreads across Kitridge's face.

"I don't know too many philosophies that condone torturing helpless things, though," she says, unscrewing the cap on her canteen, "even if they are bugs." In truth, she doesn't mind Kitridge so much, in the sense that his idiocy usually proves entertaining. Sick is sick, though, and sometimes he really makes her uncomfortable.

Like now, as he shakes his cupped hands and feels the insect bounce around inside. Hopefully, the bug is poisonous. "Aren't you a little afraid the same thing will happen to you some day?"

He squints but doesn't take his eyes off his cupped hands. "What are you talking about? I'm not a bug." Squish.

*   *   *

It was not long before Azzerello sent his minions to fetch Clarice from her cell. The jingling of chains heralded the approach of her jailor, rousing her from her pseudo-sleep. She had managed to reach some level of physical comfort with her confinement, shifting her back into a smooth indentation of the wall so that sharp stone did not stab into her spine when she leaned back. She adopted the wait-and-see approach for figuring out what to do next; it helped her conserve energy and made all her troubles seems less immediate. Even the cell looked larger and less stifling than it did when her shaggy captors first shoved her inside. With any luck, it was as comfortable as she would ever get in captivity.

A young woman stepped into the holding chamber with a pair of shackles tossed over her shoulder. Clarice felt a slight wave of satisfaction that they did not send Rich; he must have found the encounter too upsetting for his sensitive nature. This plain creature looked barely above the minimum enlistment age. She wore her dirty blonde hair tied back in a ponytail and bounced slightly when she walked. Azzerello's crew toiled in a suicidal hell, yet everybody radiated a disgustingly good mood. Clarice glowered at the girl from her seat against the wall.

By all rights, Clarice should have no chance to kill Azzerello, at least for the near future. He might be stupid enough to leave himself alone with her in an otherwise empty room, but she couldn't count on that, especially after he already made one near-fatal mistake. She would look for an opening, of course, but fully expected him to remain surrounded by half a dozen armed stooges. That's what a reasonable person would do, anyway. So, if this bubble-headed nymph came to escort her to the main chamber, Clarice vowed to bide her time and not do anything rash (i.e., kill the girl), because if she had another shot at Azzerello, she had to make it a good one.

The younger woman, whose name badge read "Tillson," handed the shackles through the bars of the cell. They were the kind with short chains linking wrist-to-wrist and ankle-to-ankle, and a long chain linking the two shorter ones. Clarice had seen them in pictures, but had never encountered them in person, so she didn't know if they had a specific name. "Put these on," Tillson said with visible reluctance. She snatched her hand back as soon as Clarice's right hand took the obsolete series of chains, and her face became drawn, as though she gazed upon an evil thing.

Part of Clarice considered refusing or throwing the chains back at the little girl, simply to get a rise out of her, but even though that might be deliciously satisfying for a half-second, it really wouldn't accomplish anything. If they sent Rich, it might have been worth it, just to piss him off, but pissing off a teenager lacked any challenge. Besides, lulling them to sleep with complacency seemed like a far better strategy. Even if he wasn't doing it on purpose, she had to credit Kole with the idea: if they tried to escort her back to her cell with nothing but an empty hand on her shoulder, she could make them pay dearly. On second thought, she wasn't Kole; Azzerello and company already saw her rip out a man's throat with her teeth, so they wouldn't be relaxing the security on her too much for the next year. Oh well…

Clarice grabbed the wrist-ends and watched the ankle cuffs fall to the floor. The shackles were made from iron or an iron-like metal that a fully functioning Wraith could shatter like glass. With a single superhuman arm, though, any effort by Clarice to escape would only succeed in breaking the rest of her limbs. How did they know she only had one cybernetic limb? Did Kole tell them?

Shackles in place, Clarice jingled toward the front of the cage, then Tillson pulled the door open. The young girl motioned Clarice into the walkway with the point of her hand-held concussion laser. There were three kinds of people when it came to holding a laser weapon: the kind who did not appreciate the weapons destructive potential, the kind who did and feared that potential, and the kind who understood the potential but did not fear it. Good soldiers needed to be confident and familiar with their weapon and, with any kind of training, comprised the third group. Bad soldiers, like Kole, generally belonged to the second group. Tillson clearly belonged to the first strain. She held the deadly weapon like a child's toy. Clarice exited the holding chamber with the child in her shadow.

Clarice turned her chin to her shoulder as she walked forward in tiny steps. "So what happened to Rich?" she called behind her. "Didn't he want to deal with me anymore?"

"No. Nothing like that. It isn't like he's the 'jailor' or anything," Tillson said, eagerly, as if they were people and this was a normal conversation. "This is only the second time in two weeks that we've had prisoners. Last time, Rich and Sharif shared duties with me; we rotate."

"Is he working on some aircrafts?" Clarice asked, recalling the stains on Rich's uniform.

"Uh, just keep walking," Tillson said.

The darkness of the hallway engulfed them. From that position, Clarice gave herself a 99% chance of overpowering and killing the girl, if she so desired. "So what's your story?" Clarice asked.

Tillson took a moment before responding. "What do you mean?"

Clarice dialed down her belligerence, slightly; it might benefit her to make nice with this girl. "Why did you decide to betray the Republic? You seem awfully young for a turncoat."

"You seem a bit old to be believing everything you're told," Tillson shot back with impressive speed. She snorted. "Turncoat? Does anybody use that word anymore? What's the minimum age for a turncoat?"

It didn't seem like a real question. Tillson showed less fear with Clarice in shackles, but that was a mistake on her part. A mechanical elbow in Tillson's face would dislocate Clarice's human shoulder, but it would do infinitely more damage to the teenage soldier; she'd be looking at brain damage or death. Azzerello would never stand for that, though. Killing Wraith One was one thing. He was barely human and fighting an opponent he ridiculously overmatched. One could argue that he deserved to die, and the rogue soldiers must have felt some satisfaction in watching the demise of that expensive piece of Republican machinery, no matter how grotesque the death. One of their own, though, and one the spritely age of Tillson... Azzerello would have to kill Clarice or else lose credibility with his goons.

Clarice shuffled forward. Better to not even contemplate attacking. Back in the Killing Box, when her hand flinched, almost by itself, and shattered Wraith One's pistol, it barely took a thought. Any mindless reflexes now would jerk the chain and take any of her other three limbs along for the ride.

Clarice and Tillson emerged into the relative brightness of the main chamber. It looked almost exactly the same as the first time she walked in, but now, her presence made all the Middesians that saw her stopped performing their various maintenance, medical, and military activities. They stared at Clarice as she passed. Amazing what one little murder-by-throat-chewing could accomplish. In front of an equal number of humans, she might have felt self-conscious; large crowds always made her uneasy. Intimidating Middesians on the other hand, gave her a bit of a charge. With humans, you were supposed to try to gain their respect. With Middesians, it was enough that they feared you. She passed by an almost completely black Middesian sitting on a bench beside the path she walked. It was mending its ragged garment with black thread and a sliver of metal, but it paused for a couple long seconds to stare at her. She glared at it until the creature's beady, red eyes averted themselves. A near smile played on her lips, as if to say, "You're goddamn right you should fear me."

She was still a little delirious from fatigue, and when Tillson spoke, it shocked Clarice back into the moment, reminding her that they'd been conversing. "To be honest," Tillson said in a low voice, "It was never, like, my life's dream to become a soldier. I wasn't doing anything after I graduated from school, so I got drafted and made pilot in, like, three months."

The near-smirk fell from Clarice's face, and she glanced backward again to make sure Tillson was serious. "You're a pilot?" she asked. "I mean, I know some of you are, but I thought the rest were just wearing stolen uniforms or something."

"We're not all pilots, but I am. Youngest ever," Tillson said. Her chin rose and her shoulders reflexively pressed back when she spoke that last part. "At least I was at the time I left. I wonder if they'll rub my name off the plaque since I quit the team."

"Excuse me," Clarice asked. Her left foot fell into a slight depression in the stone floor and nearly took the rest of her body to the ground. She faced forward when she resumed shuffling. "Did you just say, 'Quit the team?'"

"Yeah," Tillson said.

"Just checking," Clarice said with a sigh. The people in the Personnel Division really needed to update their profiling procedures for choosing pilots. It's one thing to find people who can fly an aircraft, but it's another thing to find people who won't fly off and sell that aircraft to the enemy. Rich was emotionally unstable and completely blind to the big picture of military operations. Tillson cannot seem to see the picture at all. The bombs she dropped were ripping fellow humans apart, and she still thought it was some kind of skills challenge: a game that her "team" could still win. Clarice would have loved to show Tillson footage of Wraith Two's death and forced her to look at it. "You were saying?"

"Oh yeah," Tillson continued, "so from the way Leon... Mr. Azzerello was talking, I figured joining up with him would be more challenging than bombing a bunch of Middesians that could only throw rocks back at you."

Clarice waited a few seconds for the teenager to continue, but nothing else came. "That's it?" Clarice asked. A couple dozen yards away, at the end of the stone path, Azzerello stood atop the same raised, wooden platform he stood on the first time she saw him. Instead of supervising others, though, this time he carefully tracked her approach with his cool, blue eyes, his hands linked behind his back. "You're telling me you betrayed the Republic for kicks?" Traces of the splatter of Wraith One's blood still stained the cave floor in front of the platform, despite someone's best effort at scrubbing it clean.

"Pretty much," Tillson said, shrugging. "I mean, I don't want to get into the whole morality issue, but, if we did, it certainly doesn't seem *less* moral than just... following orders."

"That's unbelievably stupid," Clarice said, shuffling along. *Is this place a bunker or a lunatic asylum?* she wondered. *What passes for a good reason to kill these days?* At least the Wraiths' motivation made sense… well, except for Wraith One's. The cavalier way in which Azzerello and his ilk slaughtered their former fellow soldiers made Clarice want to grab the closest human and shake her until she understood. *Are you blind? Don't you see what you're doing?* The outrage that seized her after talking with Tillson, though, was a different flavor than what she felt with Rich. Maybe Tillson was still young enough to make stupid mistakes with impunity… but it seemed like such a waste. "Don't you realize you could die?"

Tillson sighed this time, as though she were the mature one. "For one, this whole war of expansion crap is what's stupid. It can't go on forever. Anybody knows that."

Clarice scoffed. Rich must have fed her that line of propaganda while he rocked her to sleep at night.

Tillson paused long enough to shoot a glare at her guffawing prisoner. "And second, I seriously doubt there's anybody left in the fleet that can take me down, one-on-one."

"You're that good?" Clarice asked, glancing behind her again.

"Oh yeah," Tillson said with a sly smile. Despite herself, despite the massive gulf that separated their principles, Clarice kind of liked Tillson, on some level. Not only did the little girl possess the confidence Clarice could have only dreamed of at that age, but her head remained packed in the blissful ignorance that is the envy of anyone who ever heard the word 'duty.' Her youth kept her free from obligation.

"I thought Azzerello was supposed to be the best in the fleet," Clarice asked. They had nearly arrived at the platform. Clarice's feet carefully avoided the black streak that marked the spot where Wraith One fell. *What did they do with the body?* She wondered. Azzerello stood on the side opposite the stairs. He might have heard them talking, but she doubted it.

Tillson wrinkled her face up while thinking. She still held her concussion pistol out in front of her like an idiot. Clarice could have grabbed it and shot her in the face while the young teenager struggled for an answer. "Yeah, he is," Tillson said, "but he really doesn't count. I mean, I really don't bother to compare myself with him."

"Why's that?" Clarice asked while her feet pounded on the wooden stairs. Her leg shackles had just enough give in them to allow her to navigate the short flight. *Where the hell did they find wood to build a platform like this in such a barren region?* Yet another question to which she would never know the answer. She let the issue pass while awaiting Tillson's response.

"I'm only human," Tillson said, in a low voice. "I mean, he is, too, but not when he's flying. He doesn't make mistakes up there." She fumbled through her teenager's lexicon, trying to come up with the proper compliment, even though Azzerello still stood out of earshot. "He's like a computer... no, computers aren't that innovative." An expression dawned on her, and her bright eyes illuminated further. "He's a god. Up there, he's a god."

*   *   *

Azzerello wore a drawn expression as the two women crossed the remaining distance. He looked stiff, like someone not accustomed to trying to look intimidating or authoritative. When Clarice reached the top of the stairs, he removed a concussion pistol from its holster and used it to motion her toward the one of the benches. Somehow, the weapon looked slightly less natural in his hand than it did in Tillson's. Perhaps when you're a savant pilot, you don't have to spend much time drilling with firearms. "Have a seat," he said to Clarice. Clarice eased into one of the wooden seats around the perimeter of the platform, her back facing the middle of the cavern, and placed her shackled hands in her lap. Her eyes swept the barren table in front of her. They moved the maps since she'd been here last. So... at least they weren't complete idiots.

Azzerello turned to Tillson and said in a solemn tone, "You'd better start checking your fighter. You're going out tonight."

Without a word, Tillson's eyes widened, and a smile consumed the lower half of her face. She scampered down the steps like a child half her age running to open her Founding Day gifts. With her back turned, Azzerello broke into a smile of his own as he regarded his little killer like a proud father. He turned toward Clarice and casually hooked a thumb over his shoulder. "She's a good kid," he said.

Clarice nodded. "Nice to know you think so, since you're sending her to her death."

Azzerello shrugged, either because he didn't care about Tillson or because he didn't care what Clarice thought... probably the latter. "The Republic judged her old enough to kill and be killed, not me. Now they're the ones paying for it."

Clarice turned away, choosing not to comment. Tillson dashed down a side path, her teenage feet gliding across the ground, swerving past a Middesian hobbling along with one leg and a crutch. "She says she's good, but not as good as you," Clarice told the man she was ordered to kill.

Azzerello's smug, half-smile reappeared. "At flying war machines, maybe. There's so much more to life." His clear, blue eyes became distant. It was an easy transformation; he always appeared on the verge of drifting off into a daydream. "And who knows?" he added.

"She has decades left to her." He emphasized "decades," as if he were Garth Frusin's age.

His eyes refocused on Clarice. Some of the other male pilots in the cave had faces with more ruggedly handsome features, but Azzerello's grooming habits were impeccable, beating any member of his little band of traitors by a wide margin, including the women. Any invading stubble had been shorn from his face, and someone or something had recently trimmed his hair. She didn't notice this quality when she first met him; probably because she stood a dozen yards away and was preoccupied with pulverizing his skull. Clarice looked down at her hands and blinked. Huh… Several seconds before, while he turned and watched Tillson prance away, she could have wrapped those shackles around his neck and torn his head off. *Damn.*

"Tell me, Lt. Torrance," Azzerello began, his voice almost morose, "is there *anything*, to your way of thinking, worth dying for?"

"Yes," Clarice said automatically. She didn't have to mull it over; there were many things she would die for, which either meant that she was a very caring person, she hated her life, or some combination of the two. She thought of Jervis, for whom she would have died without a second thought. She spent many nights during her formative years praying to a higher power, asking Him, Her, or It to trade her life for those of her parents. She thought of the Republic, around which the better part of her life had revolved. She would definitely give her life to help bring order to the known universe, even though she knew Azzerello and his minions would argue differently. They would dress it up in convoluted rhetoric, qualified statements, and subjective perceptions, but what it came down to was that cowards fail to grasp the concept of self-sacrifice.

"I agree," Azzerello said, "although I'm willing to bet we differ on what we are willing die for." Clarice couldn't argue with that, so she remained silent. Maybe "coward" was an inaccurate characterization of Azzerello, technically; he certainly wasn't down here for his physical health. It certainly seemed like part of the same pejorative stew, though. He continued. "Often things worth dying for are also things worth killing for, but not always. I found the difference while I was still flying missions for the Republic."

"Look," Clarice said, holding up the palms of both shackled hands as far as the chains would allow, "if you expect me to sit here while you justify killing hundreds of your own—"

With a flick of his wrist, Azzerello discharged his weapon… about three feet to Clarice's left. It concussion blast shredded the section of bench into kindling. Clarice reflexively threw her hands in front of her face in a protective gesture. Everyone in the cavern turned to look, but he didn't acknowledge them. He continued staring at Clarice, who, admittedly, had become wide awake again. "I'm not going to kill you," Azzerello said, bluntly. His open hand closed around his gun hand as it hung loosely in front of him.

"Then what the hell was that?" Clarice said, breathlessly.

"That was a warning," he assured her. "If you try to attack me, you better hope the Wraith Squad has some spare legs lying around, but even so, I'm not going to kill you." He waited for the statement to register. "I don't know how I'm going to do it, yet, but I do not believe in executing prisoners. I'll get you home, eventually, but before I do, the thing I really want to figure out is why your Squad Leader tried to kill you, and I think between the two of us, we might be able to do it. First, though, I need you to listen. I don't expect to change your mind. I'd actually be a little disappointed if it were that easy. I just want you to try to entertain my point of view for couple minutes. It might help us reach some sort of common ground."

"Fair enough," Clarice said, reluctant to concede anything to the man. He oozed sincerity. The way he spoke made every self-serving, crackpot idea seem reasonable. It served as a charm unto itself, and she could understand how, over time, he convinced a few weak minds to follow him on this suicide course. In fact, after barely a minute, she found it necessary to remind herself of Azzerello's culpability in the death of people like Jervis to keep her own sympathies in check. Someone as young as Tillson or as guilt-wracked as Rich wouldn't stand a chance.

"Then allow me to continue," Azzerello said without condescension. He clasped his hands behind his back and began to pace. A loose board near the middle of the platform creaked whenever he stepped on it, but he didn't seem to notice. "There was a time when I would have died for the Republic. I let them strap me into a rocket and push me out the door on a day-to-day basis because, like a lot of people, I had nothing else. I was good at my job, and they treated me accordingly. Their cause was my cause, and if dying in combat and being martyred was the closest I could get to being loved, then so be it."

Were he not staring at her, Clarice would have rolled her eyes. "Love" did not belong in the military lexicon, not the section that's spoken aloud, anyway. Jervis only told her he loved her once, and even then, it came out more like a question. "You know I love you, don't you?" he said while his arms encircled her naked body. She nodded. It was enough. Jervis never threw flowery words around for no purpose, not like Rich, Azzerello, and this sorry band of bleeding hearts.

Azzerello continued. "There's an old saying, 'It's better to be loved than hated, but it's better to be hated than nothing.' I'm not sure if that's word-for-word, and I'm not sure who said it, but… well, like Captain Rich… you met him, right? Stevin Rich: blond hair—"

"I met him," Clarice assured her captor.

"Well, like Stevin, I eventually came to see first-hand the results of my selfless patriotism." He shook his head. She found herself leaning forward, slightly, in anticipation. She didn't agree with a word he said, but he certainly spoke with conviction. "As soon as the Vlorth departed in their transport ships, the remaining Middesians were to be wiped out of existence, and I was to be an instrument of that genocide."

Clarice had planned to remain polite until he finished his rationalizing but silence seemed like acquiescence, and her patience failed her. "It's a war," she moaned in exasperation.

Azzerello held up a finger. "No. No it's not," he corrected. "Not anymore. These people did not choose to fight or flee. The Vlorth made the decision to fight, however justified, and were allowed to flee. Most of these people were either conscripted or had no involvement with the war. They were going to get ground up in the machinations of the all-consuming Republican Machine just the same, though. It *was* a war; now, it's an extermination."

Clarice looked down at her lap and shook her head. *Ridiculous.* Did Azzerello and his group hold meetings to decide what metaphors they were going to use for the day? "It's unfortunate," she conceded, "but are you suggesting that they disband the Republic? The good that comes out of it vastly outweighs the negatives."

Azzerello's stopped pacing. As soon as that last sentence left her mouth, Clarice realized that it sounded like something she'd read in a government-sanctioned history book at the high school. Azzerello's head tilted, perhaps because he'd read the same book, and he took his turn looking condescending. "That's where you and I differ. I don't choose a thing over living beings."

Clarice looked up. "I've heard that one before," she assured him. "The Republic is more than a 'thing'; it's an ideal."

"Really? Which ideal is that?" he shot back, his baby-blue eyes turning steely-blue. *So, he can get angry...* "Obedience to authority. I'll give you that one. Anything else?" He sucked in air through his nostrils. "I would rather fight a hopeless battle than be part of something evil."

Clarice blinked. *Hopeless.* Did she hear that right? She expected him to cough up a retraction, but he just let his words sink in for a moment and leaned in further.

Azzerello's voice lowered to slightly more than a whisper. "Oh, I know we're going to get killed. A few of us might get away, but I'm not a fucking moron. I will die, they'll hunt me to the end of the galaxy because they have to kill me now... but I don't care. I'd rather die than live with their deaths on my head." He pulled his head to his left to indicate the mangy, dirty creatures scuttling about the chamber like rodents. He probably saw them as individuals, but to her, they remained a pack of faceless Middesians, and she could never pretend otherwise.

"Killing Republican soldiers isn't going to bring the dead ones back," Clarice said.

"Neither will killing the rest," Azzerello said, pulling himself erect. "Nothing will. That's the point. Making the same mistake over and over again doesn't justify the first time it was made. It just makes you ignorant." Azzerello spread his arms. "I will gladly say, 'I was wrong to drop those bombs. I am a weak person,' but that's all I can do. Empty gestures like that are useless, but sometimes that's all we have left to us. If there's a next life, maybe I can make amends there, but not in this one."

Azzerello fell silent and started pacing again. Clarice found it difficult to look at him; it was like staring at a sun. "No point in arguing with you," she grumbled.

"Of course not," he agreed, drawing in air and regaining his almost eerie cool. "We're both intelligent people. We see the same things, we just differ in the interpretations."

Clarice found herself nodding. If she had to publicly agree with anything he said, this seemed like a safe enough statement. He certainly seemed lucid. She even sympathized with his plight... to some degree. Not everyone possessed the strength to push the nagging doubt out of his or her mind and perform a duty. That was why not everyone was a soldier, and not every soldier was a good solider. That did not make people like Azzerello evil people, just weak, but their existence still meant that equally good people died every day because of them. The man still needed to die, if only to deliver others from the slime-trail of misery he left in his wake, and she needed to kill him, because that was her job. If he leaned in again, she would break his neck.

"Now that we have that in order," he began, "what do you know about Wraiths?" Azzerello stood in front of her, shoulders back, left hand grasping the wrist of his gun hand. He looked dignified, like Frusin did when she first saw him staring out his window. The fact that he stood in his stark, white uniform amid the drab, dank surroundings may have even augmented this impression, making him luminous. He was not at all what she expected.

"What's there to know?" she asked, quickly averting her eyes. For the briefest of moments, something about the pose reminded her of Jervis.

"Well, I heard about you crushing the laser pistol with one hand, back in the canyon, so obviously you know about the skeletal attachments," he said, gesturing toward her right arm, "and from what Lt. Kole tells me, you both got a first-hand view of the destruct mechanism in action, but what about the way they think?"

Clarice considered the question while keeping her eyes low. "Wraith Two didn't seem like she knew where she was when her power generator was turned off."

"That would be because her memory was erased when she was officially assigned to the Squad," he said.

Clarice raised her head. Her eye widened. "They do that?"

"Indeed," Azzerello said. "See, no one in their right mind thinks that Wraiths are normally functioning humans, but a lot of people make the mistaking and go in the opposite direction. They think the Wraiths' minds work like computers, where they are programmed to do certain things. That's too inflexible for a lot of battle situations. Hell, I'm sure you read about what happened to the androids they sent out during the Fultax Occupation. It was a disaster: there are just too many variables to take into account, especially on an unfamiliar surface of a foreign planet."

"Okay, so how do their minds work?" Clarice asked. *Don't get too chummy*, she reminded herself. *He could be making all this up.*

"Just like humans, with the exception of two things: long-term memory and emotion. Both are considered detrimental to a mission. The techs keep the neural framework needed for a functioning mind, and with a steady dose of chemicals and a little bit of electrical stimulation, they dump the baggage."

"Then how are they controlled?" Clarice asked. Memory erasing… It almost happened to her. If the mortar blast had damaged a few more inches of tissue, if she'd been standing half a step over, they might have decided to flip the switch and salvage her remaining tissue. She shuddered. Her memories were all she had left.

"Authority is a big part," he said. "They know who outranks them and they know how to follow orders. After all, they were soldiers beforehand. Usually only good soldiers are chosen to be Wraiths."

"At least their remains are," Clarice grumbled. She glanced up, but it was too late; the concurring remark escaped her lips before she could stop it.

"Exactly," he said before she could amend her complaint. "Partly, they are governed by intimidation, and by that I mean that remote control on your belt. Their memories aren't so good, but... I don't know if you've ever looked at the feed from the electronic eyes," he said, tapping to the place above the cheekbone where one of those black boxes with the red lights would be positioned, "but they give an onscreen readout of the necessary mission specifications every few minutes. So, even if they can't remember for shit, they don't have to. Their information gets sent back to the command ship, and the feed gets constantly updated."

Clarice nodded. Agreement on this topic seemed safe, especially since what he said was consistent with her experience. The Wraiths always did make her uneasy. Besides that, Wraith One disobeyed orders and tried to kill her. He only would have done what he did if he knew the remote would fail. It all made a neat sort of sense, except for one thing. "How do you know this?" she asked. "Did you take apart Wraith One?"

Azzerello leaned in. "What? Oh, no, we... I don't know what we're going to with him yet. Right now, we just took his remains somewhere so that the children couldn't see them. No, um, Captain Tara Ekston... the red haired woman that was up there during the meeting when you first came in..."

Clarice nodded for purposes of expediency. She could only remember that a red haired woman stood among the group, not anything specific about her, and she would have categorized the hair color "light brown," but none of that was important. "Okay. Yeah."

"Well, she used to be in the design division for the Wraith exoskeletons."

Clarice squinted. "She's a med tech designer? So how many of you aren't pilots?" She didn't actually expect him to answer and provide that type of important intelligence, but still...

"Just her and one guy who's a flight tech," Azzerello said as he alternated between standing and pacing. "See, she joined up because she was friends with Mak Telpin, who is..." Azzerello trailed off when he saw Clarice's furrowed brow. "It's complicated. Long story short, she didn't agree with some of the things going on in Wraith Division."

Clarice nodded away. Again, not to get too friendly, but Clarice didn't agree with some of the things going on in Wraith Division, either. She nearly smirked, thinking how a technician in a barren, Stone Age wasteland like this probably provided only slightly more utility than a botanist. That is, until a Wraith Squad strolls into a canyon and gets taken captive. "So what was your point, again?"

Azzerello squared himself to her and took a deep breath. "Your remote did not work on Wraith One and you have no reason to think it had been damaged from the time you used it on Wraith Two. But remember: the remote is only one of the things that keeps them in check. From what Kole tells me, you had problems with Wraith One from the time you landed." He waited for her to nod before concluding. "I think this mission was sabotaged and I think it was by someone whose orders to Wraith One would have taken precedence over yours."

Clarice ran through the short list of possibilities in her head. "You mean you think Garth Frusin instructed Wraith One to kill me?" she asked, almost mockingly. "I don't even know where—"

Azzerello held up his hands in defense. "I'm not saying—"

Clarice's chains rattled as she bolted upright in her seat. "Why would he do that?" she demanded, her voice near a shout. At first, she didn't even know who she was mad at, because the idea sounded idiotic the instant it left her lips, but then she felt the sting of betrayal again, and it hurt more than when Wraith One attempted to tear her head off. Frusin wasn't a subordinate or even a friend; she idolized the man. Beyond the fact that she could easily have died when that juggernaut attacked her, the idea that he would let that happen to anyone in his command appalled her.

"I'm not saying he did it," Azzerello said softly. Clarice huffed out a few breaths, postponing any outbursts until he explained himself. God, she was tired. "It could have been anyone higher up than you that knew about the mission."

"It was a *Top Secret mission*," she said. "The only people I know that knew about the details were Frusin and Drennon."

Azzerello squinted. "Who's Drennon?"

"Lee Drennon," she said and failed to see a glimmer or recognition in Azzerello's face. "He's Frusin's second-in-command. He was Harvath's, too."

"What's his rank?"

"He's a major," she said. Azzerello nodded in silence. "Why would either of them want me dead?"

"Or want me alive," he said with a shrug.

"What?"

"Well, it seems like there would only be two reasons to kill you: they didn't like you or they didn't like your mission. Unless you had some sort of personal relationship with one of these men, I'm voting for the latter."

Clarice chewed on this possibility for a moment. When she could not come up with an explanation that made sense, she looked up at Azzerello. "Why do you even care?"

Azzerello shrugged. "I like to know as much about my enemies as possible. I think it's generally a good practice. It might be useful to know why they would botch their own assassination attempts. Then again, it might not be useful or make any sense, but I'd rather know than not know."

Clarice nodded, satisfied by the answer. While she still had no idea why her superiors wanted her dead, at least now she could blame the mission's failure on something other than her own ineptitude… or Kole. Sitting there, it made such perfect sense why so many emotionally fragile soldiers followed a lunatic like Azzerello. It wasn't just that he was good and conjuring up rhetorical arguments to justify any action he wanted to take; he didn't come off as a lunatic at all. He was intelligent, well-spoken, even-tempered, and in all other ways, a charismatic fellow. He did all the things a good leader was supposed to do. He led by example, not by intimidation. He made dangerous assertions sound perfectly reasonable. He remained respectful to and seemed to genuinely care about those serving under him… Clarice swallowed hard… just like Jervis. Whether he actually did care or not was another matter; they were all going to die, after all, crushed by the weight of an empire.

Clarice shook her head to get rid of the idea. Azzerello gave a half-smile. "What?" he asked.

Her words came slowly. He was her enemy, after all, one that her superiors instructed her to neutralize by whatever means necessary. One that was responsible, directly or indirectly, for the deaths of someone's friends… and lovers. She swallowed. "I expected you to be some sort of maniac," she said, but what she meant was *I needed you to be some sort of maniac.*

His smile broadened, and he looked sort of embarrassed. "That's funny. I consider this the most lucid thing I've ever done."

Clarice winced. He still couldn't see. "You're going to die," she said at a low volume. "All these people, who you think are good people, are going to die. Good people on my side are going to die." She gritted her teeth, wishing she could grab him and shake him until he understood. "Why do it? How do you justify the deaths of so many good people when you know you can't win?"

Azzerello's face relaxed at the mention of death. He looked almost serene again, like when he watched Tillson scamper off. Maybe she looked the same way when she received her orders this mission. When he responded, the answer came quickly but without sounding rehearsed or automatic. He probably had asked himself the same question dozens of times. "People die in war. War is caused by conflict. In the case of the Republic, the conflict is due to expansion." He blinked several times to dispel either tears or the images forming in front of him. "If we were not here, the Republic would move on to another planet more quickly. People would still die; the raw number on the tally sheets wouldn't change, just different bodies would get turned into ash." He stopped blinking, and the electric light glinted off the moist sheen of his eyes, but no tears leaked out. "I am here because in the reality that I occupy, what is happening here is wrong… and I can do *something* about it. If denting the Republic killing machine and keeping it in check for two weeks is the sum of my legacy, then so be it. It's better than being part of the problem." He took a half-a-second to force eye contact, begging her to understand. "We have to take justice where we can get it, or make our own."

Wrong place at the wrong time, Clarice thought. War was no place for philosophers. It was more hospitable to the dense and manageable members of the citizenry, like her, people that still thought their side flew the banner of righteousness. When the world starts exploding around you, gray areas become hazardous to your health. You're better off shutting up, shutting out, and doing your job. "The Republic," she said slowly while Azzerello worked to compose himself, "is a necessary thing. It keeps order, and without order..."

He stared at her with red-rimmed eyes. Tears and pity clung to them. He knew his people would die, just like he knew people like her and people like him would never, ever understand each other. The last thing she expected him to do was nod, but they had both grown weary of the pointless conversation. "Yeah," he said with a cough, "you're right." It was a half-assed concession, even worse than her half-assed regurgitation of Republican propaganda.

"I think I'd better go back to my cell," she said, almost pleading.

"Yeah," he said, then made a beckoning motion to someone standing a good distance behind her. "I think that would be best." His voice drained itself of emotion with surprising speed. "I'll call for you in a little bit," he added, evenly, "after I've met with my... group."

They waited in uncomfortable silence as the young, smooth skinned, pony-tailed fighter pilot bounded up the steps. Clarice only talked with the man for a few minutes, and everything around her had become more fragile. She heard all the arguments before, from civilians or colonists, after one conflict or on the way to the next, but coming from a fellow soldier who obviously wasn't afraid to die for a cause... her own responses never sounded so juvenile. Normally, she would have punched him or walked away ten seconds into the discussion, but she was shackled.

She stomped down the stairs, her feet heavier than she remembered. She tried to rekindle the blinding anger so that she could complete her mission, but manufactured emotion is as obvious as it is pathetic. Her life used to hold some reason and joy in it. Leon Azzerello may not have killed Jervis, but he killed men just like him. Jervis, who moments before his death, was leading a heavily armored strike team over a hill to annihilate a group of sickly, sterile Middesians, most of which were armed with sharpened rocks… and the occasional laser mortar. She felt an unease in her guts as she shuffled, exhausted, down the stone path. Maybe it was guilt, for thinking badly about Jervis. He wasn't a bad man. On the contrary, he was one of the best men she ever met. He was just following orders.

A voice in her head, a harsh, berating voice, told her that she was weak. It told her that the enemy had brainwashed her. A second, tentative voice agreed. The second voice just wondered whether it happened a few minutes ago, or a few years.

*   *   *

From the journal of Lt. Wilson Kole:

I'm probably not the first person to come up with this metaphor (in fact, I may have read it somewhere), but life in the Republic often resembles the life of a leaf on a tree. You are part of something greater than your mere existence as a leaf and you gain your significance by keeping the tree healthy and prosperous. There exists a danger, though, of internalizing this task to such a degree that you start to think of yourself as less a leaf and more an incomplete fraction of the tree.

Sometimes, toward the end of a leaf's life, they cling to the tree until they wither and die. The tree then abandons them, leaving them to decompose into nothing. The tree has no time for sentimentality; it is busy growing. And there will always be more leaves.

On occasion, some external force tears the leaf free prematurely. The dual forces of gravity and wind currents toss the lone leaf about, transforming it into a victim of random fate. The existence proves short and death inevitable, but the fall, however brief, is exhilarating.

Azzerello drew me to him for that reason. He created a whirlwind that separated me from the tree. I had already faced death and come to terms with it during my march with Clarice. After I contributed to Wraith Two's death, I marched on, amid six trained killers, five and a half of whom wanted me dead. I had nothing but time and dread, and looking back on my decades of life, I found nothing worthwhile. Death would have delivered me from my sad, little existence. Then, we met Azzerello, someone who lived, not merely existed, and I saw what it was like to be part of a virtuous cause that I could believe in. To live the typical life, then die the anonymous death, seemed to pale in value when compared to knowing a brief but complete freedom. An existence without fear or compromise.

Clarice may have glimpsed the same thing, but she obviously had been on the tree too long. She could not conceive of living separate from it.

* * *

CHAPTER TEN:

BREATHING FIRE

The corporal watches the new lieutenant strut around the corner of the cavernous docking bay. He walks between the lines of troops, perusing them for signs of weakness or sloth, his chest stuck out. His eyes shine with a serene, laughing quality, far too confident a look for someone with less than a month of experience commanding combat troops. The late Lt. Dontz had been a veteran of some of the more dicey battles of the Darrat 16 conflict, where he served as an enlisted man. He worked his way through the ranks by proving his bravery and competence to every commanding officer he had. While not a brilliant man, he developed a reputation for toughness and fairness. He had personally pulled the corporal to safety after she stepped into the range of a vortex mine. This fresh-faced, preening specimen stepping amongst her and her fellow soldiers is an academy-bred pretty boy. She gives him a week down on the surface before he fried or went crazy. Ten days, tops.

His parallel rows of straight, intact teeth remind her of the concussion blast that blew apart Dontz's head. Dontz was wearing a flack helmet, which doesn't prevent you from dying when a concussion blast smacks you in the head, but it usually decreases the mess. This one, a stray blast from a cannon stationed a half-mile away, hit him square in the face. The helmet flew off, and from the neck up, everything liquefied and sprayed everywhere.

She shudders, remembering the strand of some sort of unidentified fluid that wasn't quite blood sluicing out of his neck stump, the way it shot upward in a long arc, and the splat it made when it landed on someone's helmet. The new lieutenant still stands several steps behind her when she lets out a silent sigh, so he doesn't notice her momentary slouch. Her last memory of Lt. Dontz probably will cling to her unto the moment of her death. Thankfully, this new lieutenant, Giles, looks too pretty to meet a fate like that.

*   *   *

Clarice dragged herself back to her cell. The metal door clanged shut behind her and massive padlock closed, sending echoes bouncing down the hall. She pressed her back against the abrasive rocks and wearily slid to the floor, back to her cell wall's lone smooth spot. Her arms wrapped their way around her knees to ward off the chill of the cave. The Wraiths sat in a similar position inside each of their cells. They looked dormant, though, not cold or tired. After a few seconds of silence, Kole called down, "Lt. Torrance?" he said. She had already started to drift off to sleep, but her eyes snapped open at the sound of his voice. "Did you see Azzerello? Did he say what was going to happen to us?"

The red eyes of the shadowy, armed Middesian in the pillbox moved about as the creature shifted and reset itself. Clarice ignored Kole and reclosed her eyes, and he showed enough consideration to not ask again. She remained in that position for a few moments, until her chin fell against her chest and she lapsed into a merciful sleep.

*   *   *

As with most lapses into sleep since the incident, when Clarice dreamed, she dreamed about Jervis. Even in the dream, he seemed far away from her, like making love to a hologram. The sensation still wrung some longing and self-pity out of her overtaxed system, especially when she woke up and realized that she did not lie in a warm bed, encircled by the arms of the man she loved, but in a cell, alone, curled up on a stone floor. Cold rock and cold iron surrounded her. Everything felt cold, except for her right arm, which barely felt anything at all.

Tears had collected in her eyes. Of course they did; a person cannot erect defenses against profound, heart-splitting sorrow while sleeping. If anything, those defenses built up during one's waking life, like an ice wall, then melted away during sleep. Clarice wiped away the escaping salt water as though it was acid, but it had already cut a path through the dust mask she wore. Without a pair of goggles to cover them, the tracks would remain in place for several hours, like a temporary badge of weakness.

She awkwardly pushed herself into a seated position and leaned against the groove in the wall that provided her the most comfort. Between the marching and the beating and the sleeping on rock, most of her body felt like a giant, aching bruise. She probably cracked at least one rib, and she might have sprained her jaw, if that was possible. Her neck was the worst, though; she could barely turn it in either direction, and it only stopped hurting when shy lay flat on her back, staring at the ceiling.

She had no idea how long she had slept. If the Wraiths provided any indication, she slept for ten seconds. Adjacent to her cell, Wraith... Four... still stared at the wall, silent as a sphinx. Kole lay supine on the floor of his cell, his hands folded behind his head as he stared at the ceiling, occasionally blinking. Clarice assumed a similar position. "Kole?" she called out, the words scraping across her raw, dry throat.

"Yeah," he called back.

"You went to the academy with Jervis, right?" she asked. "At Flint Harbor?" It took Kole a couple seconds to answer. Maybe having a conversation across four "people" bothered him, especially a conversation with such potentially explosive elements. It wasn't hard for

Clarice to pretend that the Wraiths were statues, even if those black boxes over their eyes had direct video and audio feeds to individuals who were not. "Yeah," Kole finally said.

"How well did you know him?" Why was she asking him this? Probably because the residue from the dream had already poisoned her heart and head for the time being, so she risked no additional harm in thinking about it for a few minutes longer.

Kole blinked. "Not real well." He tilted his head in her direction without sitting up and flinched out a smile. "But I doubt that I know very many people very well."

Clarice pinched her nose and tried to nod, but the pain and stiffness stopped her. What was she expecting? Maybe a story about how Jervis had saved someone's life or said something full of magic and truth during a critical part of training.

"He always seemed like a nice guy," Kole added, hopefully. "And not in a fake way, either."

The reflexive urge to nod overtook Clarice again, despite the pain. He was. He really was a nice guy. Everyone liked him. The tears started gathering again, but a shadow fell across her face and caused them to suck back inside their ducts. With some effort, Clarice pulled herself to a seated position. Leon Azzerello, in all of his white-suited glory, seemed to hover outside her cell. He stood with his back straight but not stiff, unruffled and free from the taint of emotion, like many of the good Republican officers she came to know over the years. *Of course he looks unruffled,* she thought, *he's already resolved his moral dilemma, and his life will soon resolve itself permanently in the form of a poorly maintained 840 Sprinter that gets blasted out of the sky.*

Clarice scratched her forehead and looked away, in the general direction of the Middesian in the pillbox. "What time is it?" she asked.

"Almost fourteen hundred hours," Azzerello said.

Clarice nodded, not sure why she asked in the first place. She had no idea what time she fell asleep, so she had no idea how long she slept. Whatever the duration, her aching head informed her that it was not long enough.

A Middesian stood a pair of paces behind Azzerello. Like many of its brethren in the outer cavern, its ribs protrude through exposed patches of its leathery skin. It wore a dirty, green vest and no pants. Clarice noted the missing ear and realized that it was the Middesian that yelled "Hailt" in time to keep Wraith One from ripping her head off. It never occurred to her to thank him. "So, what's going on?" she asks Azzerello.

"I've come to inform you of the results of our meeting," he said, his tone even and professional. For a flickering moment, she feared that the group of rebels had overruled Azzerello, made the logical choice, and decided to execute her. Fear of death. Wanting to live. Clarice almost forgot what they felt like. The tingle of panic felt foreign but not unpleasant. She had no time to wonder why. "We're releasing you soon as a prisoner of war."

Clarice rubbed her right eye with her left index finger. "Won't they deny having sent me?"

"Well, they tried," Azzerello said, rolling his eyes, "but... y'know... how else would you have gotten here?" She conceded the point, and he continued. "We have informed the Republican fleet, and they will rendezvous with our transport ship just above the atmosphere."

Clarice looked up and regarded Azzerello with a furrowed brow. The committee deliberated for several hours and that was the best decision they could come up with? "If you're correct, and Garth Frusin wants me dead, won't he just blast the transport out of the sky?" She didn't know whether the Wraiths' electronic eyes currently were transmitting or recording the conversation, so she tried to avoid saying anything incriminating. Then, she remembered that they were in a cave, under a mountain containing maybe ten tons of Proteum, and it would take a transmitter the size of her jail cell to force a signal through all of that.

Azzerello turned looked down at the one-eared Middesian. The Middesian gave a series of gurgles, and Azzerello responded with a satisfied nod. He turned back to Clarice. "It's been decided that Wraith... One?" He looked back at the Middesian, who nodded. "Wraith One's betrayal was engineered by Lee Drennon."

The part of Clarice that worshiped Frusin as a child badly wanted to believe in the man's innocence, but the certainty of Azzerello's statement made her scoff. "How did you settle on that one? Roll dice?"

Azzerello remained unmoved. "One of our group, Detrick Brant, used to work with Drennon in Central Command before Detrick got transferred to Aerial Operations. Right after Coppin Bay, before Detrick defected, some of his old friends at base command informed him that Drennon expected a significant promotion and to take control of the occupation when General Harvath was ousted."

Clarice nodded, slightly, throughout Azzerello's explanation. When the explanation appeared over, she asked, "So?"

Azzerello sighed, his impassive front wearing thin. "From Detrick's description, Drennon is a career military man from a military family who graduated at the top his class at Marshall Academy. Also, he's something of a narcissist and not among the most stable people Detrick has ever met." Clarice barely knew the man, but that description sounded about right. Most ranking officers could avoid leering so obviously at the subordinates. Azzerello continued. "It seems probable that Drennon, either out of spite or because he thought he had been bypassed for promotion, sabotaged your mission, which was Frusin's brainchild. Your mission required them to stall the bombing runs, so its failure would damage Frusin's already shaky position. Disconnecting Wraith One's destruct switch and programming his electronic eye to send him instructions to kill you would have taken Drennon less than five minutes. Video files can be altered or "lost," and you two were the only real witnesses. No one would have known." He gestured over to the Wraiths. "Even now, if the Wraiths were able to broadcast this conversation, do we even know who is listening, or where their loyalties lie?"

Clarice stared at Azzerello, trying to come up with an alternative analysis, but she couldn't. Middle-tier bureaucrats like Drennon tend to make a web of alliances during their years on a command ship; it's conceivable that he could control the entire situation at the edges. Besides, what was the alternative? That Garth Frusin wanted her dead for some reason? That he was tired of his pristine reputation and wanted to tarnish it with a self-sabotaged mission? Clarice grabbed one of the bars and pulled her aching body to its feet. "Even if that was plausible, what am I supposed to do? Go back and confront Drennon?"

Azzerello waved a hand. "Not at all. You need to wait until you get Frusin alone, then explain everything. Ask for a full and immediate investigation. If you don't do those things, Drennon will definitely find a way to get rid of you, and might kill Frusin."

A male voice from the other end of the holding chamber asked, "What if Drennon wants to know what happened down here?" The question came from Kole, who stood eagerly pressed against the bars of his cell. Clarice had nearly forgotten about her lone, albeit useless ally. She could only imagine what the prospect of living again did to his mental state.

Azzerello fielded the question while still looking at Clarice. "Make something up. Something like Wraith One got damaged during the aerial bombardment and lost control. He may be suspicious, but if Frusin knows you're still alive, Drennon won't outright kill you unless he has to."

Clarice smoothed back her dirty, oily hair. An officer becoming professionally frustrated and hamstringing a superior was not rare. Not at all. People that made careers out of the military can often dredge the depths of pettiness in effort to reach that next highest title. Some of them were good people at one point, but the reward of status often made its own gravy. Drennon probably never was a good man. He seemed like the sort that never morally evolved after the age of thirteen, where becoming captain of the team so that you can exert your will is more important than playing the game.

"What if Frusin doesn't believe me?" she asked.

Azzerello shrugged. "It's worth a shot."

Clarice's hands found her hips, and her right foot shifted forward, magnifying her indignance. "What do you mean, 'It's worth a shot'? Why do you even care? You don't stand to lose anything if Frusin dies."

"We stand to lose everything," Azzerello said, the spark returning to his eye. "The only chance of survival we have is an armistice where they agree to evacuate the Middesians, either off the planet altogether or to a section of the planet that isn't being bled dry. It isn't much, but eventually, we should be able to evacuate the entire population."

The Middesian flanking Azzerello gurgled again. Azzerello nodded, then said, "We'd prefer the second option. That way those that have been sterilized can at least die a natural death on their home planet."

Clarice pursed her lips and looked down. Their ultimate goals, after all this fighting and spilled blood, seemed rather pathetic. Before she could become too haughty, though, she remembered her motivations for returning to active duty: revenge and a quick death. Not exactly the stuff of high-minded lectures. Besides, she had no idea what it meant to live her entire life on the surface of a single planet. A person can become attached to things.

Clarice raised her thin eyebrows. "All that sounds like wishful thinking," she said. It was not her job to critique the plans of the enemy, but if what Azzerello said turned out to be true, her first obligation was to keep her commanding officer alive. That made Drennon the superordinate enemy… potentially.

"But possible," Azzerello said. A slight smile crept across his face. "I… sort of idolized Garth Frusin, a long time ago. A lot of us did. Obviously, my perspective has changed, but I think he's an honorable man. So long as Frusin is in power and Drennon isn't, it's *possible* that we can negotiate our way out of this. Plus, I suppose it wouldn't hurt to have the general in my debt when it comes time to negotiate." Clarice regarded Azzerello, but remained silent. The plan sounded far too radical for her to endorse, but it made perfect sense coming from the man who fought a guerilla war against an armada possessing enough firepower to destroy a solar system. "We should be able to arrange transport in the next few hours. Are you ready to go?" Azzerello asked.

Clarice inhaled to answer, but Kole interrupted her. "What about me?" he asked from the other end of the chamber.

Azzerello didn't answer, so Clarice glanced down at Kole and asked, "Yeah, what about Kole?"

"Lt. Kole will return as well," Azzerello said, then threw a cold stare in Kole's direction. Kole only slouched, as though the look had sucked a megawatt of energy out of him.

Azzerello stepped away from the cell, then waved a hand toward Clarice's cell door. The one-eared, emaciated Middesian shuffled forward to undo the lock. Within seconds, Clarice stood in the open doorway, waiting for one of her captors to produce a gun or a set of shackles. They did neither. They merely moved aside to give her a free path to the corridor.

Clarice stepped from her cell. Even though the holding chamber remained as cramped and dark as ever, she found it easier to breathe on the other side of the bars. Stepping past Azzerello caused a sensation close to nausea to sweep over her. Her feet moved forward in an uneven, almost drunken pattern. She passed by him, though, the man responsible for so much of her pain, the man for whom she endured so much for the chance to destroy. She felt the eyes of the four remaining Wraiths bore a hole in her back, demanding that she do her duty, even though she was sure that, if she turned back, their gaze would remain as passive as ever. Her right arm itched, even though that should have been impossible. Azzerello did not flinch, even though one punch would have broken his neck and crushed his skull. He looked down and kept his eyes closed.

The one-eared Middesian shambled out of the holding chamber in its short-legged strut, and Clarice followed. She told herself she let Azzerello live for the chance to save General Frusin's life. She told herself she did it for the Republic.

*   *   *

A thousand or so stars poked through the blackness on the other side of the window. The grey underside of the refurbished, PT-417 transport ship loomed over the capsule and blocked her view of another thousand stars. The deep tan of the cockpit furnishings projected a feeling of warmth to contrast the cold of space. For the second time in a week, Kole sat to Clarice's right, and they both fastened both of their shoulder restraints and prepared for disengagement. She never asked Azzerello what he planned to do with the Wraiths. For all she cared, he could turn them loose in the wild or sell them for spare parts.

The accepted interplanetary protocol for exchanging prisoners operated as follows: (1) Warring Party A placed its prisoners into a capsule inside its ship. (2) Warring Party A then jettisoned this capsule in the direction of Warring Party B's ship, while (3) Warring Party B sent their corresponding, prisoner-filled capsule over to Warring Party A's side. (4) Over the course of an hour, the capsules and their occupants move like soap bubbles toward freedom… or at least toward resumed impressment into military service. Scanners and armaments ensured fair dealing, because if one side decided to double-cross the other, they forfeit the lives of both sets of prisoners.

Azzerello did not accompany them on the transport. He did not even watch them leave to board the transport ship. In fact, after Clarice walked past the man on her way out of her cell, he seemed to disappear into thin air. This should not have bothered her; no one owes their own attempted assassin a farewell or a wish for a long life. Captors don't pack a lunch for their former captives, especially they held those captives for less than two days. Still, the parting struck her as rather unceremonious.

Clarice had never ridden in this particular model of capsule and found the seats soft and surprisingly spacious. The luxury struck her as excessive for prisoners. As the great, white, angular Republican star cruiser in the distance began to take shape, the protean tears began to sting her eyes. She looked away from Kole. *What the hell is wrong this time?* she wondered. *You're just completely unhinged, aren't you?* As she stared out the window, she assumed that it had something to do with Jervis, like everything else, and the more she thought about it, the more she realized that she was right. She never got to say goodbye to Jervis. He was right behind her, following her up the hill. She blinked. When she looked back, a man-shaped hunk of charcoal had taken his place. No "goodbye," "farewell," or "I love you," just a lot of guttural screaming.

Her hands fumbled with each other in her lap. She felt no love for Azzerello. Not even close. Certain aspects of him, though, reminded her of the man she lost. They were both dramatically different from most people. They both had courage and a sense of purpose that most people couldn't comprehend, much less emulate. The difference became especially noticeable when she visualized the stiff, soulless accountants like Drennon waiting for her back on her home ship.

Certainly, clear and obvious differences separated Jervis from Azzerello. Jervis was a good, if not great, soldier. His thoughts were clear and linear, not convoluted and crisscrossed the way Azzerello's undoubtedly were. He only bothered to think about the aspects of his environment that he could control and didn't waste time with the irrelevant, esoteric issues. Azzerello adhered to his ideals no matter the changing situation or how badly they inconvenienced him, and they controlled him and they would doom him. He did not belong in a war. He had the ability and the drive and the intelligence, but he lacked the strength and self-control. A good man, certainly... probably a better person than she was... but not strong enough.

"You okay?" Kole asked.

Clarice blinked and absently ran an index finger under her eye. Still dry. Maybe she'd run out of tears. "I'm fine," she said. "I just... It's just I'm surprised we're still alive."

"Yeah, tell me about it," Kole said, then snorted out a sardonic laugh.

His tone made her turn (her sore neck required that she shift her entire torso). Kole's downcast expression mirrored his voice. He looked just as lost as when she told him that Wraith One wanted permission to kill him. "You don't seem too thrilled about the prospect," she said. She somehow expected him to show some gratitude; even with her conflicting emotions and the convoluted nature of their escape, she felt a *little* proud to get him out alive.

Kole looked at her for a long moment, and his homely features shifted into a smile. "Yeah, you're one to talk."

Kole had never gotten snide with her before, so he let it go and merely nodded. He was probably right. She had no idea what was going to happen next, but none of the options looked promising. From the general mood inside the capsule, one would think they were headed for their own execution instead of their reprieve. "I guess I don't have anything to go back to," she said.

"Tell me about it," Kole said again, this time accompanied by an actual roll of his eyes.

Clarice's melancholy shifted over into anger, forcing her back straight. She whipped her head around in his direction, causing a stabbing pain to rifle down both shoulders. "What do you know?" she snapped. "I lost the man I loved down on that mud ball and the only reason I went down there again was to kill the man responsible... and I failed!"

"Azzerello wasn't responsible," Kole interrupted, then looked down to evade Clarice's glare.

"What?"

"Giles died at Coppin Bay," he said, looking out the front window. "That was a couple days before Azzerello defected."

"I know that," Clarice snorted, although she definitely forgot that fact from time to time. She spent nearly two weeks either sedated or borderline comatose, and her timeline of what transpired during that remained fuzzy, at best. More than that, though, Azzerello had become a convenient depository for her hate from time to time; a living target upon which to focus her rage. "Of course I knew that. I just meant... he was killing people, and I had my chance to stop him and I couldn't do it. I couldn't do it because a lot of what he was saying was true. Maybe we are fighting for the wrong side. Maybe the net worth of my entire life is a pile of corpses." She paused for a breath. She clenched her fists, searching for the magic combination of words that would send the frustration oozing out of her. She wasn't a talker, though, and her face gathered color as she watched the growing ship in the distance. They would be detaching soon, and set adrift. When she spoke again, her words came out slowly. "The most important thing in my life was Jervis. When he died I... all I had left was the army, completing the mission, doing the job. Now it's gone, too, and... I... have... nothing."

Kole nodded but continued to focus his eyes on anything but her. This time, he regarded the mostly useless control panel in front of him. "I never had anything," he said evenly, shifting in his seat so that he could sink in another inch.

Her eyes narrowed to slits. "What do you mean 'never had anything'? What does that have to do with anything?"

Kole shrugged, his eyes continuing to slide off of different objects. He looked insubstantial sunken into his oversized seat. Even standing next to a man-mountain like Wraith One, Kole never looked as childlike as he did now. "I don't know. You talk about meanings of life and reasons to get out of bed in the morning. I never had any... that I can remember. I never had anyone that loved me. I never even had a career I enjoyed. I've just been... I don't know, around."

Clarice took a second to consider whether she was insulted before responding. "That isn't pain," she scoffed. "Pain is watching the only person that matters in your life dying in front of you."

"Would you rather have never met him?" Kole asked. He said it quickly, but the question seemed genuine. "Or if you had met him, if he ignored you. The opposite of love isn't hate, y'know? It's indifference."

"You sound just like Azzerello, you know that?" She continued talking before he could further invalidate her pain. "Well, you can both take your cute little clichés and shove 'em up your ass." Maybe it was her imagination, but the temperature of the capsule had grown a bit hot for her taste. She had not bathed in days, and the sweat on her body felt like a legion of ants marching southward through a field of grime. "Apathy is what you've got, and apathy isn't pain."

"Look, I don't want to get in a semantic argument about it. I'm just saying that I wanted to –" the jolt from the detaching capsule interrupted Kole. The visual field expanded as the floating capsule cleared the underside of the rebel ship. The stars glistened in their perpetual splendor through the sea of blackness and became more numerous with each passing second as the transport ship floated over the tiny capsule like a rising curtain. With the larger floating vessel behind them, the only audible sound came from the weak hum of the capsule's undersized engine. Kole waited a couple seconds to finish what he had tried to say. "I wanted to stay, y'know," he said, sending a timid look her way, as if expecting her to snap at him, "but guess even they didn't have any use for me."

Their capsule finished clearing the transport ship and drifted across the void. Clarice gave Kole a disapproving glance, mostly for effect. In actuality, she felt a little sympathy for Kole; she just wasn't good at expressing that sort of thing. Even though it wasn't a nice thought, she had to admit, he described himself perfectly: he *did* strike her as one of those people who was just "around." No one special. No one worth noticing unless you needed someone to hold a door or draw fire.

In his position, she might have wanted to stay behind. She had yet to calm down, though, and could not resist getting an extra dig in. "Why stay?" she asked in a mocking tone. "So you can give your life 'meaning'? So you can run off and get yourself martyred in the hope that somebody will love you for it instead of crawling back to civilian life, where you'd be just as big a nobody as you were when you left?"

Kole set his jaw and looked like a man either preparing to cry or spit. Clarice hoped for the former, then the hollow, churning feeling of shame settled into her guts. *Nice one, Clarice. What did he ever do to you? Accuse you of not being the only person with a broken life? Maybe next time, you can hold him down and spit in his face.* Jervis never would have done that to a subordinate. Not in a million years. Before she could make an awkward attempt to take the words back, Kole's answer came.

"Exactly," he said.

They drifted on in silence.

*   *   *

From the journal of Lt. Wilson Kole:

I wonder what would have happened if Clarice had killed Azzerello when she had the chance, when they spoke while she was in shackles. I wonder how she would have felt. They would have shot her to pieces, of course, but I can't help feeling that in the brief instant that followed, before the concussion blasts tore her apart, she would have felt some sort of peace. Not because she did the "right" thing, but because she stayed pure... That is, she stayed completely defined by one set of values. There would not have been any conflict among her thoughts. There would not have been a feeling that her actions were betraying alternating sets of beliefs. She would have been an obedient military drone to the end and would have rationalized doing what she did as being the duty of a soldier in the greatest damn military force in the galaxy. Ambiguity is such a bitch.

  Instead, she let him live and continued to straddle the fence all the way to the end. She told herself that she was doing it to protect Frusin, that it still constituted part of her duty, but that was just a functional lie. Deep down, she probably knew that the decision would nag her for the rest of her life (however long that was), but to her credit, she refused to take the easy way out. She accepted the mental and emotional baggage that comes with not knowing what you are doing is officially Right or Wrong. She kept questioning instead of sinking back into the warm comfort of certainty and belonging. From my cell in the cave, I saw the look on her face as she walked past Leon Azzerello that last time, with no shackles to slow her down, and, in a weird way, I think that letting him live and not killing herself may have been the most heroic moment of her life.

*   *   *

CHAPTER ELEVEN:

HEROES

The soldier stares down at the brown blood on her gloves. The stains run all the way up to her elbows. A stain of similar size and color starts at her beltline and runs up to her sternum. She sits motionless on a squat, flat rock, but all around her, more than a dozen soldiers swirl about with practiced regularity, wordlessly readying the camp for the night. Some dig trenches, some set up perimeter motion detectors, some ready the tents. Her attention, though, only allows for the blood.

"Torrance," a male voice says from behind her. She doesn't look up. "Corporal Torrance," the voice repeats, louder and sharper this time.

Although the more self-aware portions of her mind remain adrift, reflex forces the soldier to her feet and snaps her to attention. Her head faces forward, but her eyes track the figure moving around her left side. The strong, chiseled features of Lt. Giles slide into view. Lt. Giles, with the intense, blue eyes and the blond, close-cropped hair, the large, straight teeth and the I-beam posture. He might as well have walked straight out of an Army recruitment video.

"Yes, Lieutenant," she says, her throat feeling dry and raw in contrast to the numbness that envelops the rest of her.

"What seems to be the problem?"

"Nothing, Lieutenant."

He sets a hand on her shoulder, and she quivers. "At ease," he says softly. No other soldier stands within earshot. "Have a seat." Her eyes dart toward him, and he nods, reassuringly. She eases back onto the chair-like rock, but her knees refuse to stop shaking. Giles remains standing and looks at her with his cool, blue eyes for a couple of impossibly long seconds. "It's the blood, isn't it?"

"What?" she asks before noticing that she has begun to absently scrub her gloved hands.

"It's okay," he says, leaning forward and resting his hands on his knees. "It happens to all of us, eventually. It's one thing to blow them apart from one hundred yards, you just pull a trigger and watch them fall. It's almost too neat. When they're right on top of you, though, and you have to use the knife..." He simply shakes his head, either because he doesn't need to describe it or he doesn't know how.

She clasps her hands in front of her to keep them from moving. "I don't know what it is... I just... I can't—"

"It's happened to everybody... everybody who survives long enough. Hell, I'd be more worried about you if you didn't react this way." She briefly glances up at him, and he gives her a reassuring smile as his hand returns to her shoulder. "The key is," he tells her, "you can't think of them as humans. It was just a Middesian. You hacked one of them to pieces, and the others didn't even stop to notice. They just don't have the same regard for life we do."

She nods as he shifts around to her left. She feels his hand migrate from her shoulder to her back. The pat turns into a rub, his fingers gently running back and forth between her shoulder blades, but only for a moment. He slowly pulls his hand away, and she continues to stare at her gloves. The talk helps, though; it isn't human blood that clings to her hands.

*   *   *

The gust of cold, sterile air hit her first. Rather than make her bristle, the sensation brought back memories of her version of home. Clarice stepped off the transport capsule's boarding ramp and into the familiar confines of the command ship's cavernous auxiliary hangar. A few of the mechanics and maintenance personnel milled about in their practiced manner. Even the familiar, high-pitched beep of the mechanical loader made the world slightly more inviting.

Before she could feel too comfortable, Drennon and three armed guards marched into her field of vision from the direction of the starboard entrance. The three guards wore the same blue uniforms as everyone else, but she could tell they were security personnel because of the concussion pistols strapped to their belts: only security was allowed to carry arms beyond the hangar doors. Clarice wasn't worried, as long as the guns remained in their holsters. Once they left the hangar, it wouldn't matter; in a tight hallway, they could have all the guns they wanted, and she could take out three of them in as many seconds. She had no idea what would happen next, but she tried to remain mentally prepared for anything. She did her best to relax away the disgust from her facial muscles and remain impassive at the sight of Drennon. Hopefully, Kole would do the same.

Drennon, as he waddled forward in his tight-assed strut, wore the wrinkled brow of someone genuinely concerned. "Lt. Torrance," he said, closing within a few feet of her. Even worried, he looked like he came out of a mold. Not a hair out of place. "Are you alright?"

Clarice half-smiled and tried not to overdo the fake gratitude. She wanted to appear glad to see him, but not too glad. He was a superior, not a pal. "I'm fine, Major. We're both fine."

"Did you see him?" Drennon asked eagerly. "Azzerello, I mean?"

"Yes, Major, but we were never close enough to attempt a kill," she said, rattling the words off like a machine. Despite the long drift in the capsule, she neglected to rehearse her explanation in its entirety. If she kept the plot simple and refrained from out-thinking herself, though, everything would be fine.

Drennon eyed her an extra half-second before nodding. "I apologize if you're still a little... frayed," he said, glancing about him, "but General Frusin wishes to see you immediately. After that, I'm sure you're both in need of a shower and a bed."

The allusion to sleep... in a bed, no less... made Clarice's shoulders wearily sag forward. *Yeah, sleep*, she thought. *Thanks for reminding me.* Hopefully, she wouldn't have to kill anyone for a few hours.

Drennon turned and led them down the main hallway out of the hangar, Clarice flanking him to his left. Kole stayed an arm's length behind her, and the three members of the security force trailed in their collective shadow. *Why are they even here... officially?* she wondered.

Though not as mangled as her neck, Clarice's thighs ached horribly from the two days of constant marching over uneven ground, followed by the day of sitting on the stone floor of her cell. Kole limped along to her right, probably in even more pain than she was, given his complete lack of physical conditioning. He labored to drag his feet forward and match their lethargic pace.

Drennon turned back to Clarice as he walked. "So, what happened to the Wraiths?" he asked. He glanced forward long enough to maneuver past a pair of maintenance personnel manning a hover lift before returning his gaze to her.

"Four of the six are still down there," she said with confidence. "One and Two bought it after an aerial attack on the way there. We had to destroy Two, and One flipped out and actually tried to kill me." As they passed a door with a black-tinted window, Clarice glanced at the reflection of the security detail. Their weapons remained holstered, which was good… but they were still a security detail, which meant that something needed securing.

"Really?" Drennon asked, his thin left eyebrow rising to an awkward angle. "That's odd." He seemed sincere, sincere enough to make her consider that he might not have anything to hide. Maybe Wraith One really did sustain some sort of damage when the concussion blasts came raining down. Maybe something shorted out his destruct switch in addition to altering his behavior. She'd endured the entire bombardment while hiding under the wrap and couldn't see anything… but, no, that entire scenario seemed like a stretch. Especially since he started in with the threatening stares and general bad attitude the moment they stepped off the landing module.

Clarice nodded solemnly in agreement. "Odd" would indeed be one way to describe it. Drennon deferred to Kole over his right shoulder as he continued walking, but Clarice could not see Kole's nonverbal response. Drennon faced forward to navigate down the empty hall. "Well, you'd better be right," he said, "because General Frusin is not a happy man." He twisted toward Clarice and flashed his mouthful of straight, white teeth as if they were old friends. "Just between you and me, I don't blame you two. The whole mission was stupid… just suicide." He shrugged. "Maybe he's mad because you made it back."

Again, if Drennon was acting, he gave a marvelous performance. *Maybe Frusin did orchestrate the whole thing*, Clarice considered as the six adults squeezed into the elevator. He would have no motive, though, at least not one Clarice could conceive of. He had nothing to gain because there were no promotions to be had. He wasn't a rebel sympathizer because… well, the words "Garth Frusin," "rebel," and "sympathizer" didn't fit together at all. She had difficulty envisioning Frusin as anything other than an old warrior who defined himself through his code of professionalism, personal integrity, and service to the Republic. Sabotaging his own mission would sacrifice that code for no apparent gain. By the time the doors parted and they stepped into the hallway containing General Frusin's quarters, Clarice had securely replaced the blame on Drennon. "Drennon is a petty man who sabotaged the mission out of spite" struck her as a far more plausible scenario.

The three officers entered the General's living quarters, and the doors slid closed behind them, leaving the armed escort outside. Almost a week after moving in, Frusin's furnishings had not risen above the bare-bones level. A larger conference table stood as the only noticeable change: a rectangular, wooden plane sporting twice the surface area had replaced the economical, square thing Clarice had sat at the night before she deployed to the surface. Frusin stood in the same position Clarice found him the first time they met: in front of the window, staring at the stars with his one good eye. *Is he posing, or is there something out there that interests him?* she wondered. Frusin turned to them, his face warped into a scowl that brought every age line on his face into stark relief.

Frusin stuck his fists on his hips and shoved his chin forward. The expression came from a bygone generation and made the general look even older. "Can one of you screw ups tell me what in the hell happened down there?"

Drennon stepped forward before the other two could reply. "Lt. Torrance claims that Wraith One malfunctioned after sustaining damage from an aerial bombardment and attacked her. This sort of event is not *completely* unheard of, and this may have contributed to the mission failure."

Frusin's tanned brow wrinkled like a wadded up tissue, and he stared at Drennon for a long moment. "Yeah, I would say a soldier attacking his commanding officer might contribute to mission failure," he growled. "And what do you mean 'malfunctioned'? I thought you told me these things are foolproof."

Drennon's gaze dove to the floor under Frusin's harsh stare. "Well, compared to normal soldiers, they are. They don't fear or tire or get sick, but any machine has a statistically significant failure rate. I dare say, though, that the Wraiths are ten times more reliable than our best fighters, and anything that could significantly damage a Wraith would probably have killed a normal human."

The corners of Frusin's weathered lips almost lift into a smile. "You dare say?" Frusin said, squinting. "I dare say Azzerello's still alive down there, attacking our extraction operations before they can even get set up, and we haven't come close to one hundred percent occupation of that damn planet. Now he's got four cyborgs down there... what if he reprograms them... or figures out some universal district mechanism?" Drennon took a breath, as though to answer, but Frusin pressed on. "Mother of God, man! That mission was risky enough without having to worry about your own people trying to kill you! What the hell am I supposed to do now?"

Clarice's eyes focused on the back of Drennon's hairless neck. The moment he stepped forward, Drennon became the focal point of Frusin's considerable frustration. The old man rolled back into active duty amid the inevitable speculation that his methods were outdated and that he couldn't adapt to modern warfare. He was proud and cranky and old and, more than anything, not used to losing, and now, his entire legacy risked ruination due to one man. Azzerello did not stand before him, though, so Frusin needed a substitute. Also worth noting: Unless Drennon had stepped forward, that substitute would have been Clarice.

Frusin began to pace as he ranted, pausing only for the particularly nasty and personal sections of his tirade. While he had his back turned, Clarice took a half step back toward the doorway until she found herself even with Kole. They exchanged a glance that said, "Thank god I'm not him," while Drennon received the sort of verbal lambasting normally reserved for a first-year cadet who wired a laser cannon backwards. Drennon endured each assault on his competence and personal pride with complete impassivity, except for the occasional nod of agreement. Clarice once saw a man flogged with a leather strap after an undisclosed failure on the battlefield, and she could imagine Drennon internalizing all the winces that crossed the nameless man's face every time the lash flayed his back.

"Goddammit," Frusin thundered, his face the color of a smoldering ember. "I give you one responsibility, and you botch it! You didn't have to design it! You didn't have to think it up! You didn't have to supervise it! The only thing you had to do was assemble the parts like you were told, and you... you send these people down there with a machine that almost gets them killed. Wait, no. Not even 'gets them killed'; the thing loses its shit out and almost kills them itself! Son, I served with your father, in the same goddamn company for five years, and he probably would have disowned your sorry ass for this one!"

Her internal pendulum changed direction, and Clarice found herself evaluating the merit of Azzerello's causal theory. Drennon may be a smarmy, rank-grabbing jerk, but for some strange reason, he saved her from taking the blame for her failure, and in so doing, risked everything important to him. After all, if he took the fall for this one, it would destroy his career, and blaming lower ranking officers for failure was a time-honored tradition in the Army of the Republic. Her mission was to kill Azzerello, and she failed it, partly due to incompetence (e.g., choosing the wrong Wilson Kole) and partly by choice; she had a couple chances to break his neck and simply stood by, just as she stood by now. Despite the rationality behind her decision to remain silent, she *should* be the target for Frusin's verbal tirade. Azzerello and his minions… and Clarice, for that matter… could only speculate on Drennon's character, and they could have speculated wrongly. In their desperation to explain a complex and confusing situation, they might have seen what they wanted to see.

"Mother of God!" Frusin continued, spit flecks flying. "You were one of those academy-bred wastes of space that was supposed to stick to being a glorified office boy. How the Hell did you ever make Major? Do you even know what it takes to survive down on the surface? When it gets hot? Do you have a clue?"

Clarice knew she should step in and tell the truth… just move her right leg forward, followed by her left leg, open her mouth, and say, "Sir, this was my fault, not Major Drennon's." It would have been the right thing to do. She could have completed the mission on multiple occasions, most recently, when she walked past Azzerello that final time. She let her feet rise and fall, carrying her past her target as if he were just some civilian and not the sole objective of her mission. With similar impotence, Clarice now stood dumbly while Drennon withstood the verbal barrage meant for her. The least she could do was shut up and not throw unfounded accusations about sabotage and betrayal at the man. In his mood, Frusin might have believed them. So, she showed remarkable consistency and did the least she possibly could.

*   *   *

The warm water from the shower flowed over her, carrying away the days of grime that had accumulated in every crevice of her body. She had gone longer periods of time without showering, and in warmer weather, but she had never felt more grateful for a shower. Part of it may have been the metaphorical need to "get clean" after this whole, sordid mess, but mostly, she just wanted to physically feel good. Gradually feeling more and more disgusting over several days, then removing that disgust in less than a minute, feels relatively fabulous. Nothing had brought her genuine pleasure since... well, nothing had brought her genuine pleasure in weeks.

Clarice stepped out of the shower and hit the button for the hot air jets. The comfortably warm air shot out from all four corners of the shower alcove and dried her within seconds. The reflection of her dry, naked body lingered in the mirror, and the sight did not appall her as badly as she expected. The finger-shaped bruises running under her jaw-line were barely visible if she kept her chin low, and the large, blue-green discolorations on her abdomen and back would go away in a few days. The scrapes and scars dotting her skin were no worse than what a typical round of surface duty might produce. Her problem was one of hair. The hair on her head had grown a bit long for her taste, the light brown ends split and frayed and would almost beg an opponent to grab at them in a fight. On the other end of the spectrum, she badly needed to assault the field of leg hair sprouting up. Neither condition violated military protocol; they were just housekeeping issues she needed to tend to.

Clarice's hands smoothed her hair back against her scalp, and she leaned in to examine her face in the mirror. She looked older than she should, mostly in the eyes. Creases lined the outer corners, while slightly discolored bags of skin collected under the lower rim. Maybe it was a passing thing... she'd endured a lot of sleepless nights recently, but maybe she had seen too much. Maybe the life events afflicting her had dug in and made a permanent mark, and like a parasite would continue sucking the life out of her. Whatever the cause, she knew that, after the initial occupation ended... and assuming she survived it, she would walk away from the military life and the bloody business it entailed.

The idea of working at a desk, pushing buttons and staring at a hologram projector for half of her waking day, never appealed to her before. People grow up, though, and people slow down. She wanted some stability, some predictability, at least for the near future. To wake up some morning with the confidence that no shadowy forms lurking behind a rock would fire an incendiary blast through her guts that day seemed like the sum of all celestial bliss. To take a walk on a cool day and not endure the tragic sight of a flash of mortar fire arching across the sky would be something even greater. She studied the collection of skin below her eyes that had started to lose its battle with gravity. She needed to feel young again. She rarely enjoyed her youth, but at least she felt hopeful for the future. It would be nice to get that back, at least for a little while.

Plus, she just wanted to get the hell away from Middes and never come back.

Less than an hour ago, Frusin excused Kole and her so that he could talk at Drennon alone. While walking down the hallway, Clarice explained to Kole that she planned to not tell Frusin about Azzerello's petty theory implicating Drennon, and she explained why. Kole replied with a single nod and continued to match her stride for stride. It was obvious that he didn't agree with her decision, but then again, he bought into the righteousness of Azzerello's quest a bit more readily than she did.

At a four-way intersection in the hallway, Kole turned to her. They both looked like they had spent the last five days digging trenches barehanded. Kole extended his chubby, hair-choked left hand. It looked like a Fangorian flesh spider with a few missing legs. "Well," he said awkwardly, "thanks for, um, getting me out of there alive."

"It was mostly luck that any of us got off that planet... and mercy," she said while shaking his hand, with its awkward, weak grip.

They had endured a lot together in a short amount of time… he watched her rip a guy's throat out with her teeth and still respected her… so the gesture didn't seem like enough.

Kole held onto her real hand a bit too long before releasing it. "Don't sell it short… the effort, I mean," he said, looking at the blue carpet. "You'd have been perfectly justified in letting them kill me. You took a stand and, for whatever it's worth, it saved my life."

Clarice suddenly found the floor equally interesting while remembering how close she came to letting Wraith One have his way. Even the hypothetical mess it would have caused would haunt her for the near future. "Maybe technically," she said to Kole, "but there are ways of treating people that supersede 'technicalities.' Besides, Jervis never would have let one of his people die."

Kole looked up toward the soft, hallway lighting while considering the point. He smiled as he bit his lower lip, and his mouth shifted into an involuntary smirk. "Yeah, I guess so." He shoved his hands into his pockets and trudged down the hallway before stopping to look back. "Hey," he said, still smirking, "if you ever need to talk about anything, you know where I live."

"I do now," Clarice said as she nodded, waved, and returned the smirk. "I hope I never see you again," she muttered under her breath after he turned around and stepped out of earshot. It wasn't personal; he seemed like a genuinely good person, the type of person who, given a chance, would make other people's lives better. Certain people reminded her of certain things, though. Wilson Kole reminded her of her great failure: he reminded her of everything she wasn't.

*   *   *

A dull thumping startled Clarice out of her daze. Someone was knocking on the door to her quarters. She stepped out of the bathroom and started toward the door before remembering to grab her bathrobe from its hanger. As she pulled the robe's belt tightly around her waist and cinched the neck, she noted how soft the fabric felt on her clean skin. She probably wouldn't have noticed the sensation before the mission, but deprivation helps you appreciate the little things.

Her living quarters had maintained an acceptable degree of orderliness despite (or because of) her bone-crushing depression. The edges of the bedspread remained tucked under the mattress because she had wanted to get clean before getting rest. Otherwise, her bedroom usually looked presentable, mostly because she didn't own anything. Clarice pushed the black button to the left of the doorframe, and the door slid open. She had a short list of people she expected to see standing in her doorway, and Lee Drennon was not on it. Yet there he stood, a bit haggard, as though he had just escaped General Frusin's quarters on his hands and knees. The eyes remained sharp, though, the hair rigid, and the sardonic smile still clung to his lips.

"Major Drennon?" Clarice said, absently clutching the neck of her robe. In another life, she might have found Lee Drennon attractive. In this one, though, she always detected something lurking under his calm, well-groomed appearance. Although she would not go so far as to call him sinister, he was an altogether different entity from the one his boyish charm conveyed. Maybe she'd seen too much to get taken in by superficial charm, in general. Down on the surface, you figure out what's important pretty quickly. "Won't you come in?" she said before she could think better of it.

"Thanks," he said, casually, and sauntered past her. He seemed too smug for a man who recently absorbed so much abuse. Maybe she imagined that entire scene in Frusin's. Maybe Frusin got tired and let him off easy. Maybe he was drunk. Drennon plopped down on Clarice's, standard issue, two-cushion sofa and spread himself out onto it like a Darrattian starsquid.

Something felt seriously amiss as Clarice stood by the doorway, but he would surely tell her soon. He was fully dressed while she wore nothing but a robe, but given his lack of surface experience, she had little doubt that she could subdue him in seconds, even without using her exceptional arm. The door automatically squeaked closed behind her, and Clarice flinched. Still holding her robe closed to defend against Drennon's wandering stare, she asked, "To what do I owe the pleasure of _"

"Were either or your folks military people, Torrance?" he asked, casually, as though they were two people seated at the long bar of a cantina and not a commanding officer lounging in his subordinate's private quarters.

Clarice shook her head. "No, Major. My father repaired low altitude aircrafts and my mother was a translator on Alteth 4."

Drennon nodded, seemingly satisfied with their choice of occupations. He paused in mid-nod and raised an eyebrow. "Alteth 4… wasn't that the mining colony that—?"

"Yes, Major," Clarice said, suppressing a shiver.

"That's right; I remember that from your file." Drennon scratched his forehead so he would not have to look at her for a moment. "My daddy was a military man," he said as his eyes refocused. "Tail gunner on an XT-1250 transport. Hard work. Hard-working man. In ten years, never made it past corporal. I guess he didn't have the capacity to spread on the fake charm like I do."

Clarice gave a silent nod, not sure where Drennon was headed. Had more time elapsed since the scene in Frusin's office, she would have put money on the possibility that Drennon had become intoxicated in the interim. She couldn't smell anything on his breath, but that wasn't her most precise sense.

"I can spread it on thick, too," Drennon said, folding his hands behind his head. "Some people can't. It makes them uncomfortable, but it doesn't bother me in the least. Why do you suppose that is?" Before Clarice could cough up some neutral crap about the Republic needing all sorts of talents, he continued. "But all that is neither here nor there. I didn't come here to tell you stories about my daddy. I didn't even come here to tell you why you didn't kill Azzerello." Clarice's eyes widened and she began a token protest, but Drennon cut her off. "Oh, I know what happened," Drennon said with a loose-wristed wave. "I had the electronic eyes on all the Wraiths broadcasting back to me on a closed circuit. I don't care that you didn't do it, though. If Frusin asks, I'll tell him we didn't get anything because of the cave, which is true enough. Being in that cave made it more difficult, but we combined all four feeds. It only gave us a picture without sound, but I got the gist of what happened down there." He allowed her to absorb that information for a few seconds before adding, almost as an afterthought, "Hell, I wanted the mission to fail."

Clarice's eyes narrowed and gave him a look she never gave a superior officer while they were facing her. "You were the one that ordered Wraith One to kill me?" It started as a demand, but ended as a question.

Drennon rolled his eyes in exasperation. "Like you hadn't figured that one out already." Clarice snorted and looked away, feeling like she should act but not sure of what to do. Drennon saw this and added, "Don't take it personal, Torrance. It was all a matter of positioning. Hell, I'm not the one that shot you down to that dirt clod in the first place."

Her hands shifted to her hips. "So are you going to turn me in?" she demanded. "Did you the second I left Frusin's office?"

"Absolutely not," Drennon said, shaking his head, almost as though the question wounded his fragile pride. "If I had, you can rest assured that you never would have finished that shower. I'm just here to ask one question..." he held up the index finger of his left hand, for emphasis, "... and make one request." He held up an index finger of his right hand.

Clarice's arms folded across her chest, but she remained silent. So far, he had nothing on her that she could not top. Even if he showed Frusin the alleged video images from the electronic eyes, he would have to explain how he got them and why he didn't show them earlier.

"I'll take that as a reluctant 'okay,'" Drennon said and shifted forward on her couch. "First, I'm dying to know: why did Azzerello send you back? Why didn't he kill you?"

What would happen if she admitted that Azzerello had guessed about Drennon's sabotaging the mission? Maybe nothing. She had no idea. The whole situation unnerved her, to the point that she wondered if some stress-induced fever-dream had afflicted her. Assuming Drennon actually sat in her quarters and she was still sane, half-truths usually provided the safest route through touchy situations. "He hoped releasing some prisoners would convince Frusin to let him evacuate some Middesians," she said after a long, awkward pause.

"A real bleeding heart, that one," Drennon said, his tone decidedly condescending. He glanced over his shoulder at the lavatory, then looked back at her, almost as an afterthought, and added, "But the bastard sure can fly. You ever see him fly?" Clarice started to shake her head, but Drennon waved it away. "Eh, that's neither here nor there. My second question... I know I only asked for one, but this is just because my curiosity is piqued." He paused for a breath before continuing. "My second question is: in the General's quarters, why did you lie about Wraith One?"

"He would have taken your word over mine," Clarice blurted out. Another half-truth.

"Frusin?" Drennon asked beneath a furrowed brow. "So you were waiting to get him alone?"

Clarice shrugged, embarrassed by her naiveté as she offered up the real reason. "I decided against it. I was beginning to think my theory was wrong and maybe you weren't trying to kill me."

"That's sweet," Drennon said, smirking, "but you couldn't be more wrong." Again, Clarice started to wonder if this whole conversation wasn't some bizarre hallucination that her shattered mind had conjured, but Drennon reached in the pocket of his jacket and removed a small, black remote control with gray buttons. It looked like the one Clarice carried with her down to the surface... even the size was identical... except that only two buttons dotted its exterior, not seven. "Do you know what this is?" he asked.

Clarice slowly nodded. Despite her recent shower and the sub-normal room temperature, sweat broke out across her forehead and the back of her neck. Every pore dotting her flesh stood ready to perspire, except the fake ones on her right arm. "I think so," she said.

"Can you guess whose power source it's hooked up to?" His smile deepened until it became a grimace.

"Mine," she said, numbly. It was not a guess. His thumb touched the larger, bottom button on the control. He sat almost ten feet away. She would need to shoot herself out of a cannon to reach him in time.

"Good," he said. "We'll see if you can go three-for-three. What is your mission?"

She pulled her gaze away from the deadly piece of plastic long enough to see Drennon's green eyes gleaming in the low light. He actually seemed to enjoy himself, on some infantile level that she failed to fully understand. He reminded Clarice of Kitridge did all those years ago, letting the panicked bugs bounce around for a few seconds before smashing them in his greasy palms. "I don't know," she said. She could hazard a few guesses, though, and all of them were vile.

Lee Drennon frowned in mock disappointment. "You're going to kill Garth Frusin for me."

*   *   *

From the journal of Lt. Wilson Kole:

I still don't know why Clarice didn't say anything to Frusin while we were standing in his office. She said she wasn't sure she was correct, but I'm not satisfied by that answer. I often wonder how things would have turned out if she had spoken up. For my part, I was just waiting for them to finish so I could finally get some rest. It seems pathetic for a grown man and a professional soldier to be thinking such a thing at such a critical time, but I was a soldier in-name-only, and I honestly didn't care if Frusin, Drennon, or Azzerello all died; I was still alive and off that graveyard of a planet. I also happened to be hungry, tired, and filthy in no particular order, and biological needs are the first ones that cry out for attention. That's not an excuse; just an explanation… and I didn't see resolving this spat of palace intrigue as my responsibility. I thought that Clarice was better than that, though… better than me.

Whatever she decided, her expertise in the area of life-and-death decision-making far exceeded mine. In fact, I had endured feelings of utter ineptitude for several days, and as we stood there, as the tension of in the room mounted and Frusin started yell and I started to realize that they moment for speaking up had passed, I found myself searching for a stray death ray to shield Clarice from, just so I could feel useful.

I think I would have done it, too. Even at the time, I knew I would come to regret that moment of indecision.

When we said goodbye right after the meeting, we were both relieved to be out in the hallway, and I did something that made Clarice smile. I don't remember what it was, exactly; something about the characteristically awkward way I spoke or acted must have struck her as funny. I just remember the way she looked when her lips parted for that brief moment, and her teeth made a rare appearance. She smiled like a person guilty of a crime. It wasn't much, but the fact that I could make her smile made me feel a little less worthless. I hadn't felt anything for so long... unless you count self-loathing punctuated by sheer terror... I think I would have done anything for her. I felt like I owed her so much, because even though her effect on me was probably inadvertent, she had given me hope.

*   *   *

CHAPTER TWELVE:

VILLAINS

The thermal readout of the binoculars registers every inch of the flat, barren landscape in a cool blue. Nothing large and living has ventured within a mile of them. The scout lowers the binoculars and rubs her tired eyes. Night will be falling soon, but for now, a deep pink sky and red dirt greet her. "Nothing," she says, sliding back down into the depression where she and her fellow soldier made camp.

"Just like five minutes ago," Lt. Giles says as he peels the top off the heated ration. He takes a healthy whiff of the cooked meat product before returning his gaze to her. A slight smile flickers across his face that indicates how truly hungry he must be. "Relax. The perimeter detectors are set up. We'll know if anything is coming for us long before it gets here."

"I'm sorry, Lieutenant," she says, tucking her binoculars into her rucksack. She leaves them turned on, though, just in case there's a rustling or chirping sound that needs investigating. "It's just… I just haven't ever been on a scout mission before with so few people."

He smiles, amused. She doesn't feel insulted, though; he's one of the few officers she's encountered who doesn't use mockery or belittlement as a motivational tactic. "Just relax," he says. "Take off your ruck, come over here, and get some food."

She lets the rucksack slide to the ground. When she eases toward him, the sound of the gravel grinding under her boots seems magnified by a factor of ten. There isn't any wind this evening, and the sounds carry far. She maintains a respectful distance between their bodies, nearly three feet, as she folds her arms across her chest and searches the rapidly darkening sky. How cold will it get after the second sun finishes setting? She has spent several weeks on the surface, but always in the tents with ten or more soldiers. She can't actually remember seeing the second sun set. Out on scout missions, though, soldiers are only equipped with individual heat units, designed to keep the temperature of her extremities above the danger level. A vast gulf rests between danger and comfort, though.

To her left, Giles eats his half of the heat ration off the end of his knife. He probably has body heat to spare. *She shakes her head, trying to force the impure thought out of her mind, not wanting to make herself vulnerable to disappointment. She clamps her eyes shut, draws her knees toward her chest, and drops her head. Giles has a penchant for sending himself on dangerous advance scouting missions; the troops find it endearing, if not particularly responsible. Why did he have to pick her to go along, though? She was fine interacting with Lt. Giles as long as it took place in the presence of other soldiers. Now, everything she considers saying strikes her as horribly inappropriate..*

Something lights down on her thigh, and her eyes fly open. It's a hand. His hand. She didn't hear him move, but he silently crossed the three feet to her. He slowly draws closer with each passing second. In the twilight, the white of his eyes and teeth stand out. "Do you trust me?" he asks.

She closes her eyes and doesn't feel so cold. "I trust you."

*   *   *

The flat, gray ceiling suspended above her had not moved in the last half hour. Clarice lay atop her bedspread with only her sweatshirt and shorts to protect her against the cold, dry, processed air pumping through the vent. A thin pillow lay crammed under the base of her skull and her hands lay uselessly limp at ear-level as she stared through the dark at the ceiling. She could barely see it, but knew that it was there. From time to time, her mind blasted images onto the blank canvas. All of them dealt with her dilemma. None were good.

It turned out that Drennon was not joking when he told her to kill Frusin. She also assumed that the remote in his hand was not a joke, either. In fact, for someone who spent so much time grinning, he really had no sense of humor at all. They spoke for several minutes after the remote appeared, but his eyes never left her. He barely even blinked. Drennon lived for so long with an inferiority complex that paranoia had become his default setting, and Clarice would not have the same opportunities to take him down that she had with a trusting doofus like Azzerello. He maintained a roughly eight-foot distance from her at all times, enough distance that he could punch the buttons and fry her before she got halfway to him. There were things that could happen to a person far worse than dying... Jervis was one example, Wraith Two was another... but Clarice badly wanted her death to have some sort of consequence, and death-by-remote would be every bit as useless as it would be humiliating. She could almost visualize the sneer that would stretch across Lee Drennon's face as he stood over, watching her liquefied flesh collect in a puddle. If she allowed him win, that would be the last thing she ever saw.

The one thing in her favor was that Drennon sort of needed her. Getting Wraith One to try to kill her was a small matter: a commanding officer ordering a machine to execute a subordinate, but Frusin was Drennon's superior, and the same order wouldn't make it through the Wraiths' failsafe measures. Clarice, though, had enough of a brain left to ignore rank and enough machinery to do the job right, and unlike a normal soldier, she had a destruct switch, which gave Drennon leverage over her. The best of both worlds. So, she wasn't irreplaceable, but definitely a convenient tool.

Her tongue licked the front of her parched lips. She wanted some water but did not feel up to moving. She could not tell anyone about the plot against her, except maybe Wilson Kole the Lesser. Kole knew the truth, didn't seem to have a lot of reverence for the chain of command, and he seemed to really like Clarice... almost too much. Kole... her one ally. Could she pick a more useless ally in this situation? He had yet to kill anything more menacing than a plant, and any uncertainty on his part would allow Drennon to live and cause them to die.

She shuddered at the thought of Kole dying painfully. The image materialized in the darkness above her: Kole clutching his stomach after catching an incendiary blast, writhing from the waist up, tears pressing out from between his closed eyelids. A low-caliber incendiary weapon would burn through your guts, but the wound cauterized almost instantly, so it took a long time to bleed out... hours, sometimes. In the beginning, Clarice thought of Kole as a pain in the ass: a weakling with a head full of useless trivia. Then he became a mascot, or at least a pet, to be cared for and protected. He was a good person, though. Azzerello probably would argue that it was better that someone like Frusin die than someone like Kole. Frusin entire existence was that of a cog in a machine. Whether the machine represented order or senseless consumption, it would chew onward with or without Frusin. The Balance of the Cosmos, on the other hand, seemed dangerously short of good people.

Drennon assured her that she would not get caught. His conspiracy ultimately required that someone take the fall, though, and "not getting caught in the near-term" and "living a long and prosperous life" were two different things. He also might be lying about his plans.

What if he ordered her to kill Frusin, then killed her so that he could look good by saving the life of the soon-to-retire general? It would be the closest Drennon ever came to heroism. He certainly was lying to her about something; she estimated that 30 percent of what he said was a lie. When he told her Kole would die a slow and painful death if she did not follow the order, though... that statement seemed genuine.

Even after several hours of thought, following the order still looked like it headed toward either disgrace or execution. A still worse scenario continued to play out in her head, though. Even if she assassinated Frusin, what would stop Drennon from keeping his thumb on that button and keeping Clarice around to deal with all the other political enemies he was bound to make? What if he developed ways of making her do... other things?

She would lose this game unless Drennon got careless and screwed up. Everyone eventually made mistakes, but Clarice feared that the necessary waiting required more patience than she possessed. The prospect of death failed to frighten her; she just wished she could do the right thing. What was "right," though? She tried to think of advice Jervis might give her if he still lived and stood before her, but nothing came to mind. Maybe that's because he wouldn't have had any advice to give. He was a brave, honest man, but he placed far too much faith in his superiors. That's one of the traits that made him a good soldier, but not all useful traits translate across situations. Coercion in the form of an implanted destruct mechanism might not have been necessary with Jervis.

Azzerello would have told her to jump on Drennon and keep punching until the acid hit her. The thought drew a slight smile out of her. His style seemed to be a complete lack of style: you know the right thing to do, so just do it. The fight would have been hopeless, but it would mean that, at least she would not let doubt and fear beat her...

with the added bonus of maiming Drennon. To Azzerello, the internal victories, the ones over ourselves, were the most important. Clarice wanted something more tangible, though.

She could go talk to Kole, but he might offer to help. If he involved himself, he might screw up any plan she shared with him, and he would die. She did not want that; dying was the job of a soldier.

She could easily overpower a member of Drennon's security staff, take his hand laser, and fire off a shot at Drennon. Hand laser's required aiming, though, and she may not have time to aim... and a hit might not be a kill. She couldn't go over Drennon's head because no one was currently over his head. Clarice's eyelids stretched to their widest point. She swung her legs over the side of the bed and sat up so fast that she had to blink back spots. *No*, she corrected herself, *one person is still above Drennon*. One person still had the authority to swiftly and completely neutralize him... for now.

Clarice sprung from the bed and opened her closet without turning on the light. She would tell General Frusin about the plot against him. If she accomplished that, she would probably die, but at least Frusin could send out an order and have Drennon in custody within minutes. It seemed like her only way to salvage a quasi-victory. It might even be the right thing to do.

*   *   *

Clarice wasted time getting dressed into her full uniform before skulking down to the General's quarters. No armed patrols roamed the hallways, but two stood outside the Frusin's room. She wasted over a minute time pleading with the guards stationed there and had to tell them that she needed to speak with the general about a life or death situation before they agreed to wake him. One of the guards disappeared into the General's quarters while the other patted down Clarice thoroughly (a bit too thoroughly for her taste). The door slid open, and the second guard emerged. He nodded toward the guard with the busy hands, and they stepped away from the doorway to allow her entrance.

The small reading lamp above Frusin's bed produced the room's only light and lengthened the shadows. The General's room sat nearly devoid of furniture and so resembled Clarice's own, except for the framed photograph that sat atop the nightstand. It showed the great man with a woman of roughly the same age and a young boy with his blond hair cut military style. It looked about ten years old, taken back when it was easier for Frusin to maintain his ramrod straight posture. She did not remember seeing the family photograph the last time she entered the room, when the General dressed down Drennon. Maybe he put it away when he had company.

Clarice stared past Frusin at the people in the picture. What did the man in the photo want back then? How did he react to becoming a colonial governor? The woman in the picture smiled a workman-like smile, but her teardrop-shaped eyes betrayed a strain. Maybe Frusin retired at the peak of his powers to attempt to save his family. Maybe she died or left or they could no longer bear one another's company and that prodded him back into active duty. The blue-eyed boy, perhaps ten, showed a toothy grin and looked genuinely happy. He would be military age now. *Is he still alive?* she wondered. *Does he hate his father?*

Frusin cleared his throat, and her eyes darted toward him. He stood in front of her, leaning against the back of a chair for support. Except for the white stitching, his black pajamas appeared to be made from the same material as his eye patch. Clarice wondered if this was intentional. He'd been staring at her during the couple seconds it took for her to peruse the lone photograph in the room. Now, his scowl hovered in front of her. The lighting and the fact that he'd awoken mid-slumber made him look positively ancient. "Well?" he barked. "What's the goddamn emergency?" Clarice suddenly remembered that he did not summon her.

Clarice stood in full, on-ship uniform, while Frusin looked like a grumpy resident of a retirement colony. His knobby knees poked out from the loose pajama pants, and a few wispy hairs adorned the exposed section of his liver-spotted chest. The General looked frail, like a formerly fearsome reptile that had lost its shell, and this embarrassed Clarice even more than the fact that she interrupted him. Part of her wanted to offer to step outside so that he had time to gird himself up and become impressive. "You see, General…" she began, suddenly forgetting the tactful, persuasive warning she had rehearsed during her march over.

"Two sentences," Frusin said without inflection. "Whatever you have to say, sum it up in two sentences and leave an old man alone to get some rest."

Clarice inhaled and held the breath while she arranged the words in her head. "Major Drennon has ordered me to kill you." *One sentence. Not bad.*

Frusin's leathery brow folded in on itself even further. "Come again?" he asked, probably wondering whether his hearing had failed him.

Clarice checked the closed door behind her. Word travels fast on a command ship, and this meeting had already taken far too long. "Major Frusin," she began, then corrected herself. "Excuse me. Major *Drennon* told me that if I didn't kill you, he would detonate the power cell implanted in my neck."

Frusin's eyes closed and his fingers dug at the bridge of his reddish nose as though trying to manipulate the strings of an undersized harp. "Why in god's name would he do that?" he demanded when his fingers stopped moving and he could accost her with his full glare.

"I-- I don't know for sure," Clarice said. She somehow hadn't expected to have to explain her position. In her head, the entire process had consisted of warning the general and waiting for a security detail to swarm Drennon's quarters. "I assume it's because he wasn't chosen to lead the occupation after Harvath... I mean, General Harvath."

Frusin tilted his head to a condescending angle. His eye blinked once. "You expect me to believe that Major Drennon, your commanding officer, would threaten the welfare of the Republic in an occupation vital to its interests out of spite?" Clarice thought it might be a rhetorical question, so she remained silent and wide-eyed. He looked over her shoulder and barked, "Guard! Get in here!" Frusin refocused on Clarice and scoffed. "We'll clear this up right now."

The door made a swishing sound as it opened, and one of the guards stuck his square head around the corner. Frusin strode forward, as if he wore full parade regalia rather than black jammies, until he stood a few steps from the door. "Fetch Major Drennon," he commanded with the confidence of a man who didn't have a deadly explosive implanted in his neck.

The door started to slide closed, leaving Clarice and Frusin in the dim light and silence. She felt naked, standing with her back to the window, or at least strangely underdressed. It would be her word versus Drennon's, and he outranked her, so she would lose. End of story. No one could chalk up the dispute as a misunderstanding, because either someone ordered you to kill the commander of the fleet or he did not. Then, the guards would magically whisk her away to a prison cell where she would patiently wait for Major Drennon to kill her at the first available opportunity. Implausible as he found Drennon's motivation for wanting him dead, Frusin should have thought about why Clarice would lie about such a thing. She had only a few minutes to convince the General that —

The door squeaked as it reversed direction and reopened. "No need," Drennon's voice said from the doorway. He stepped from around the corner like a man strolling through an arboretum. He wore a zip-up fleece and civilian trousers: casual-wear, but he certainly did not look surprised to be standing in General Frusin's quarters in the middle of sleeping hours. As usual, his black hair looked like a sculpture. Clarice's mental timer that marked need for action started buzzing ahead of schedule.

Frusin blinked hard, as if making certain he was awake. Clarice could sympathize; she half expected Jervis, her mother, or her old physics teacher, Mr. Gemmel, to come walking through the door next. When he opened his eye and Drennon still stood before him, fully dressed and unannounced, Frusin asked, "What in god's name is going on here? I demand some answers right this instant."

Drennon ignored the General's order and looked over Frusin's knobby shoulder at Clarice. They maintained eye contact for only a second, however, because Clarice's gaze dropped to the plastic remote control barely visible in Drennon's right hand. "Do it," he said. "Right now."

Clarice's heart rate bounced ever upward. Of all the alternatives, she never thought this one would actually occur. Frusin turned back toward her. The faces of the Major and the General hovered in alternate visual fields. Frusin's hard-set jaw slackened, and his eye stared off at nothing while he methodically made sense of the situation. Drennon's features showed no confusion. He stared hard at Clarice, unblinking and impassive.

Frusin's eye narrowed. His head swung back toward Drennon. "Do what?" he demanded, although in his aged, sleep-clogged brain, he had to know that Clarice had given him all the intelligence he needed. "What is going on here?"

"Do it!" Drennon said, louder this time, as the request became a demand. His thumb depressed the first button.

Clarice's fists clenched and unclenched as the images of Wraith Two's slow-motion disintegration swirled in front of her. More than the stench or melted flesh or anything else, she remembered the glassy eyes. Dilated pupils. Crisscrossed veins. Then they burst and ran down the front of her face.

"Guards," Frusin called out, his voice more angry than panicked. He didn't recognize the danger, even after Clarice's warning. "Guards!" he repeated, unaware that he was no longer in control.

Drennon depressed the second button. Whether the sensation was real or merely something generated by her imagination, heat radiated from the back of Clarice's neck, just under the skin. Even if the sensation wasn't real, inside her, a river of incendiary fluid sloshed against a tiny floodgate, waiting for to burst forth and consume her flesh, along with the precious technology.

Clarice had no time to contemplate the pain she would feel as she died. The instant she felt the heat on her neck, a chill rippled down her booby-trapped spine, and her right arm turned her slightest thought into action. She lurched forward and planted a petite fist into the side of General Garth Frusin's skull, and it hit with the force of a sledgehammer. He was staring at the closed door, awaiting the arrival of his security force, and never saw the blow coming. The punch struck Frusin's skull with enough force to snap the older man's neck with an audible pop, but not enough to tear his head completely off or cave in his skull. The general's feet lifted off the floor, and his head hit before his feet landed with a thud, but the mess was minimal. Clarice didn't plan any of that. She barely felt her arm move. She just got lucky.

Drennon's thumb still rested on the first button but he has yet to depress it a second time. He watched Frusin's body bounce off the floor, flip, and hit the wall. His lifeless limbs flailed like an oversized rag doll. When the sequence of thumps ended and a trickle of blood oozed from the general's mouth and eyes, Drennon turned to Clarice and smiled. "There. That wasn't so hard."

Clarice stared at Drennon with wide eyes. The voice in her head screamed *Kill him kill him kill him kill him!* but he stood almost six feet away and, with a lone button left to push, could fry her before she laid a finger on him. Her back remained rigid, and her lungs refused to draw air until the remote control vanished into Drennon's jacket pocket. After a few long seconds, the hot sensation in her neck ceased, and she could breathe again.

Drennon nodded politely and took a quick step toward the door. "Wait a minute," Clarice hissed. "Wait just one goddamn minute."

Only when she stepped toward him did Drennon react. He stopped, and his hand reemerged from his pocket, holding his remote. "Yes?" he asked, nonchalantly.

Clarice held up her hands defensively and scanned the late General's living quarters. "What are we going to do about this?"

Drennon flashed a tightlipped smirk. "Nothing. Don't worry about it; the guards are on our side. They're the ones who told me you came here."

Our side. The words echoed in Clarice's head and sent a wave of nausea through her. "Why didn't you have one of them do it?" she asked when she felt confident that she could keep her meager supper down.

"I can't afford for them to get caught." Drennon pursed his lips. "Don't get me wrong: you're not any more expendable than they are, and you won't get caught. If a member of Frusin's personal security detail was caught, though, it would be an obvious conspiracy and it would eventually lead back to me. On the other hand, I couldn't use any of the Wraiths because they have that nasty rule about following orders of the highest-ranking person. Which left me with you. This way, if worse comes to worse and the accusations start to fly, I can always claim you've been brainwashed by Azzerello." He shrugged. "I'm just paying attention to all the angles."

Clarice raised her eyebrows. "Well, glad I could be of service," she said, sarcastically.

"No you're not," Drennon said, automatically but without malice. "Hell, you'd kill me right now if you could… slowly and painfully. But you can't, so why bother worrying about it?" Drennon glanced past her, at the digital clock on Frusin's nightstand. Clarice followed his eyes. The clock stood next to the picture of his family during happy times. The glowing, red numbers spelled out "0254." "Listen, you'd better get back to your room."

"How do you plan on handling this situation?" Clarice asked. *No, don't walk away! Do something!* a voice from deep inside her screamed, but her numb body and the more functional, self-preserving parts of her brain remained in control. The two of them kept her stumbling forward toward relative safety.

"A concussion blast to the temple will destroy evidence of the real cause of death, and we can doctor the video and make it look like a suicide." He shrugged, as though it were the most natural thing in the world. "See, I've been planning this for a while. Old man. Dead wife.

Estranged son. Failed at the only thing he was ever good at. It's believable enough."

Clarice stalked toward the door. Drennon slid against the far wall, matching her step for step. He kept his cushion of space constant and the remote pointed at her. "What's next for me?" she asked. "Am I supposed to be one of your thugs now?"

Drennon scratched his hairless, pointy chin with this free hand and thought it over. "No. No, I think I've got a different job for you now."

"What?" Clarice asked through clenched teeth. She could not think of a worse task than this one. Drennon probably could, though.

"I'll be in touch." Drennon waved his free hand toward the door. "You really ought to get going."

Eyeing Drennon carefully, Clarice eased out of the living quarters of the idol whom she killed.

*   *   *

Clarice lay in bed, trying not to sleep. If she fell asleep, she would drift into a reality where she was not profoundly screwed, and the shock of waking up and re-entering her real life would feel all the worse. She focused on frightening thoughts, like the probable range of that remote. Drennon told her 100 yards when he gave her the one for the Wraiths. In all likelihood, that was a conservative estimate, based on interference she could expect to encounter on the surface. If it operated like a typical detonator, it had something like a quarter-mile range in space, which meant Drennon could incinerate her from the comfort of his quarters, and all he would have to worry about is whether the fluid spilling out of her would burn through the floor onto the person in the room below. Thoughts like this brought the requisite dread, but even they could not keep her awake. She nodded off, the dreams came, and for an hour or so,

Jervis still lived, she had survived the army, and no chemical bomb sat planted under the flesh of her neck. Waking hurt every bit as badly as she anticipated. When she tried to breathe, it felt like a twenty-pound weight pressing on her chest. Fortunately, the numbness permeating every inch of her living flesh kept her from sobbing.

For the next twenty-four hours, Clarice stumbled through limbo. In the wake of the failed assassination of Azzerello, she remained assigned to Special Operations, but with no mission, and therefore, no responsibilities. She drifted about the ship when she couldn't stand her quarters any longer, waiting for Lee Drennon's voice to come thundering over the intercom like an angry deity.

Every one of her fellow soldiers seemed to know that Frusin had died. Maybe Drennon released a fleet-wide announcement earlier in the day, only she was too lifeless to hear it. She walked past her comrades with impunity, legions of soldiers with no idea that she broke the neck of a living legend with one mindless, reflexive right cross. During her roaming, she learned that the Military Council scheduled Frusin's funeral for almost exactly sixty hours from the day she killed him. It would coincide with a temporary, fleet-wide bombing halt, to honor the great man. The military made a grand production out of the deaths of the famous and visible. They played music and read long eulogies before blasting the corpses of the great ones out the hangar door to rejoin the cosmos. If you were a nobody, they just kicked dirt on your body or set fire to you. During one of her passing stretches of lucidity, Clarice wondered if she would live long enough to attend Frusin's funeral. She already felt like a ghost.

A gray haze stuck to the hallways. She plodded along, each foot slapping the blue carpet in succession. Although she still craved death, her relationship with it had fundamentally changed. It was not a vengeful wish, like when Jervis died, when she wanted to stop the pain and transfer it to a faceless enemy. Then, she wanted to use her body as a blunt instrument of revenge. Now, her dreams of heroism were dashed, and she just wanted to disappear from existence to keep from inflicting more evil on other people. She imagined getting hold of an incendiary pistol, sticking the barrel in her mouth, and squeezing the trigger. What would the barrel taste like? The idea calmed her, like a baby sucking on a pacifier. If she didn't die soon, she knew Drennon would force her to do something else repellant. Jervis's death stripped the worth from her life. Now, it had somehow gotten worse, transforming her existence into a perverse, negative image of all she had aspired toward. Now, the only ability she possessed was the ability to cause harm.

Azzerello must have felt the same way before he reached his breaking point, as if a series of distant, devastating explosions measured the worth of his life. He saw something that awakened his conscience to the pain he had inflicted, and once the veil rises, once the sight of what lies behind it burns its way into your memory cells, you cannot replace the veil. Clarice admired the confidence of a man, who when faced with reality, decided to respond by pitting his skills against the most powerful military force in the known universe. Her own pain motivated far less ambitious goals. She would kill Drennon. She didn't know when or how, but it didn't matter: she would wait as long as she had to, she would do every awful thing he commanded, but he was human and he would slip up. When he did, she would dredge a final ounce of pleasure from her existence by watching him die as slowly as she could manage. Then, if necessary, she would allow herself a suicide. It wasn't much of a life goal, but it allowed her to continue drawing breath.

The constant barrage of artificial lighting made it difficult to gauge the exact passage of time, but at some point during her wanderings,

Clarice ran into Kole. The voice on the intercom had just dismissed one set of soldiers from the mess hall, and they spilled out from all three sets of doors by the dozens. In seconds, the wide, hitherto-empty hallway she shuffled down filled with young, ignorant soldiers. They all seemed so much younger than her. She kept her eyes low as she instinctively sidestepped a series of them. One pair of legs, though, shifted in her direction, cutting her off as she tried to slide around. Her eyes ran up the length of the stocky body. The instant they reached the squat nose and pockmarked skin, she recognized Wilson Kole.

When the look of recognition flared in her eye, his face broke into that ugly smile with the crooked teeth and pinched eyes, but after a second the corners of his eyes drooped in concern. While in his cell down on Middes, Kole overheard Azzerello explain his plan to Clarice. He also stood beside her yesterday (or was it the day before?) when she failed to confront Drennon. In the hallway, amid the stream of healthy, young bodies rushing past them, he looked at Clarice as one might look at a person with a terminal disease. He was pretty smart... certainly smart enough to fill in the blanks and complete the chronology of recent events.

Kole grabbed her elbow, her left elbow, and she suppressed a potentially lethal flinch. He leaned in. "Do you want to talk?"

He really was an ugly man. Not at all heroic. She realized she was staring and forced herself to respond. "No thanks," she said, unable to look into his beady eyes. "They'd kill you. Besides, it's too late to talk."

"I don't care if they kill me," he said, barely moving his lips. Hips and shoulders from passing crewmen jostle them both. Clarice tried to pull her elbow away, but Kole held fast. "You did it. Didn't you?" he asked softly. It wasn't an accusation. His tone made it sound as if his real question was, "Did they force you to do it?"

It felt good to have someone show you that they care about you beyond what your rank demanded. It had been a while. The corner of her mouth lifted into a sad, sweet smile. "Of course not. I don't know what you're talking about." Kole looked at her dazed, like a lost child, because he had no clue what to do or say. She wanted to tell him everything, of course, not because he could help her, but because they had been through things down on the surface, and in a weird way, he knew the person she had become about as well as anyone left alive. More importantly, though, he would understand that she wasn't a monster, and she needed that worse than anything. She looked down at her elbow. His fingers did not dig into it. They almost caressed the knobby bone. "I really need to get going," she said.

Kole slowly, silently released the captive joint. An awkward pause ensued. The torrent of bodies reduced to a trickle. Clarice turned and allowed herself to stroll away, caught up in undertow of humanity. She didn't look back. She continued to wander, awaiting the sound of Lee Drennon's incorporeal voice.

*   *   *

At some point, Clarice slept. The next morning, she received an intercom message telling her to report to Drennon's office at 0900 hours. She didn't exactly know where Drennon's office was located, and actually went to the wrong place in her first attempt, but eventually learned that he was now using Garth Frusin's old quarters as his office. Maybe he liked the view...

Arriving five minutes late, she found that the room still reflected Frusin's rugged sensibilities, but then again, Drennon had only occupied it for a matter of hours. An uncomfortable, angular chair occupied the spot where Frusin's head had thumped against the floor. She wondered if so much as a stain remained of the great man, or if they'd replaced the carpet. Drennon sat at the far side of a dark, rectangular wooden table that occupied the center of the room. Clarice stood on the end closest to the door. Half a dozen other warm bodies occupied the room, bureaucrats with, hopefully, scant knowledge of the more shady goings-on in the ranks. The three men and one woman sat on either side of the long table with their backs straight and chests puffed out, two other men operated the computer system set up in the spot where Frusin's bed used to be. Some of the additional occupants had more hair and a smaller waistline than others, but all the men gave her the same, toothy smile when they noticed her. She had no idea who knew what, and whether they knew it about her, because they all looked like men staggering drunkenly over the line that separated righteous from self-righteous.

I had only been two (or three?) days since Frusin fell, but one had to like the cover-ups chances of succeeding. The major issue was one of distance. Sure, the Council will investigate the death, but it would take days or weeks for that person to arrive. Meanwhile, the crime scene would grow cold, and the locals, people with whom Drennon had spent years cultivating relationships, would do their best to impede, delay, and obfuscate. These people may not even know why they were doing it, other than that they owed Lee Drennon a favor.

Drennon motioned to Clarice to walk over to his desk. From his casual expression, no one would know that matters between them had grown exceedingly complicated. "You're probably wondering why you're here," Drennon began.

Clarice nodded silently but assumed that the request would involve another execution/assassination. After hearing the twenty-second version of events, she could feel her heart beating again. When she spoke, her voice sounded like it came from under a foot of water. "Major," she said to Drennon, "I do not understand why we are changing courses of action."

"Because," Drennon began, his hands spread about shoulder's width and gripping his end of the table as if he were about to either stand up or tip the table over, "Frusin was a fool. He was too proud to admit defeat, and in the end, he knew it." Drennon's behavior bordered on flighty at times while he operated in the shadow of his commanding officer. Sitting at the head of the table, though, he seemed immersed in his element. After following his slime trail for almost a week, Clarice knew his true nature well enough to recognize that this all amounted to an act, his image of how he thought a leader should behave, but it was a good act, and one that most soldiers badly wanted to believe. He had become someone not to mess with, and he played the part to the hilt. He then regarded the men and woman who used to be his equals but who were, for the time being, his subordinates. "We are not admitting defeat here, people. Make no mistake about that. We are merely giving the remaining resistance a means to flee so that we can obtain the resources that are the reason we are here in the first place."

Clarice kept her shoulders pressed back and focused all her effort on keeping her jaw rigid so she would not smile. *If I did start smiling*, she wondered, *would I recognize the sensation?* So much time passed since she heard or saw something that did not make her want to gut herself that the first mildly positive event nearly made her burst with joy. Drennon's only reason for making such a concession was out of fear that the Military Council would terminate his interim command after one week. He knew he could not beat Azzerello in that time, but to keep his command, he had to do something bold and elaborate, something that would make it foolish to remove him midway through the process. Her smile continued to force its way into the open, though, because despite the legion of fates aligning against him, the occupation was ending and Leon Azzerello and a pile of spare parts had beaten an intergalactic armada.

Drennon affixed his gaze to Clarice, which made it that much harder to conceal her emotions. "Lt. Torrance, you are going to oversee the delivery of the first of the nine transports Azzerello requests. It will take place tomorrow at 0600 hours." He paused and squinted, maybe trying to place what was wrong with her reaction. "Your duties will consist of letting Azzerello's pilot dock with the transport, make sure they know how to operate it, take the pilot's docking vehicle, and return to the command ship. Any questions?"

"Just one, Major," Clarice said. Drennon stared impatiently, his eyes smoldering in the shadow of his brow. He probably spent hours looking in the mirror, trying to perfect the look because he thought commanding officers used expressions like that. Something distinctly hateful lurked under it, though. He probably didn't like being called "major," even though, until the paperwork went through, that term remained technically correct. "Why have you chosen me?" she asked.

The six officers in the room twisted their faces toward Drennon to varying degrees. He cleared his throat. "I didn't. Azzerello did."

Clarice nodded. The decision flattered her, but it failed to do her much good in the short term. If the opposition liked you, your side started asking questions. A thought flickered in her mind: what if he wants me to join his side? It seemed a little late in the game for that, but it was possible. There was life after war-time, after all, and the scattered population of wounded, sterile Middesians would need all the help it could get. What would she say, if given the opportunity to betray her side? "Yes," of course; there was nothing left for her up here except for death and regret.

"What do you make of that?" Drennon asked. Even though they were pretending not to look, the eyes of the six other officers swung back in toward her as though hooked to a pendulum, forcing her vision to refocus.

"I don't know, Major," she lied. At the very least, Azzerello rightly worried that Drennon would double-cross him, and he probably trusted Clarice more than he trusted anyone else in the fleet (whatever that was worth). There was Kole, of course, but he probably didn't possess a transport operator's license.

Drennon eyed her as if to say, "Nothing you do matters because I can let you live or die as I see fit." Aloud, he said, "Carry on, Lieutenant."

Clarice kept her steps slow and short as she exited the room. No need to look happy. No need to draw attention. If a hand had fallen on her shoulder, though, she probably would have bolted down the hallway, because it felt like she was escaping.

*   *   *

From the journal of Lt. Wilson Kole:

Hope. Hope is the only reason to do anything. If life has turned bad, you persist because you hope it will improve. When life is good, you hope it will stay that way. Even if you know on a rational level that no marked change will result from something you find yourself hoping for, you still hope for it because the expectation makes life bearable.

For example, I had not been enjoying my life when Clarice Torrance knocked on my door that fateful day. Soon, however, while slogging across the surface and dodging laser fire, the possibility of returning to the dull routine of my existence transformed into a blissful, unreachable dream by comparison. Self-fulfillment seemed a distant worry compared to a bed, a shower, and solid food. The mild pleasures of sterile space living wore off in less than an hour after waking from my sleep, but the anticipation might have kept me alive while down on the surface.

When I heard of Azzerello's success, though, I felt my version of true joy. The previous day, I had seen Clarice in the hallway, and it would not have surprised me if I'd learned that she'd been drugged. I thought she would be dead by the end of the week, either because of Drennon or by her own hand. When I heard about the cease-fire and what came after it, though, I knew in my heart she would be all right. We both would. If Leon Azzerello could manage to defeat the Republic, I could survive the existential void of my life and she could survive whatever the likes of Lee Drennon threw at her. It felt like, from that day forward, Azzerello's triumph would remain a source of inspiration of what persistence and courage can accomplish, no matter what circumstances threw at us. An immortal source of hope that someone like Frusin could never be.

In a way, the memory has provided precisely that. Thinking back, though, maybe Drennon saw it the same way I did. We weren't out of the woods yet, because the woods were so much bigger than any of us imagined.

*   *   *

CHAPTER THIRTEEN:

PHANTOMS

The woman lifts her head from the rigid, standard-issue pillow and stares over her shoulder, through almost a foot of blackness, at the lean, muscular outline of her lover. Only a sheet covers them, but his warmth envelops her, walling off the sterile cold of the climate controlled room. She has grown used to the sensation, but has never grown tired of it. "Jervis?" she asks. "What's going to happen to us?"

"What d'you mean?" His arm descends across her body, settling on her abdomen, providing her with an extra degree of protection.

"I mean after the occupation. It is almost over isn't it?" She recognizes the pleading quality in her voice. It isn't the voice of a soldier. Normally, she would work to extinguish that sound of encroaching weakness, but the role of soldier is fast ending for her.

"I don't know," he admitted, seemingly unconcerned. "If I don't stick with the Army, there are a lot of jobs on the economy for a former officer: security, management. I think I will stay in, though. Sit back and watch the action with the rest of the C.O.'s." He leans in and kisses her sore neck without opening his eyes. "Wherever I go, though, I want to be with you."

That is exactly what she wanted to hear, so she closes her eyes and smiles, feeling safe in his arms. Soon, she will have to drive these memories away, though,

hopefully for the last time. In a few hours, they will board a transport ship, and that
ship will take their unit to the surface. She doesn't follow the politics of the occupation
much, but from what she understands, the last reserves of enemy strength have gathered
for a final stand, in a place southwest of the Wharrib Mountains. It's an entirely
landlocked area, but due to a mistranslation, everybody in the army calls it Coppin
Bay...

*   *   *

Piloting a transport was not an easy task. As the name implied, it transported troops, vehicles, and artillery, and a transport pilot needed to reach places where scores of troops were located, which meant that the vessels were bulky, armored, and hollow. They also tended to be shaped like torpedoes, and this made them perfectly suitable to drift about in the void of space. In order to perform a docking maneuver, however, a pilot needed considerable skill at manipulating the massive, hollow phallus back and forth, inching it in any of the three dimensions at the same time, without carving a chunk out of your docking partner. Even though she received an operator's license restricted to ship-to-ship commutes, Clarice's experience was mainly restricted to simulators. She had never actually piloted a full-size transport in real life before receiving the assignment from Drennon. Fortunately for her, the job only required that she find a point on her view screen and drive her transport in a straight line.

After detaching from the external docking tunnel, she steered the behemoth in the general direction of Middes. Not too difficult; it was the big, brown planet with flecks of blue that took up half the sky. Despite a primary specialty in infantry, Clarice was not a complete idiot when it came to piloting bulky vehicles; in addition to her minimal experience with transports, she'd operated a hover-loader when she helped load freight down at Ground Base 5, and, more to the point, she took a couple

classes on operating a HG-283 Field Trawler at one point while
contemplating a life outside of the military. The instructions Drennon
gave her fell well within her area of expertise: aim the nose of the ship in
the direction of the planet, and an enemy ship will eventually intercept
you. To her thinking, Azzerello probably refused to offer a pre-arranged
meeting point so that he could track the ship from its point of origin...
and to prevent Drennon from doing the same.

Clarice set the accelerator at a steady pace and settled in as the
great, brown orb took up more and more of her visual field. She felt a
pleasant tingle of anticipation, for the first time in weeks. Sure, she'd
experienced the biological, panic-driven excitement that comes from
having a cyborg try to rip your head off, but this was something
qualitatively different. Azzerello clearly selected her for the duty because
he trusted her, but was that the only reason? The more she contemplated
the idea, the more she considered that he might want to offer her a
chance to switch sides. Somebody with her infantry experience would be
valuable, wherever they ended up, and he and his little, unkempt band
would need all the help they could get. Temporarily halting the
occupation was an achievement but only the first step of several they
would need to take. Even with a few transports full of Middesians, where
did he plan to take them? What habitable planet would want refugees
with no resources, except to use them for slave labor? Azzerello would
never abandon his adopted people to a life of slavery. So, what then?

And what about Azzerello, the little girl whose name Clarice
could not remember, and the guy that used to dump all that sterilizing
agent on the enemy? The Republic would give them a healthy head start
because it would be happy to get them off the planet, but it would not
leave the source of such shame to fester. Drennon would have them
hunted down, imprisoned, and publicly dismembered, all to send a

message to potential dissenters that you cannot cross the Republic and survive. In the air, Azzerello was reputed to be as good as they get, if not better, but he was a destructible instrument of flesh, and it only took one mistake. God help her, but she wished them all luck. If they failed to accomplish any more than inspiring her to keep drawing breath, to fight on for the sake of fighting, than at least that was something.

Clarice shifted in her seat and readjusted her grip on the Y-shaped control stick. *What if Azzerello does offer to let you join?* She shook her head. He won't. She absently checked her instrument panel. All the gages seemed to be in place. She scratched her real forearm. She smoothed her hair back. Still, the possibility refused to leave her. What if he did? If he did, if he stepped out of the airlock and said, "I'd like you to join our group and fight the Republic," she would have a hard time turning it down. Lost causes made for good water in which to drown personal demons. It may not aid in speeding Drennon toward a painful death, but it might make him lose his appetite for conflict, temporarily. In all honesty, though, power-hungry yes-men weren't hard to come by. In a bureaucracy, when one Lee Drennon died, another rose, phoenix-like, to take his place. Joining Azzerello would continue the cascade of defections and may, in the long-run, hurt the whole of Drennon-kind more than erasing a single stooge from existence.

Something about the prospect nagged her. It sounded great, in theory… in her brain, but when the time came… if the time came… could she overcome the feeling in her guts and really do it? To betray the Republic was to disown the only real family Clarice ever knew. She needed the army for a long time, to tell her what to do and to pat her on the head when she did it right. She even loved the army when she loved a man in the army. He was gone now, though, killed as much by the adolescent power-mongers like Drennon as by laser mortar fire. She still loved her family, it still had the potential to bring a benevolent order to the universe and provide a haven for people like her, but the family had gone astray. Only action, not acquiescence, could direct it down a different more righteous path.

But he won't ask.

A blue light blinked away on the right side of the orange-tinted instrument panel. The gentle, steady blinking meant that no flying objects were trying to intercept her. Harmless enough, but it reminded her of something. She scanned the walls. Her cockpit design was typical for any vessel larger than a fighter, seating three comfortably and five uncomfortably. The rest of the transport was the size of a stadium. What if Drennon planted a bomb on the ship? Her eyes scanned faster, foolishly hoping the phantom saboteurs left a telltale bundle of disconnected wires in plain sight in the only occupied part of the ship. Drennon certainly would not mind seeing her blown apart or sucked into the airless void. A more likely scenario involved him waiting to detonate any device until Azzerello received the ship. She would be flying back toward the command ship by then. Better that this phantom bomb erase her from existence than for Azzerello to think she had become party to a betrayal.

Clarice took a deep breath and wrung the steering controls with both hands. Worrying didn't help anything. Besides, Azzerello was smart, smarter than her, and had no doubt already considered the possibility of a double-cross. All these possibilities were out of her control and not even real threats at this point. If someone had planted a bomb on board, she had no way of finding it. If Drennon wanted to detonate a bomb, he would wait until the ship had changed hands. He wouldn't waste a bomb large enough to blow apart a transport on her, not when he could press a pair of buttons and watch her flesh melt.

The myriad details that might go wrong continued to invade Clarice's thoughts and accumulate until the blinking blue light changed to a solid green and a single-passenger vessel blipped across her radar screen. Seconds later, she received a visual confirmation of the ship through the cockpit window. It appeared to be a black, three-winged, Republican vessel, probably a CAL-14. Definitely stolen. Probably booby-trapped. Any complications with the reception of the transport would no doubt result in a faceful of retaliation by Azzerello's camp.

The CAL-14 drifted closer, cautiously. Maybe Azzerello sat behind the controls. Probably not, even though he struck her as the sort of man who would not issue orders he was unwilling to carry out himself (she knew someone like that once...). He needed to stay alive, because without him, there was no Cause. Drennon would never send an overwhelming force down with Azzerello alive. Oh, sure, if he sent enough ships, they could burn a hundred miles of planet in every direction, but even if Drennon won with that kind of strategy, he had to think about the cost. What if he lost a hundred ships? He'd be lucky to get a position repairing photon torpedo tubes. With Azzerello gone, Drennon would have the Republican fighters scrambled within the hour, and they would crush the resistance like a paper cup. A more likely pilot would be the girl who had barely crossed over into puberty, the man with the load of guilt so heavy that only a violent death would relieve it, or one of the nameless other traitors... or revolutionaries, depending on how one looked at it.

The other vessel drifted close enough to the transport that Clarice could initiate the automated docking procedures. She pushed a few buttons to set the timing coordinates and pulled the lever that engaged the auto-pilot. Over the course of minutes, the CAL-14 slowly drifted across the blue viewing screen to her left. When the image of the little ship became parallel with the image of the big ship, a mechanical, grinding sound echoed through the docking bay behind her. Seconds later, the grinding stopped with a thunderous click, announcing that the two ships had successfully docked.

The ships internal gravity was engaged, so Clarice unhooked her chair's Y-shaped safety harness and scrambled toward the back of the ship. She told herself that Azzerello would not be standing on the other side of the docking door. He would not point at her and say, "You. Come with me." She would not escape the yoke of Drennon and the Republic so easily. She knew all this, but her heart still bounced against her rib cage. Hope fueled her, and it possessed a more savory flavor than revenge. Maybe the onrushing juggernaut of time would trample her along with everyone else, no matter how fast or far they run, or how much or how little harm they inflict. Maybe righteousness brings no external reward, and when we make the choice to not commit acts of evil and to tread as lightly as possible, we satisfy only our own criteria for living. Clarice made the mistake of compliance, and now, walking down the narrow corridor to the cargo hold, she sought absolution.

She strode past the blinking lights and wavy, electric lines, only vaguely aware of what most of the gages did. The corridor ended with a locked security door. She turned the handle, and the room opened up before her. The sheer size of the domed cavity caused her to stop and nearly strain her neck as she looked up to the ceiling. Row upon row of stasis pods lined the walls, all the way up, and the equally numerous rows of seat/beds stretched back to the recesses of the chamber. Azzerello and his team could comfortably fit over twenty times the population of the cave inside this thing. She shook her head and continued toward the inner docking door.

A hand-sized keypad situated beside the door awaited the access code Drennon gave her. "6-1-4-3-2-3," she mumbled through a surprisingly dry mouth, punching each number with her index finger as she said it. What if the man himself stood on the other side of the outer docking door? What would she say? Anything but shameless gushing would do. She did try to kill him, after all. Besides, shameless gushing would make her look extra pathetic, and dignity might be the only thing of worth she had left. Hopefully, she wouldn't have to talk: he could just ask her, and she could nod, and that would be that.

A hissing resonated as the door to the airlock shifted several inches away from her. Then, it mechanically shifted to the right. Clarice stepped into the brightly lit chamber and took a deep breath in a futile attempt at composure. So many possibilities danced in her head that she could scarcely focus. A rectangular, metal door stood several feet away. *This is it*, she told herself, *my chance to make things right*. The last thought struck her as a bit unvarnished, but it sounded correct in her head. Something beeped from the other side of the door, indicating that the person in the CAL-14 had entered the correct access code. The other door opened with a hiss, then slid to Clarice's left. A disheveled, male Middesian stepped through the doorway into the airlock. He wore a dirty, green poncho. This, and his slight hump and dry, cracked snout, made him vaguely familiar, but only vaguely.

Clarice swallowed the lump in her throat. Not even a human. Not even someone she could apologize to. The Middesian nodded at her, and she responded with an automatic nod. "Where's Azzerello?" she asked.

The Middesian squeaked back at her using vocal chords that could not hope to replicate human speech. She stared, dumbly. The sound that he generated could have contained minute details as to

Azzerello's whereabouts, or could have called her mother a whore. A few awkward seconds of silence and inactivity follow before the Middesian shuffled forward and squeezed through the narrow gap between Clarice and the door. It brushed against her left side for less than a second. She never noticed it before on all the corpses she left down on the surface, but their fur was surprisingly soft.

She took one step toward the CAL-14's airlock but stopped. She would be returning to the Republic, and in all likelihood, she would never see a Middesian again. "I'm sorry," she called behind her, not even remotely concerned whether Drennon watched and listened to her on a video feed.

The Middesian's tiny steps continued to carry it into the cavernous main chamber of the transport on his way to the cockpit. Her apology either came too late or in the wrong language.

*   *   *

From the journal of Lt. Wilson Kole:

A person never gets as close to death as they do in war, not without actually dying. Notice that I did not say that "a person never gets as close to dying"; humans always hover precariously close to dying from a variety of sources. In war, though, you marinate in the presence of death. From the moment you sign away your freedom, death clings to the air. It permeates your lungs and pushes out your pours. Even if you never leave the safety of your command ship, you see the chunks of humanity they bring up to sew back together and you meet people that you will know for long enough to miss them when something incinerates them.

A close companion to death in instances like this is guilt. If you hang around for a while, you feel guilt for living while others die, be it friend or enemy. If you happen to be the one doing the killing, eventually, you start to feel like not only are the people you killed no worse than you, you might even start thinking they are better. Giving them the benefit of the doubt, you can't say for certain if they've killed anyone, while you have at least one notch… and counting. That's why machines and psychopaths make the best warriors. No guilt.

Watching the Middesians in the cave for however many hours, Clarice saw that the enemy acted just like us: they bleed, they screamed, and they loved. The second the enemy grew a face, as soon as Clarice saw the Middesians as individual beings, the seeds of guilt germinated within her. I don't know how the math works, if you have to save someone for every person you killed or if the former number is ten times the latter, but you often see people trying to make amends for the damage they've inflicted in ignorance. The guilt never totally leaves, of course, but while you perform your good works, you think you're lessening the moral burden on yourself.

Clarice went on the transport looking for a deal that would allow her to make amends. She did not find one. I think she came back to the command ship knowing that there was only one way to end the pain.

*   *   *

CHAPTER FOURTEEN:
MISS WORLD

The far edge of the loading ramp strikes the ground, spraying dirt in every outward direction. "Let's move out!" Lt. Giles bellows. His eyes sparkle, and his lips pull back into a half-smile, like they're about to do the most natural thing in the world. He winks at the soldier closest to him, and she smiles nervously as she hurriedly files past. She takes a deep breath and grips her rifle tighter. As she nears the top of the ramp, the sky opens up before her, and the bright blue trails of the laser mortars arch across the blackness.

Stomp stomp stomp. *The military-issue boots thunder down the metal ramp and kick up dust when the reach the ground. The transport drew fire on the landing, and the pilot had to set them down in a crater. Steep inclines surround them. They are safe unless the enemy starts advancing, but that's not what their field regulation programming says: it says that low elevation = danger. The soldier submits to the pull of her training and moves along in-step with the rest of the group. This time, though, it feels different. She doesn't want to shoot anything. She just wishes she could discharge her weapon into the air and walk back to the ship... or fast-forward through this scene and get on with her life, her real life, the life she always knew awaited her if she worked hard and lived virtuously, a life with some security and a sense of belonging.*

Ten seconds and a hundred feet pass. A flare ignites overhead and bathes the land in a crimson glow. The soldier finds herself flat on her belly. She raises a flat hand to signal for those behind her to hold. She waits. Distant explosions rip through the night. Her right hand wrings the handle of the concussion rifle, and she leads the crawl up the hill.

"One more time," she thinks.

*   *   *

Clarice bolted upright in bed, her skin clammy and her chest heaving. She'd fallen asleep above the thin layer of blankets but still awoke covered on sweat. Outside, in the hallways, someone knocked on her door for at least a second time. She had barely left the bed in the last twenty-four hours, just in case any of her few acquaintances on the ship asked her how she was doing. The sudden, explosive movement of sitting up left her light-headed.

Clutching the damp bedspread for support, Clarice shifted her legs off the end of the bed, first her right, then her left. She'd made plans to move hours ago, and now that the moment had arrived, she felt totally disoriented. She remembered watching the transport ship recede into the starlit space, but after that, everything kind of melted into a blur. She returned to the command ship, and the safety and shadows of her quarters beckoned to her. There, she waited for Drennon's call. Keeping a sense of perspective while in orbit could be difficult, under the best of circumstances. There was no day and no night, so you had to force yourself to watch clocks. There were no seasons, so you had to watch for calendars, holiday decorations and the like. If you didn't, days bled into weeks, weeks bled into months, and so on.

The situation Drennon forced Clarice into was far from the best of circumstances. He had forced her into the role of a killer, and killers don't fill their days with the same things that give meaning to the lives of non-killers. They don't make pleasant chitchat, catch up on reading, or water the plants: they sit in the dark, waiting on a knife's edge for a chance to fulfill their function at a moment's notice. Only time would tell whether the role involved killing others or killing Drennon. Until then, nothing to do but eat, breathe, shit, and kill… and the hours were beginning to bleed into days.

The knocking on her door continued. Someone knew she was home and would not be departing any time soon. Dressed in shorts and a sweatshirt, she staggered toward the slivers of light filtering into the room that demarcated the top and bottom of the door. Her feet tangled themselves in a pair of pants lying on the floor, and Clarice started to fall. The butt of her right hand slammed into a section of wall adjacent to the door, arresting her momentum. She braced herself, took a breath, and said, "Bathroom light." Her throat felt raw and cracked, but it did its job and the bathroom lights flickered on. The luminance coming from the far right corner of the room provided one with enough light to navigate through the room but without hurting one's eyes… if one had just spent twenty-plus hours immersed in darkness.

Clarice kicked the pants away from her legs and in the direction of the bathroom. With her eyes tilted groundward, she noticed all the scars crisscrossing her arms and legs that the low light illuminated. Typically, they just blended into the scenery of her body, but since she hadn't seen her body in a while, it struck her as a hell of a lot of scars. Almost too many to count. Almost one for every corpse she created. Still more under her clothing, to be sure… like that gash that ran in an arc from her navel to her left hip. That was her most impressive one; she got it when an Advance Walker exploded and a flying hunk of metal took a bite out of her. A few staples and some field dressing, and she was right back in the fight. Her body read like a star chart of her life since she left high school, mapping the abuse that her body had absorbed. They were everywhere, except on her perfect, pristine right arm.

Clarice shook her head to clear it. Her thumb depressed the black button beside the doorframe, and the door slid open. A deluge of bright hallway light poured into the room and hit her eyes like a small explosion. The image of Kole's asymmetric face crept its way between her squinting eyelids. She stared, uncertain of how to respond. He wasn't the last person she wanted to see, she supposed, and motioned for him to step inside. A moment after he stepped across the threshold, the door slid closed, sealing them inside the musty coffin. Clarice had only to say, "Bathroom light off" before the effect became complete and the protective, non-judgmental blackness returned to envelop her.

Clarice drunkenly stalked back to her bed and crawled onto the mattress. She molded the pillows under her head and shoulders and let her feet flop open. Kole pushed a small pile of clothes off the only chair in the room, a cushionless plastic model in the far left corner. He then picked up the chair and brought it a few feet over to the side of the bed, rotating it so he could face his quarry. He waited in silence while his bug-eyes adjusted to the dark. Clarice pulled her blankets around her. If she forced herself any further from the edge of the bed, she would have made a Clarice-shaped imprint in the wall.

Kole waited in silence for several moments, perhaps expecting that she would ask him his business. She did not oblige him, so he took the initiative. "I heard you were the one delivering the first transport to Azzerello," he said, straining his eyes to make sure she was still there. "How'd that go?"

"Didn't crash," she said. Her voice sounded better after a second usage, not nearly so raspy. Still, her throat could use a tall glass of water.

Kole nodded, perhaps asking himself why in the hell he chose to visit her at this point. "You think the war's over?"

Somewhere in the darkness, a real shoulder and its mechanical counterpart shrugged. "I don't know. I've been told that war ended several weeks ago."

"Yeah," Kole said. "I suppose in the official history it did. We can't have people thinking the Army of the Republic ever encounters –"

"He wasn't there," Clarice said forcefully, relieving Kole of his obligation to fill the silence.

"Azzerello?"

She ignored the obvious instead of saying something snarky that she might regret later. "He wasn't there. He had some Middesian come instead. It wasn't the one with one ear," she said, gesturing toward her ear, "so I don't even think the thing understood what I was saying."

"Maybe not," Kole said. "What would you have told him if he'd been there? Azzerello, I mean."

Clarice scanned the ceiling for the tiny camera lurking up there. She couldn't see it, but only a fool would think that they were really alone. The Special Operations division possessed surveillance equipment the size of an eyelash that could fly through the air. Using the ventilation system, they could access any room on the ship except for a few areas that had self-contained air supplies, so she never bothered to conduct a thorough search of her quarters. It wasn't like she could dismantle it; Drennon's people would know what happened in an instant, just like they could know every word of this conversation, Kole's pulse rate, or the core temperature of her crotch, if they wanted to. "Same thing you would've if you'd delivered the transport," she said.

Kole licked his lips, measuring his words carefully. Maybe the cameras were on his mind, too, or maybe he just didn't want to sound clichéd. "I'm sorry. I know you wanted… to make things a little less wrong. I guess we both have to keep paying for our sins."

Clarice's crumpled form pulled itself upright. "Sins?" she scoffed, feeling more awake than she had since the airlock door closed on the transport. "What sins do you have? Did you ever even fire your rifle while you were on the surface? Ever?"

"We're both guilty," Kole said, calmly, "of thing that happened down there… and since." The invading eyes and ears weighed on him as he struggled to avoid saying anything incriminating. "If it hadn't been you—"

"It sure as hell wouldn't have been you," she fired back. Her voice sounded almost comically creaky. "You don't have anything to apologize for. The only reason you want to jump sides is so you can be a part of something and don't have to bear your half-assed life, and that stinks, man, but don't go pretending we're carrying the same weight. Don't you even dare…"

"I'm sorry," he said when he was sure she was done. "I didn't mean it that way. I-I just don't want you to feel like you have to deal with this all on your own. You can talk to me—"

She snorted out a laugh. "Well, thanks, Willy, but I can't. The walls have ears, y'know, so I say we both compliment the all-powerful Republic and you can go back to being a mouth-breather and I can get back to killing people." She sniffed in the darkness as the rest of her started to unravel. "Y'know… y'know how much time I've wasted talking to you? I could've killed half a dozen people by now… just ripped out their throats with my bare hand." Her left hand dragged across the front of her face, absorbing a few of the tears that had collected there. "Damn," she said through clenched teeth. "If Jervis could see me now…"

Kole licked his lips. "He, um, he wasn't perfect either, y'know?"

Her head whipped toward him. "What?"

"I said he wasn't—"

"I know what you said," she snapped, her voice cracking. "I know he wasn't perfect. I never said he was."

"Well, you act like he'd be disappointed in you or something. You do it all the time." His words came slowly, carefully. "It's like you think he would've done a better job."

"Well, you never served under him," she told Kole. "Did you?"

"No," Kole admitted, shaking his head. He bit his lip, as if he was suddenly anxious. Maybe he was wearing a microphone or a booby trap. Maybe he was worried she might kill him. She didn't care anymore. Lying in that Med Tech table a week ago, she couldn't fathom that her life could get any worse. It can always get worse, though. Even now, she could come up with half a dozen ways her life could get significantly worse in the next five minutes.

"I guarantee you this," Clarice said. "If he was in my position, he would not be sitting on his ass, balling his eyes out."

Kole stared at his hands as he folded them in his lap. "I was at Flint Harbor with... Jervis," he reminded her, rotating his index finger in a clockwise fashion. "He and I didn't know one another that well, but I do remember that once when I was walking around the hallways of the barracks... I don't even remember what for... and I went into one of the stairwell and saw Jervis there, crying his eyes out. Just sobbing, like a little kid." Kole shook his head. "Hell, we almost were kids. I remember it because we'd just run some war games, and Giles' team lost. It wasn't his fault, but it was somehow supposed to build solidarity if the instructors reamed the mission leaders in front of their group." He shrugged. "Jervis was always so confident and... self-assured. It just surprised me how much he was keeping inside."

Clarice took several slow breaths, picturing a younger version of Jervis, sobbing in the stairwell. She found the image sort of unnerving. She wished she could have gone to him and told him that it was okay. "What was the point of that story?" she asked, but even she noticed that her voice had grown softer.

"I don't know," Kole admitted. "Maybe it's supposed to illustrate that everyone has doubts, even if they don't show them. It's also about the only story I have of him. I thought you might like to hear it." They sat in silence for several seconds. The only sound came from Clarice's labored, uneven breathing and the drone of the ventilation system. "Would you like me to leave?"

She didn't want to be alone, but she enjoyed looking pathetic in front of an audience even less. "I would. I really would."

Kole put his hands on the armrests, as if he was about to rise, but stopped and replaced them in his lap. "Can I say something first?"

Clarice sighed. "I... suppose."

Kole licked his lips, and his breathing became deliberate, like someone working up the nerve to do something, or say something. "I think I'm in love with you," he said through an imperceptible mouth.

Deep in the darkness, Clarice's face muscles slackened, and her mouth dropped open, slightly. Although aware of her expression, she could not seem to draw her lips together. He might as well have picked up the chair that he sat upon and beaten her over the head with it. He seemed like such a nice, sensitive, asexual man. Why did he have to complicate their perfectly innocuous relationship? She knew that attachments often develop between people who endure highly stressful situations together, so maybe she should have anticipated it. She didn't feel the same way, of course, she was certain of that. It might have been the only thing she felt certain of. She liked him well enough, and she trusted him… but she didn't really respect him… and god knows she didn't find him attractive. And now, as if she did not have enough problems weighing her down, she had to take time away from her descent into self-loathing to crush the heart of one of the nicer people she ever met. What in the world did he hope to accomplish by dumping that one on her?

Before she could tiptoe through the unpleasantness, Kole added, "I know you don't feel the same way." The words came out in chunks, as if he had memorized what he wanted to say after the inevitable rejection, but forgot as soon as he started to speak. "I know I'm not what you're looking for. I knew that as soon as I saw the way you looked at Azzerello. In a weird way, I felt it, too, because as soon as I saw him, I thought, 'Wilson, there's a man that's everything you're not.'" He pressed on, maybe to keep her from talking. "I know you don't love me… and you don't even have to say anything, because I'm okay with that. Really."

Despite the invitation of silence, Clarice felt compelled to say *something*. She licked her lips and tried to keep her sub-standard voice from sounding too cynical or condescending. "If you know how I feel, why are you telling me this?"

This time, the words rolled out of Kole. "I'm making you feel uncomfortable and I'm sorry for that, but we're both in a lot of danger and I might never get the chance again, and if I keep it to myself, it's like I never felt what I did… what I do." He paused for a breath. It calmed him by a fraction. "I'm not mad or bitter; it's no more your fault for not wanting me than it's my fault for not being what you want. It still hurts, though, in all honesty." He nodded for emphasis. Light from somewhere reflected off his dewy eyes. "Hurts, because any way I look at it, I wasn't good enough."

Clarice shook her head, almost on reflex. "Wilson," she said, calling him by his real first name for the first time.

His shadow stood up. "Look, I didn't come here for pity. I... it might not make sense why I came here, but I want you to know that I love you and... I admire you and the type of person you are, even if you feel like nobody else does. I don't know. That might be all there is to say about it."

Kole's retreat was almost graceful as he backed toward the door and somehow kept from falling over the miscellaneous articles of clothing scattered about the floor. His voice sounded flat, and his facial features were a dark blur, so she could not tell if he was crying or angry or merely numb. "Goodbye," he said, "and take care of yourself."

The door slid open at his approach, and he became a darkened silhouette against the brightness. She raised a hand in a pathetic attempt to both wave and block the invading light from pounding through her pupils. His back faced her by this point, though, and the gesture went unnoticed by everyone but her and whoever might have watched her room through the surveillance camera.

When the door slid closed, Clarice blinked and glanced around the darkened room. She drew a couple breaths. Nothing had changed. She still felt the same as she did before Kole came into her room, almost as if she had hallucinated the entire encounter. "How odd," she mumbled to herself. He may not have wanted pity, but no other emotions registered.

Clarice shifted atop the mattress and lay her head on the pillow. Kole acted as if she was in love with Azzerello. She disagreed, but in all likelihood, she probably could have loved someone like him in a perfect world. No one could deny that Leon Azzerello had his moments, not even his enemies. She never pursued people because of their integrity in her younger days, but since descending into this maelstrom of deceit and betrayal, its value grew daily. You cannot love if you cannot trust. Azzerello had more than integrity, though. Kole had integrity, and it did not raise him nearly high enough in her eyes. Azzerello had looks. He had personality. He had a presence. Standing next to him was standing next to greatness. Of course, that coin had a flip-side: would a man like Azzerello love a weak-minded drone like herself? Probably not, but that wasn't something worth dwelling on at the moment.

Part of her wished she could have told Kole she loved him and meant it; it would have been a nice thing to do. They were in for a world of trouble, and in their own way, they had developed a sense of intimacy, but it would have been nice to have something mutually acknowledged as tangible, even if it only lasted for a little while. For his sake, as well as hers. Eyes weighed on her, be they real or electric. The cold breath of death tickled the back of her neck. It would feel better to have someone to cling to on the way down.

Clarice crawled out from under her warped layer of blankets. She began to dress herself.

*   *   *

From the journal of Lt. Wilson Kole:

I'm just going to say it: I always thought Jervis Giles was an asshole. Of course, I didn't say it to Lieutenant Torrance, because I did love her, and I thought we were both going to be dead within a few hours. The story I told Clarice that night in her room was real enough, but I didn't tell the whole thing. In the full version, I pushed open the door to the stairwell, and there he sat: a pathetic wreck of a human being, after being chastised for his failure, his head nearly hanging in his lap. It took him a second to notice me as I was slowly trying to silently back out the door, but when he did, he stared at me with those pink, haunted eyes and said, "What're you looking at, pig-man?" I have an ugly nose. Everyone notices it, but even in the army, most people have enough grace not to lord it over me.

I never liked him much, even before that. He was one of those people who the fates had blessed with looks, charm, a delusional level of confidence, and all the other things that I would never have, and he took it for granted, wielding it like a cudgel over us lesser humans. Azzerello had all those qualities, too, but he wasn't a prick about it, because Azzerello also had dignity. Giles would have been lucky to spell "dignity." To me, he was always a laughing, taunting idiot of a man. When I saw him and Clarice together on the ship, she became something of an unattainable object for me. I never spoke to her before she accidentally selected me for surface duty, but I'd think about her from time to time, and by "think," I mean "fanaticize."

Giles and I had attended the same academy together, almost ten years before he died. Maybe he'd changed with the passage of time and the accumulation of experience. Maybe he was closer to the man she believed him to be than the man I remembered. I'd like to think Clarice wasn't being used or deceived. It's also possible that I caught him in a vulnerable moment, and he was just lashing out. Maybe he was a prick to everybody but her. I don't know. I can't figure it out. I'm glad I told Clarice the story, though... the edited version. She liked to think about him, and this gave her an image of the man she loved and revealed the sensitivity she'd convinced herself lurked inside him. "See?" she could always say. "Everybody knows he was as wonderful as I thought."

For me, the incident defines Giles as someone who was so hard up for approval that he'd spill his guts to get a pat on the head. I have no idea what his childhood was like, or what made him that way, but I developed the impression that he was a yes-man in training, and what made him a good officer was that he wanted it so damned badly. Sure, there was charm and charisma and all that necessary stuff that goes into being a leader of men, but the willingness... his eagerness to put himself and everyone in his command into peril made him a valuable commodity to his superiors. I think he was pathetic, not because he was crying but his reason for crying: the master had denied him its approval.

From the way she talked, I got the distinct feeling that Clarice thought Giles and Azzerello had a lot in common. I find that funny, because if Giles reminded me of anybody, it was Drennon.

*   *   *

CHAPTER FIFTEEN:
MAN OUT OF TIME

The patient stares at the ceiling as her remaining arm lies limply at her side. The white room and the bright white light should hurt her eyes, but her eyelids stay peeled open. Her mouth hangs slack, and the breaths come slow, loud, and regular. She wears a hospital gown, but for all she knows, she still lies swaddled in her fatigues and body armor.

Amorphous shapes drift back and forth on the other side of the observation window to her left. If she bothers to look, she will see two medical technicians in white coats, conversing as they examine electronic readings and type the information into their handheld computer tablets. The younger and taller of the two wears a neatly trimmed beard. The older is clean-shaven and balding. Their muffled voices penetrate the transparent barrier, but the soft, flowing music and her lack of focus prevent any meaning from coming through.

"Damn, Janick," the older Med Tech says to the younger. "How much sedative did you load her up with?"

The younger consults his computer tablet and shakes his head. "The last sedative we gave her wore off three hours ago. She didn't show any reaction, so we didn't see any reason to give her more."

"Damn." The older technician rubs his chin and stares out the observation window.

*   *   *

Clarice rushed from her room when the siren started blaring in three-second bursts. Her mind and body had already awakened; Kole had left over three hours ago, but his visit began the slow trek out of her malaise. In the last hour, she'd even gone so far as to take a shower and eat a month-old energy ration she found in her closet. When the alarm sounded, signaling the scrambling of fighters, Clarice shifted into a gear beyond awake. Her combat instincts took control, urging her to go somewhere, but she had no default location to guide her. Normally, an infantry officer would rally to the predetermined area, specific to where his or her platoon quartered. When Jervis died, his superiors temporarily split up the platoon and sent the remaining members in different directions, plugging the gaps left by deceased soldiers. Due to the sensitive nature of her post-injury duties, she remained on loan to Special Operations and had no idea what her superiors expected her to do.

She ran through a few scenarios in her head, involving both what was happening and what she could do about it. She drifted through a hallway intersection, weaving in between bodies charging from four directions. Scrambling the fighters meant one of two things: (1) the makings of a major combat operation had developed on the surface or (2) they were under attack. Both seemed impossible. As for her options, should she locate Major Hilbold, who would have been her old commanding officer during her time or infantry? Or should she go to Drennon's quarters? She shuddered at the latter thought. If given the choice between reporting to Drennon and doing nothing, Clarice preferred to do nothing. Seconds after resolving to return to her room, turn off the lights, and open that bottle of grain alcohol she found in her closet (next to the energy ration), she remembered from her days of rehabilitation that the infirmary lounge sported an impressive viewing deck. She trotted down the left-hand branch of the hallway, rushing just fast enough to avoid getting run-over.

Clarice swam past an onrushing soldier, bulky and balding, who looked vaguely familiar. She slithered between a couple more uniformed teens who wore matching anxious expressions. It seemed as if everyone in this level of the station had congregated at the far end of the hallway and now rushed in her direction. Everyone in this level of the station except Kole. She never saw him.

They were scrambling the fighters. All the serviceable fighters in Carrier 219. Usually that only happened when an enemy squadron approached in an attack formation. She grabbed the shoulder of the next soldier who rushed past on her right. He has the standard, unremarkable, square jaw, crew cut, and dull, blue eyes of an Army of the Republic poster soldier. Including equipment, he must have outweighed Clarice by at least one hundred pounds and would have dragged her down the hallway with him had she not grabbed him with her mechanical arm. As it was, she nearly lifted him off the ground.

"Whuzza?" he gasped as his momentum stopped with alarming brevity. "What the hell?"

The fact that he wore body armor and carried a helmet branded this bewildered man as, at most, a corporal or second lieutenant, so she could ignore any of his questions. "What's going on, soldier?" she demanded as he regained his balance. "Why are they scrambling the fighters?"

Stray bodies continued to jostle the two soldiers as they stood clogging the hallway. "It's the Middesians," he said, and for a moment, Clarice interpreted it to mean that the Vlorth had returned to save their doomed brethren. She inhaled, and fresh wave of adrenaline surged through her. The corporal, whose name badge on his left breast read "Dale," then elaborated. "Major Drennon has ordered a full assault on the Middesian transports." Her expanded chest deflated, and she felt like she couldn't stop exhaling. *What... the... hell.*

This young man didn't sound particularly frightened or bloodthirsty. The words exiting his mouth contained a matter-of-fact tone. He was just following orders, like all the other good soldiers. Part of her, though, badly wanted to hit something. *Just unclench your fingers, Clarice,* she reminded herself, *and let the poor kid go.* Clarice's hand fell away from Dale's jacket, and she heard her voice say, "As you were." Corporal Dale stood still long enough to salute, then rushed down the hallway, a couple dozen seconds behind his original schedule. Clarice stood for a moment, dumbly staring at her empty fingers. Where was she going, again? The observation deck. She ran in the opposite direction of Dale, her remaining path much clearer than when she began.

*   *   *

The observation deck. She last saw it while lying on her back during the days that followed her surgery. She remained unresponsive for several days, so the staff would guide her out here on one of the stabilizer beds and let her stare blankly at the stars. The deck consisted of a collection of overstuffed chairs and genetically engineered ferns situated beneath an enormous, transparent dome. The architects of the observation deck intended to provide a restful place where damaged men and women could stare at the heavens. For Clarice, though, in the wake of Jervis's death, each point of light might as well have represented a Middesian that needed killing. The cosmic beauty failed to bring her peace now, either. Her body tightened like a clenched fist as the legion of fighters hurtled past the dome. Each gray metal monstrosity rocketed overhead with such speed that their rear thrusters left a series of red and orange blurs. Despite the impending tragedy of the situation, or because of it, Clarice had to stop and stare at the red, arching afterimages.

The bubble-dome design of the deck made half the sky visible and enabled Clarice to see all the fighters, dozens upon dozens of them, converging upon a transport that lumbered away from Middes like a great, white Fultaxian Fruit Worm. The transport needed to leave the gravitational fields of Middes and its three moons in order to use its hyperdrive. The one-hundred-plus fighters would blast it apart before that happened. Clarice never personally witnessed fighters attack a vessel as big as a transport, but imagined something like a slow decomposition of the vessel. The undersized guns would pepper the outer hull and scrape away chunks at a time. Eventually, the transport would split open, and those inside would explode from the pressure shift or slowly asphyxiate while the black void swallowed their bodies.

Clarice's breath returned, but the anxiety igniting her nervous system prevented her from sitting down. Battle frequently made her nervous, but at least when she was involved in the battle, she could do something to relieve the tension. Here she could only watch, like some helpless civilian. Her chin descended to its normal position to relieve the strain on her neck, and for the first time, she noticed that she wasn't alone on the deck. Fellow soldiers, most clad in the light green hospital gowns, stood with their necks craned toward the heavens. A few wore white robes and slippers, but she could still see that they sported a gamut of injuries, from missing limbs to missing chunks of flesh. The infirmary technicians did a great job patching them together, though, and they'd be receiving their replacement limbs soon enough. *Not much scarring*, she thought with a knowing smirk.

After a quick scan of the assembled soldiers, she could separate most into two groups: the ones who still believed in the fable of a righteous Republic and the ones for whom the veil had been lifted. Both groups had sacrificed equally, but they made sense of the suffering in different ways. Clarice could distinguish between the two with expert efficiency, because at various times, she'd belonged to both sides. The first group kept a constant tension in their jaws and in their spines, and they would watch the carnage all the way to the end. They believed in the unmitigated righteousness of the Republic, and the obliteration of the enemy would validate that belief. Their suffering only made sense if it represented a sacrifice to a worthy cause.

The second group of soldiers showed less tension. They watched, but with trepidation. Eventually, their expressions would become sick and worried with each explosion from either side, and later, when they tried to sleep, those images would haunt the darkness. They saw the cosmic theater as only the latest manifestation of a cycle of pointless death. Their suffering had no grand design behind it; it resulted from desperation, lies, and naiveté. Just like Clarice, neither group knew how to alleviate their suffering, so they both simply watched the events unfold.

As the swarm pursued the hulking transport into the blackness, the glare of the engines meshing with the stars, a single, barely visible fighter peeled away from under the transport and veered in a tight, horizontal arc to face the oncoming mass. From such a distance, she couldn't identify the model, but the wings of a fighter unmistakably shifted upward, exposing the side cannons. Attack position. Clarice strained her eyes in search of any accompanying fighters but failed. The lone fighter made no attempt to escort the transport and remain in the protective umbrella of its plasma cannon. Its collision course with the mass of enemy fighters made fleeing an impossibility. "Dear God," Clarice muttered as the lone fighter dove toward the cluster of one hundred Republican fighters.

As the lone fighter grew closer, Clarice could definitely see that it was a Republican model, maybe a type of Heckler. That would aid the pilot immensely because any random shot it took would be a shot at the enemy, while the Republican ships might hesitate a split-second to make sure they were not firing upon one of their own. Also, with minimal, somewhat random between-ship spacing, any Republican shots that missed the lone fighter would threaten other Republican ships. Even if these factors increased the lone pilot's chances of survival tenfold, though, the odds merely increased from one-million-to-one to one-million-to-ten.

Clarice crossed her arms and drummed her fake fingers on her real bicep. Odds. What were the odds she would still be drawing breath? The blast that killed Jervis came inches from incinerating half of her vital organs along with her arm. Wraith One came a few pounds of pressure from decapitating her on a couple occasions. How many times had mere luck protected her from death? How many individuals… Republican, human and otherwise… had to die and would continue to die in her place before death found out that she was long past due? Odds were useless. One could not live life based on odds. People do what they have to do to feel righteous enough to make it through the day, they can't just do what is economical and play the percentages, because if they throw themselves into the fire, there always exists a *chance* that the flames will not consume them, but guilt that accompanies apathy or compliance will consume them every time.

The fighter plummeted into the onrushing torrent of ships, twisting and slithering through any available gap, maneuvering the machine in ways that its designers never conceived of. From her position, several of the turns seemed to be at a ninety-degree angle, which is, of course, impossible. Green blast after green blast exploded from its wing cannons and side cannons, perhaps randomly, perhaps not. The intent mattered little since laser blasts could scarcely ignite in that cloud of metal without hitting something on the way out. The same applied to the dozens of enemy shots. Most Republican shots hit something, as evidenced by the handful of fighters spiraling outward, away from the swarm. None hit their desired target.

Almost impossibly, the lone fighter sliced its way out of the back of the mass of enemies. The upper row of Clarice's teeth pressed against her lower lip, and her eyelids clamped shut. *Think depressing thoughts*, she warned herself. She forced Jervis into her thoughts, and the way his charred body collapsed onto the dirt and rocks, just to keep any expressions of joy from surfacing. Beyond the danger inherent in cheering for the enemy in front of a group of injured soldiers, it would be disrespectful to those brave soldiers in space and under the dome. Still, even her suppressed celebration made some of the surrounding, robed soldiers eye her uncomfortably. Their hard stares prodded her. At the edge of her peripheral vision stood a bald man with a dark complexion. He reminded her in a strange way of Wraith One as he glowered and shook his bald head in disapproval. Everyone lifted their heads skyward again, though, so she did the same. The lone rebel ship had made a looping, 180-degree turn and accelerated into the floating mass of firepower.

Surviving a head-on attack of such a number of ships was remarkable. To accomplish the feat a second time, when a single, stray blast from a laser cannon could send two halves of the ship hurtling in opposite directions, involved something beyond skill and something beyond luck. It would stand as a testament to the power of divine intervention. Unfortunately, whatever deity in charge of the Greater Middes area of the universe failed to watch over the lone, fearless pilot. Roaring forward at the ship's maximum speed, he (or she) cut three-quarters of the way through the fleet of ships, now having lost a quarter or a third of its number. A distinctly unremarkable burst of cannon fire blew through the side of his ship. The flare from the wreckage burned out in seconds, sucked away by the void of space.

Despite the dubious purpose and anticlimactic demise, everyone in the observation chamber threw up their real and fabricated limbs and cheered, some with less gusto than others. Clarice found herself clapping. It might have kept her from becoming sick or getting killed. Her languid hand felt like a side of meat slapping against its mechanical counterpart as tears rolled down the sides of her face. She did not wish to see the sixty ships cut the transport to pieces, but with the sickening urge of a voyeur, she rotated her eyes skyward yet again. Strangely, her eyes found nothing but blackness, stars, and all those tiny ships.

The transport had escaped.

*   *   *

Clarice stood in front of the mirror wearing a formal dress, the kind with ruffles that wrapped around her so tight she could not have slid a piece of paper between the fabric and her skin. The hemline failed to reach her knee. She only wore shorts on leave, and she hadn't taken leave in some time, so the cold air made the exposed skin of her legs tingle unpleasantly. Drennon had sent a hairdresser down to her quarters to curl her hair, swirl it, and wrap it above her head so that it cascaded downward in gentle, auburn waves. It looked lovely. So lovely that it dredged up memories of Founding Day dances, and part of her felt like crying when she looked in the mirror.

She had no idea where the dress came from, or the hairdresser, but it was a big ship full of highly skilled people. She never wore dresses. She never even planned to wear one when she and Jervis married. She hadn't worn a frilly formal dress since she was a teenager. She felt like something on display, which she supposed was precisely the point. Only the color of the dress was familiar. It was royal blue, of course: she about to attend a banquet in honor of her commanding officer.

Clarice walked to Drennon's command office in the awkward, unnatural gate that the dress shoes demanded, and told the guard outside the office that General Drennon wished to see her. She examined his square face and, even though he didn't look particularly familiar, decided he must have been one of the troopers standing outside the door the night Frusin died. The guard stepped into the room to check with Drennon. She wondered if Drennon eventually would promote this cretin for letting him kill Frusin… letting *her* kill Frusin. Why not? The full-blown colonization had commenced down on the surface of Middes and everyone of consequence was either getting stinking rich contracting their services out to the mineral companies or getting drowned in enough awards to sink a transport craft. It truly was a great day for the Republic.

The plain-faced guard returned and, as he spoke with her, made no effort to disguise his efforts to stare down the front of her dress. *Small breasts are still breasts,* she told herself, *and some people can't help themselves.* "The General will see you now," he said, smirking, as if he knew something she only suspected. "Enjoy the evening, Captain Torrance."

Clarice gritted her teeth and stepped past the guard. Garth Frusin, Jeb Harvath, and about a dozen other better human beings and generals than Lee Drennon had held high-level meetings in that very room in the past. The room looked exactly the same as when she last saw it; blue carpet with the Seal of the Republic emblazoned on it, the large, wooden desk, the semi-circle of uncomfortable, wooden chairs facing the desk. Drennon's presence drained the room and its furnishings of all dignity, though.

Drennon looked up from between two stacks of papers sitting on his desk, probably authorizing a parade in his honor. His hair was perfect, as usual. He seemed to have been preparing for this banquet from the moment she met him. "You sent for me, General," she said, adding his title after a half-second of debate. Standing at attention was precarious in heels.

"Torrance," he said, almost surprised, as if he had not sent for her specifically so that he could ratchet up the torture on her soul for a few more hours, "you look ravishing. Truly. I realize that the Army goes for the homogenous, asexual look, but I always suspected that, underneath that standard issue haircut and fatigues, you were a lovely woman. I'm glad I was right."

Clarice saluted him with her mechanical hand. "Congratulations on your promotion, General," she said. She had become so numb to the experience of toadying that it no longer disgusted her most of the time. More likely, her constant level of disgust had become normalized. Thinking about some activities, though, could still drive her to revulsion. When Drennon looked at her with white teeth and shining eyes, she knew they were thinking about the same thing and experiencing diametrically opposite reactions to the images that were conjured. "I trust that this will not be the last banquet in your honor."

"Thank you, thank you," he said, his sly smile staying locked onto his features. "And congratulations on your promotion, *Captain* Torrance. I couldn't have done it without you. And I want you to know, I'd like us to put our animosities behind us and become... friends."

She winced, imagining his cold clammy hands touching her shoulders, his breath on the back of her neck, telling her that if she just shut up and went along, she could make Major in a week. Could he ask the technicians to whip up something that would paralyze her instead of killing her? That was highly likely, and it seemed like something he would think of. If not, handcuffs would do the trick on someone with only one mechanical appendage. "I'm glad I could help," she lied, then added, "I just wish I could've done something to stop that transport full of Middesians from escaping."

Drennon shrugged, but his smile deepened, as though maintaining it now required effort. "Oh well. They're off the surface and Azzerello's blown to bits. What more can a general ask for?" Drennon rose from his chair, buttoning the top button of his shirt. "We should be getting to the banquet."

"Are you sure it was Azzerello?" Clarice asked.

Drennon paused before he could stand fully erect. "It was him," he said, his eyes rotating in her direction, in case she wanted to argue.

Clarice gave an elaborate nod, as if merely humoring him. Leon Azzerello was dead. She knew that. He wanted to die a noble death more than anything. Maybe in a perfect world, he could have lived a normal, happy life, but there was nothing left for him, no place for him, anywhere. With all the guilt he carried, driving that ship into the swarm of fighters, twice, was the only thing that could deliver him from his own conscience. Thinking about Azzerello and his death, Clarice could not muster the customary sorrow that she generated for a fallen comrade. It was too late for him, or anything else... and there were far worse fates than dying a noble death.

As if on cue, Drennon walked around the side of his desk, fishing in his pocket for something. "I want to talk with you about something before we get into more polite company."

"Yes, General," she said. She did not want to address him by that title. She had always respected people she called "general," and habits die hard. Drennon removed the deadly remote from his pocket and waved it in her field of vision. She would have felt greater surprise if he had not.

"It's a basic cleaning job," he said, coming to a stop at the corner of the desk to her right. "See, the only people that know the specifics of how I rose to my position are a couple guards, a security technician... oh, and your little friend, Lt. Kole."

Clarice's eyelids spread to their widest point. Since Jervis died, she had done few things that she considered "right," but she did keep Kole alive. Although an arbitrary victory from a professional standpoint, that stood out as the kernel of solace that kept her warm at night.

"Oh, don't look all dramatic," Drennon chided. "You know you'll do it." He wiggled the remote in front of her, pinching it between his thumb and forefinger. It hovered slightly over an arm's length away. He was a sadist, just like Kitridge, just one with better hair and more ambition. He liked to torture people, not insects, which was the only reason he kept her around. She wasn't particularly attractive, even for a career soldier, and she was downright morose, but he got a charge out of how wildly uncomfortable she felt around him, which made her presence priceless. He reached his free hand out and slid his fingers over the outside of her thigh. "You'll do a lot of things, thanks to—"

Clarice's artificial hand flicked out. Had she time to think about it, she never would have done something so foolish, because her brain would have done the math, and a normal, human limb could not have struck in time. The arm reacted by itself, though, the second the emotional part of her brain noticed an opening. Such a simple end to such a complex situation. It had been in front of her the whole time. She just had to stop holding on to the future and allow herself to react; she just had to be willing to die. She heard the plastic remote bounce off the wall before she saw it. It landed intact on the spot of the carpet sporting the Great Seal of the Republic. Clarice and Drennon stood frozen, staring dumbly at one another. A squeaky laugh escaped Drennon as the air rushed from his lungs, and his invading hand retracted like a withering vine. He glanced at Clarice, with bared teeth and dead eyes. He started to dive to his left. He didn't get far.

Clarice's hand flashed out again and snared Drennon by the neck. This time, she remained fully aware of every aspect of her decision as she pulled him in front of her... slowly, deliberately... as his limbs flailing helplessly. Her arm lifted him off his feet like it was picking up a bag of dirt. Her plastic and metal fingers crept to his jaw-line, where fingertips that could crush steel caressed human bone. She allowed his feet to touch the ground, then kept going, forcing him to his knees. Drennon's pale, sweaty face stared up at her. He knew exactly how much trouble he was in. His Adam's apple bobbed sporadically under the skin of his throat, as if a small animal that had climbed into his neck and desperately sought an escape. A light squeeze, little more than a flinch, would shatter his jaw and summon forth a scream that would satisfy her right down to the core of her soul. Not yet, though. Drennon had something to say.

She slid her hand from his jaw down to his throat so that he could talk. "You don't want to do this," he choked out. At least he was *trying* not to blubber. It must have been difficult. During his pathetic life, he'd slithered around so much that he had scarcely dealt with direct confrontations, much less something *this* direct. Slithered... like a tiny, insignificant little worm. He may not have been the cause of all the grief in her life, even her recent life. Nothing more than a cog in a corrupt machine, really. He made a great substitute, though, and he would suffer because no other cogs presented themselves. One person can't kill a galaxy-wide system, but one person could certainly kill the hell out of its representative.

"You kill me," he gasped. She felt him swallow. The drops of his cold sweat rolled over the skin of her fake hand. "And you'll be convicted of treason before the day's out. They'll detonate that implant in your neck and you'll die howling." She shuddered, and he pressed on, the words coming out in short bursts. "They say it's like being boiled alive from the inside. They say it's the most painful thing a person can experience. I know you saw what happened to Wraith Two. That stuff eats right through human flesh."

Clarice pressed on his throat until he bent backward at a painful angle. Her fingers stayed planted on either side of his neck. *This is it*, she thought, somewhat serenely. *The end of my life.*

Drennon's throat bobbed again. Strands of his normally perfectly coiffed hair hung in his face, and he looked pale and... what was the word? Frazzled? *So, he can feel... pain, anyway, and fear for his own, sorry life.* Did he ever love anyone? Did anyone ever love him? She never talked with the man, not in the sense of having a real conversation; someone was always either giving orders or lying. She has no idea if anyone would miss him. She could be the bigger person and let him go. On one level, it would be the right thing, the magnanimous thing, to do. He'd certainly learned to never touch her, and she might be granting a reprieve for someone's husband or father. Besides, the machinery of the Republic was corrupt and would be corrupt as long as it continued to exist. Too many people had invested in its continued health for her one action to change anything. The only battles a person in her position could win were small battles waged in the inside. Azzerello taught her that. Drennon's replacement probably would be no more of a high-minded saint. Stooping to the level of your enemies made you no better than those enemies. Trite, but true.

She stared, and listened to the steady beat of her own heart. *What are you thinking, little man?* Drennon's fear ran out of him in his sweat, tears, and respiration. Her fingertips soaked it up, and the sensation traveled the length of her wonderful arm, eventually reaching her tongue. His fear tasted as ripe and juicy as a piece of fruit after living on concentrates. She was who they thought she was... that night, when they called her into Frusin's office. She was desperate... and petty... and willing to die for a cause. Drennon just made the mistake of assuming that she couldn't change the cause she was willing to die for.

She took a step to her right, then another, and her fingers dragged him along. He scrambled along on his hands and knees to keep up. When she took them within a half-step of the remote, Clarice squatted down and reached for it with her left hand. The heels made it awkward. If Drennon had leapt forward, he could have knocked her down, but he risked her crushing his windpipe. So he stayed frozen, because he didn't have magic limbs that turned the flicker of thought into bone-crushing reality. Her real fingers closed on the remote. Little. Black. Plastic. It looked so damn harmless. "The most painful thing a person can experience," she repeated aloud, softly, looking at the simple, basic black housing and the two cute, gray buttons.

Clarice's human thumb depressed the first button. Nothing. She pressed the second, and a familiar warmth grew in her neck. It failed to frighten her this time. It had come to comfort her, like an angel massaging her neck. Her hands began to tremble, and she feared that the shaking metal and plastic appendage might cave in Drennon's neck involuntarily. As her thumb pressed down on the final button in the sequence, she dragged Drennon under her chin.

"What do you know about pain?" she snarled.

Drennon's hands pried madly at her fingers. He might as well have tried digging through the side of a mountain with a spoon. Had he the time, he might have marveled at the craftsmanship of the mechanical limb as much as Clarice did. Drennon started screaming before the drops of acid hit his skin. *He might get away alive*, she thought in one of her final bursts of brain activity, *get away with nothing more than a melted face*. Beyond the pain, that would entail the loss of sight, taste, smell, and vocal ability. He might leave behind enough nerves and raw materials for the techs to assemble a Wraith. Leaving Drennon to exist in a mind-wiped un-life would satisfy Clarice just fine. Sometimes, people have to make their own justice.

THE END

www.ingramcontent.com/pod-product-compliance
Lightning Source LLC
Chambersburg PA
CBHW031103260626
47172CB00001B/191